A PROUD STAND

Sitting Bull took the lead. "I have killed many whites," he began, "but not without provocation. They have taken our land, they have killed our women and children, they have come where they were not welcome, telling those who have always lived there that they would have to leave. I am willing to listen to what you have to say, and I am prepared to be peaceful, but not if it means giving up everything my people need to live."

De Smet listened respectfully, occasionally asking a question or two. "I am not here to make peace," he said. "I cannot do that, but it is something I want to see happen. I think it would be a good thing if you were to meet with the peace commissioners at Fort Rice. This war is a terrible thing. It is terrible for the whites and it is terrible for the Lakota. The cruelty is causing pain to everyone involved, and it would be a good thing if it could be ended now."

Sitting Bull said nothing.

Also by Bill Dugan

Duel on the Mesa
Texas Drive
Gun Play at Cross Creek

War Chiefs
Geronimo
Chief Joseph
Crazy Horse
Quanah Parker

Published by
HarperPaperbacks

Sitting Bull

War Chiefs

BILL DUGAN

🔲 HarperPaperbacks
A Division of HarperCollins*Publishers*

This is a work of fiction. The characters, incidents, and dialogues are products of the author's imagination and are not to be construed as real. Any resemblance to actual events or persons, living or dead, is entirely coincidental.

HarperPaperbacks *A Division of* HarperCollins*Publishers*
10 East 53rd Street, New York, N.Y. 10022

Cover illustration by JimCarson
Back cover photograph courtesy of Culver Pictures

First printing: April 1994

Printed in the United States of America

HarperPaperbacks and colophon are trademarks of HarperCollins*Publishers*

❖10 9 8 7 6 5 4 3 2 1

Sitting Bull

War Chiefs

Chapter 1 ═══════

Many Caches, Missouri River Basin
1831

THE BABY WAS STRAPPED to his cradleboard, his arms free to waggle in the air like feathers in the wind. The tipi was tall, so tall that its top was lost in shadows, even when the bottom was rolled to let in the warm breeze in summer. His birth name was Jumping Badger, but everyone knew that the name was only temporary. When he grew older and went off for his vision quest, he might come back with a new name from *Wakantanka*, the Great Mystery. Or perhaps he would do something great in battle against the Crows or the Hidatsa or the Assiniboin, and he would take a new name to celebrate his exploits. But for now, Jumping Badger would do.

The baby's father, Sitting Bull, had taken his own name from an apparition, not on a vision quest, but on a hunting expedition. Gazing at the new addition to his family, Sitting Bull remembered the occasion as vividly as if it had just

1

happened that morning. It is not often that holy things happen, even to a holy man like Sitting Bull, but there was no doubt in his mind that what had happened had been a sign. Even a man who believed in nothing would have been impressed by the visitation. And a man like Sitting Bull, who at that time was known as Returns Again, was no ordinary man. He came from a long line of warriors who were also holy men, and was schooled in their ways. He took both medicine and the warpath seriously. He was called Returns Again in those days because he was fearless in battle, never content with making a single pass at the enemy, but coming back again and again until the battle was won.

Thinking back on that night, he still felt chills, the hair on the back of his neck prickling as if some invisible hand whipped him with a pine branch, the needles stabbing into the skin with every blow. It had started as an ordinary hunting expedition. But after three days on the plains, with just a single buffalo to show for their efforts, he and the other three warriors had camped for the night.

They had known even before the sun went down that they were in for some heavy weather. The clouds had thickened, catching fire, then swirling in dark masses, as if they were tumbling in a torrent, the sky all but disappearing. The four men huddled around a fire when the cold wind came and slashing rain hissed through the trees like angry snakes. Everything had changed. It was dark . . . darker than usual. There were no stars to be seen because the clouds were so thick and black, hanging just above the tops of the trees.

Returns Again knew enough about the hostile world of the plains to know that they were in for a bad night. And there was just the hint of something ominous in the sky, as if it were preparing itself for something.

Despite the risk of discovery, they had built a fire. It was better to be warm in the sudden biting cold than to worry about enemy warriors who, if they had any sense at all, would be huddled around their own fire, if they were unlucky enough to be away from their own tipis on such a night.

Returns Again fell into a fitful sleep, huddled in a buffalo robe spread on the ground. He was as close to the fire as he dared to be, close enough that he could smell the steam rising from the rain-soaked fur of the buffalo skin. They were camped beside a creek, farther away from the bank than usual because the waters might rise if it continued to rain. In the darkness, the sound of the rushing current drowned out everything but the wind in the trees that rattled the brittle cottonwood leaves, already losing their green with the advancing autumn.

Gray Horse sat up to keep watch, his back against a tree, while the others tried to sleep. But the weather was so much on their minds, so insistent in its ferocity, that sleeping was difficult. The night wore on, and the rain continued.

It was just an hour or two before dawn when Returns Again sat up. He had heard something in the distance, out on the open plains . . . an indistinct sound, possibly the hooves of a horse pounding the sodden earth, or maybe a buffalo. He got to his feet, careful to fold the buffalo robe to keep it dry, and took his bow in hand. Slipping the quiver over his shoulder, he left the campfire and went to find Gray Horse. He found him slumped against the cottonwood trunk, wrapped in a robe, so still he might have been dead . . . had it not been for the sibilant shudder of a snore, he would have thought so.

For a moment, Returns Again thought about waking his comrades, but the sound out on the plains was not threatening, just mysterious. He moved further away from the fire, now little more than glowing embers that hissed now and then as wind-blown water spattered the cherry coals, darkening them as curls of steam rose up to mingle with the rain.

He stood quietly, not sure what it was he was listening for. He was sure only that he had heard something. He listened for several minutes but heard nothing more. Only when he had decided to turn back did it come again, the thud of an uncertain hoof on the long grass. Squinting through the rain in the direction of the sound, he saw nothing. He was about to move toward it when he heard a sound behind him and turned to see Gray Horse, bow in hand, an arrow notched but not drawn.

"What is it?" Gray Horse asked.

Returns Again shook his head, then held a finger to his lips. He pointed into the night, and Gray Horse leaned forward to peer through the darkness. But he saw no more than Returns Again had.

Then came the thud of another hoof, then another, then a third. It sounded as if whatever it was was

coming closer. It could be a scout from a band of
Crows, or maybe a Shoshone. It could be a hunter,
lost in the storm, groping his way home. Maybe an
elk or a buffalo. It was heavy, not a deer or a
pronghorn. Either a horse carrying a man or a full-
grown buffalo, Returns Again decided.

Gray Horse leaned close enough to whisper, "We
should wake the others."

Returns Again shook his head impatiently. "Did
you hear it?"

Gray Horse nodded.

"What was it?" Returns Again asked.

"I don't know. But I think we should wake the
others. I don't like the sound of it."

"Go ahead, then."

"Wait here until I get back."

But Returns Again was in no mood to wait. As
soon as Gray Horse vanished in the darkness, he
started to move away from the trees and under-
brush. He could still hear the creek burbling
behind him, but the noise of the hooves was more
insistent now, and closer.

He looked up at the sky, thinking there might be
a break in the clouds, maybe a little moonlight to
let him see more easily. But the mass of clouds was
unbroken, like a ceiling of slate stretching to all
four corners of the earth. He moved into the tall
grass, feeling the resistance of the water-soaked
blades against his leggings. Despite the chill, he
wore no shirt, and the rain pelted his skin now like
icy needles.

The wind whispered through the trees and moaned
back from the darkness. He moved cautiously until

he was fifty or sixty yards away from the brush, but still saw nothing. The sound of the hooves had stopped now, and Returns Again was baffled. He listened for several moments, then turned back toward the campsite. He encountered Gray Horse on the way back and told him that the sound had stopped and that they might as well go back to sleep. "It will be morning soon, and maybe we will see what it was when the sun comes up."

Gray Horse seemed uncertain, but Returns Again knew things other men didn't, and Gray Horse decided that he might as well take the suggestion. When Returns Again reached camp, he threw a couple of pieces of wood on the fire. Even though they had tried to protect it from the weather, the wood was damp, and for a few moments it hissed and sputtered as the water boiled off. Then the bark caught and light flared up, widening the circle of comfort among the trees.

Gray Horse lay down wearily, curling up as if to sleep, but no sooner had he closed his eyes than the sound of hooves could be heard again. This time the noise was loud and steady. Accompanying the thud of hooves was another sound, almost like water running, but not quite. It sounded a bit like an old man talking in his sleep, but not quite that, either.

The four Lakota warriors, their bows gripped tightly, arrows ready, moved away from the fire-light and pressed in among the trees. Suddenly, so suddenly it seemed almost as if it had not walked but just appeared, a huge buffalo bull stood in the circle of light. The thudding of hooves stopped, but the other sound, now like someone muttering, continued. It was babble, the kind of noise a crazy man makes when he thinks no one is listening.

Gray Horse drew his arrow all the way to the fletching, but before he could let it loose, Returns Again stopped him. "Wait!" he hissed. "Listen!"

Gray Horse looked at him as if he had said something crazy, but he relaxed the tension on his bowstring, still keeping the arrow notched, ready to draw it full and loose it in a split second.

"That buffalo is medicine," Returns Again whispered. "He is talking to us."

Gray Horse was not convinced. But he knew Returns Again understood medicine, knew that he was *wichasa wakan*, a holy man, a man who understood the spirit world. Returns Again had had visions and dreams, and he could tell the future that no man had yet seen. If he said the buffalo bull was talking to them, then they had better listen.

The four warriors stood as if frozen, listening to the strange mutter, trying desperately to understand it. It might be the buffalo god talking, and ignoring it might be dangerous. But try as they might, they could not interpret the sound. Gray Horse was getting impatient, but as soon as he made a move, Returns Again held up a hand. In the firelight, the great bull looked as if it were made of metal, not quite gold, but not quite flesh and fur, either.

The flames flickered, casting waves of highlights on the animal's thick hide. The dark eyes of the huge beast glistened, and its heavy head swung back and forth, the sharp horns reflecting fire and winking out, then bursting into flame again. The bull was making the same sounds over and over again, as if repeating a message in annoyance, one that should have been simple and easily understood. The sounds grew more strident, as if the bull—or the buffalo god himself—were frustrated by the thick-skulled dimwits he confronted.

Finally, Returns Again raised a hand and looked at the sky. "I understand," he whispered. "I know what he is saying."

He leaned closer, as if to make sure, and the bull went through the same strange muttering once more. Then it turned and disappeared as suddenly as it had come. For a few moments, they could hear its snort and the drumming of its hooves in the darkness, then the hiss of rain washed the echoes away and there was nothing but the wind again.

"What did he say?" Gray Horse asked.

At first, Returns Again didn't answer. It seemed almost as if he hadn't heard the question at all. But finally he walked to the fire and sat down. Without looking at Gray Horse, he said, "The buffalo was talking about the four ages, childhood, youth, maturity, and old age—Sitting Bull, Jumping Bull, Bull-Standing-with-Cow, and Lone Bull."

"What does it mean?"

"I am not sure. But I know that these are names, names that I can use, names that I can give to others. This is strong medicine, these names are *wakan*, holy names, and I must use them carefully."

"There are four of us," Gray Horse said. "Maybe each of us should have one of the four names."

"I don't think so," Returns Again said. "I think that if *Wakantanka* had meant that, all of us would have understood the buffalo. But I know that the first name is the most important, and I will keep it for myself. I will have to wait until I know more, until I can see more clearly, before I know what to do with the remaining three names."

That had been many winters ago, but he could still see that bull, gilded by the flames, just as clearly as if it were standing there in the tipi with him now. And looking at Jumping Badger in the cradleboard, the tiny arms waving, he wondered whether one of those names had been meant for his son. But everything took time, and he would have to wait. For now, Jumping Badger would be good enough for the boy. If he were meant to have one of the *wakan* names, time would tell.

Chapter 2 ═══════════

**Missouri River Valley
1833**

THE CRADLEBOARD WAS BEHIND him now, and Jumping Badger's world was beginning to expand. His legs were sturdy and his curiosity insatiable. At first it was just the tipi. While Her Holy Door tended to beadwork, she let her infant son have the run of the lodge. Everything seemed to fascinate him. Sometimes he would sit by her side for hours on end while she worked with porcupine quills, decorating a dress, or holed soft leather with an elkhorn awl to make a pair of moccasins. Then he seemed still to be a part of her, no more detached than her shadow, his hands mimicking every move of her own.

Other times, she would hear him behind her, rummaging in the baskets stored against the walls of the tipi. Then she knew she would have no peace, because he would toddle to her, hand outstretched, with a piece of cloth, a scrap of buckskin, a fistful of beads gotten in trade from the Cheyenne, who had gotten them from the Flatheads, who had gotten them from the Nez Percé.

Those times required patience, which fortunately Her Holy Door had in abundance. She would take the cloth or beads, sometimes having to unclench the tiny fingers forcibly, and explain what it was, what it was used for, and where it had come from. Sometimes she thought maybe she was telling him too much, giving him more information than he needed. But there were times when the dark eyes would stare into hers, and she would think that he understood more than she was telling him.

Just starting to talk, he asked many questions, stumbling sometimes, reaching for words just beyond his command. In frustration, he resorted to stabbing fingers, jumping up and down, and bellowing, while she tried one thing after another, trying to guess what he wanted explained. But there was never a doubt in her mind that he wanted explanations. He seemed to need to understand things in a way other children did not.

Her other child, Good Feather, was six years older, so dealing with a child's inquisitive forays was nothing new. But Jumping Badger wanted to know more, and sooner, than any child she had ever seen. At night, lying next to Sitting Bull, she would think about her son, asleep at last, his insatiable thirst for knowledge finally quiet for a few hours. It seemed to her then that he was not ordinary, that he was meant for something she could not see or know.

Sitting Bull got his share of questions, too, and as the boy started to wander around the camp, poking his nose into other lodges, watching the women work with the buffalo hides, or the warriors make arrows, bows, or lances, Sitting Bull wondered whether his son might be just like him. Part of him was glad when he thought this, and part of him hurt a little for the boy. Knowing was not easy, understanding harder still, and knowing what to do with the knowledge was the hardest part of all.

The world was so vast and so complicated, just making sense of it could give you an aching head. But Sitting Bull understood that knowing was important, that it might make a difference for his people one day, and that most of all it could not be denied. If your mind craved knowledge, it would have it at any cost.

He remembered when Jumping Badger had walked for the first time, his short legs barely able to support his weight. Every step seemed like agony, and took an eternity. Barefoot on the buffalo robes in the lodge, tiny toes curled, a leg would tremble, the whole body above it tilting because the boy did not yet know to let his knee flex, and finally it rose an inch or so and darted forward another inch to slam down again into the soft fur of the robe.

Step by step, arms outstretched, a look of wonder on his face, the fledgling toddler had made his way from mother to father. And when he had started back, squirming at first in Sitting Bull's hands as he tried to assert his independence, then breaking

free, he had veered off toward the fire pit, lost his
balance, and tumbled on his face. Excited, he had
not cried, but started to crawl like a turtle until he
reached the pit. Her Holy Door rushed to him,
reaching to pick him up, but Sitting Bull had
stopped her with a quiet word.

The boy reached for the orange flames, tinged
with blue, that danced above the embers. The tiny
fists had clapped through the fire for an instant,
then were drawn back. Jumping Badger looked at
his hands for a long moment, then at his father and,
when no explanation had been forthcoming, at his
mother.

Only then did he start to cry. Good Feather
rushed to pick up her brother, collapsing on her
rump with the boy in her lap. Gently, she uncurled
his fingers, saw the slight reddening, and knew that
he had not been badly burned. The girl looked at
her parents, a smile on her face. "He's all right,"
she said. Then she continued, "But it takes him so
long to do everything. He doesn't eat food without
looking at it. He turns a berry over in his hand to
see every side of it before he eats it. He plays with
beads, moving them one at a time, sometimes all
day long. I think maybe Jumping Badger is not a
good name for him."

Sitting Bull laughed. "What would you call your
brother, then?"

Good Feather shrugged noncommittally. "I don't
know. Everything he does is slow. He was even
slow to cry when he burned his hands. Maybe
that's what we should call him. Slow."

Her Holy Door wouldn't hear of it. "Jumping

Badger is a perfectly good name. I don't see why we should change it."

Good Feather would not surrender easily. "Did you see how long it took him to cry when he burned his fingers? That was slow, wasn't it?"

"He didn't understand what had happened," Her Holy Door argued.

"But he *was* slow, wasn't he, Mother?"

And so the name stuck. By the time he was three, more people knew him as Slow than as Jumping Badger. And he continued his explorations at the same solemn and studied pace. On walks with his father, he would wander off to examine a flower. If a bee paid a visit to the blossom, then darted off in search of another, Slow would follow it, his own route as jagged and indirect as that of the bee.

On his own, he would walk up the hill behind the village to watch the prairie dogs popping in and out of their dens. Sometimes the older boys rigged snares, arranging a rawhide loop around the mouth of a den and then lying patiently, waiting for the hapless inhabitant to pop up, then jerking the rawhide noose to catch the plump rodents. As soon as he had mastered the tying of the loop, he began to catch prairie dogs himself.

Already he was running fast enough to belie the name Good Feather had given him, and he loved to race with the older boys, always keeping up with them, but not yet long-legged enough to win.

By the time he was four, he had discovered the wonders of the riverbank. He would sit for an hour at a time, watching fish dart toward the edge of the river, hang placidly in the current, and break the surface to make a meal of an unwary skimmer or mayfly. He especially liked the young fry, swarms of them like waterborne gnats. He would dangle his bare feet from a flat rock and feel the tickle of the tiny fish as they nibbled at his toes and ankles.

But tadpoles were the best of all. In the sluggish pools, clogged with weeds and water lilies, he watched them wiggle their way among the roots. Once Sitting Bull had explained to him the connection between tadpoles and frogs, he grew even more fascinated, spending whole days in late spring and early summer hoping to see one change into the other.

There were times when his patience was exhausted and he was convinced his father had been teasing him. Not once had he seen a tadpole become a frog. How could it be true? But Sitting Bull had never lied to him, and what he said was always so. This could not be an exception. He just needed more patience.

Late in the day, lying on his stomach with his arms folded under his chin, staring through the glaze of sunlight on the surface, he would sometimes fall asleep. When Good Feather came to fetch him, he would grow irritable, throwing pebbles at her to try and chase her off. But she always prevailed.

One thing never changed. There was always something new to learn, and he couldn't get enough information about the ways of nature. More and more, when Sitting Bull was not out hunting or on the warpath, father and son would go off into the hills. Instead of planning lessons, Sitting Bull waited to see what the day would bring. If they stumbled across a deer, they would watch it for a while, tracking it, studying its ways, Sitting Bull pointing out how to tell when the deer knows it's being watched, how to follow it, and how to tell the difference between the hoofprints of the deer and the elk and the pronghorn.

If they found a bird's nest, Sitting Bull would climb the tree, Slow on his back, and together they would examine the nest and, if there were any, the eggs.

Once, Sitting Bull brought Slow along when he needed eagle feathers for a new warbonnet. Finding a suitable hollow in the ground, one that would hold them both, Sitting Bull wove a blanket of grass and brush large enough to cover the hole and sturdy enough to hold the weight of the eagle. Then he trapped a rabbit in a snare, tied its legs with a rawhide thong, and fed the loose end of the rawhide through the grass thatch. After directing Slow to crawl into the hollow, Sitting Bull followed him inside, then made a hole in the thatch just large enough for his hand to fit through.

"What do we do now?" Slow wanted to know.

"Now we wait. If you want an eagle feather, it is better not to kill the eagle. But you can't go to him, you have to let him come to you."

"How?"

"Wait and you will see. You must be quiet now, Slow." Sitting Bull covered his lips with a finger. Slow stared up at the thatching. Now and then he caught a glimpse of the terrified rabbit. Once or twice it tried to hop away, but the rawhide held it securely.

It seemed to take forever. It was hot under the grass roof, but Sitting Bull sat patiently. Slow was learning how to control himself and tried to sit on his haunches without speaking. Eventually, the flutter of wings could be heard and a huge shadow passed over the hole in the roof. The rabbit squealed and tried again to pull itself free, but it was too late. The shadow reappeared and the flutter of wings grew loud in the hollow. As the eagle sank its talons into the rabbit, Sitting Bull reached through the hole in the thatching and grabbed the great bird by the ankles.

Standing up, he reached around the edge of the grass mat and plucked several feathers from the eagle's tail, taking care not to come within reach of the razor-sharp beak. The eagle beat its wings, trying to pull free, and gave a terrible cry. Sitting Bull was almost done. After plucking one more feather, he let go of the bird, and it took off with several frantic beats of its broad wings.

Slow watched as the bird rose into the air with an angry squawk. "Isn't it easier to shoot the eagle?" he asked.

Sitting Bull laughed. "Yes, it is. But if you shoot all the eagles, where will we get the eagle feathers when the birds are all gone?"

"I never thought of that."

"You should think of such things," Sitting Bull cautioned. "Take only what you need, and leave more for another time."

The eagle was circling overhead, watching them, one eye on the wounded rabbit.

Sitting Bull handed the feathers to his son and bent to set the rabbit free. It dashed off, its terror more than making up for its weakened state. The eagle dropped like a stone and once more sank its talons into the rabbit. After a baleful glare at Sitting Bull, it started to tear strips of fur and flesh from its now-lifeless prey.

"Why did you do that?" Slow asked. "Why did you let the eagle have the rabbit?"

Sitting Bull laughed and explained, "The eagle has given us some fine feathers. We promised him a rabbit and he should have one."

"I still think it is easier to shoot the eagle—as long as you don't shoot them all!"

Sitting Bull nodded. "When you are old enough to gather eagle feathers, you get them the way you want to. This is the way I learned from my father. It was good enough for him and it is good enough for me."

"Sometimes things change," Slow argued. "Sometimes there is a better way."

The boy was right. Sitting Bull just nodded. "As long as you know when something is better, not just new," he said.

Chapter 3 ====================

Platte River Valley
1839

SLOW WATCHED AS THE buffalo robes were tied in
bundles and bound to travois. He stood quietly, trying to stay out of the way yet close enough to hear
the men talk. What he heard confused him.

"Are you sure," his father was asking, "that they
want buffalo robes at the white man's fort?"

Four Horns nodded. "I have heard this many
times. I know that many tribes travel to the worn-
out fences and bring furs. In exchange, they get
tobacco and metal knives and looking glasses, coffee and sugar—white man things."

"I am not so sure we need such things," Sitting
Bull said. "We have always managed without them.
I don't know why we should change now. We will
just make ourselves need the white man, and will
forget how to live without him."

Four Horns smiled. "We used to say that before
the Chippewa traded beaver skins for the white

man's guns. Then when they had guns and we did not, we had to move. I still remember the old men talking about such things. I think maybe now that the Blackfeet and the Crows and the Hohe are trading to get guns, we have to do the same."

Sitting Bull wasn't so sure. "If we get the white man's guns, then we will always need to trade with him. We will need the powder and the balls and will have to get them from the white men, or from other people who got them from the white man. We will be dependent on one enemy to be able to fight another."

"But you say yourself," Four Horns reminded him, "that our enemies are getting such things. If the Crows have guns, we will need guns, too. Already, Elk-Who-is-Afraid and Standing Deer have been killed by the guns of the Crows. They are getting the guns from across the mountains, from the Flatheads, because the white men come down from the Grandmother Country and trade guns and knives and beads for beaver pelts and horses."

Sitting Bull nodded. "I will go, but I still don't think it is a good idea."

"I don't think it is a good idea, either," Four Horns agreed. "But I think not doing it is a bad idea. And when you have to choose between a bad idea and another one that is not a good one, the choice is still clear. It is not even really a choice."

"I don't like killing more buffalo than we need, just to get skins to trade to the white man."

"We have nothing else he wants, except maybe our land, and we will not trade that, not for all the guns he has. And I say again, if we want to keep our land, if we want to keep hunting the buffalo, and living the way we have always lived, soon we will need guns to do it. That is just the way it is."

Slow was still confused. He understood trade, knew that sometimes even the Crows and the Hohe would enter into a truce with the Hunkpapa so they could exchange goods. But they didn't stop being enemies, they just stopped fighting long enough to trade things. Sometimes, too, they went to the Pawnees, and traded horses or buffalo skins for the maize the Pawnee grew near their villages. But trading with the white man was something different, something new.

Slow had seen only one white man, and he had not been that white. Burned bronze by the sun, with many dark whiskers on his face, he had spoken a strange language to his companions, and a creaky kind of Lakota that was just good enough to make himself understood. The white man had had only some cloth and some glass beads to trade. The beads were pretty and lasted longer than the quills that Her Holy Door used to decorate moccasins and clothing. The man had not wanted skins, only meat, because he had been traveling for a long time and had used up the food he had brought with him. Slow had been six years old then and could not understand why the white man had not hunted for his own food. Sitting Bull had tried to make him understand that some white men didn't hunt but ate food that others hunted for them, and that they grew food out of the ground the way the Pawnee and the Mandan and Hidatsa did.

To Slow, that had seemed a strange way to live.

But he knew already that the Crow did not live exactly like the Hunkpapa. And the Arikara did not live like the Crow or the Hunkpapa. If it worked for the white man, that was fine . . . but only for the white man. As he had grown older, spending more time with his father and with Standing Bear, the medicine man, he learned more about the *wasichus*, which is what they called the white man. But he still didn't think he understood them, really, and wasn't sure his father did either. It was one thing to learn about what someone did, and another altogether to truly know it, to *understand*. And Slow wanted to understand.

As soon as the buffalo skins were packed on the travois, the lodges were disassembled, and a half hour later they were ready for the long trek to Fort Laramie. The fort was on the western edge of Lakota land, and it would take several days to get there.

On the way, Slow listened to the men talking about the fort. Few of them had actually ever seen it, and it was difficult for him to visualize. As near as he could picture it, there was a high wooden fence surrounding buildings where the white men kept their trade goods and lived. But that wasn't much to go on.

He listened, too, to the talk about the buffalo skins. Sitting Bull said they were good skins, taken in the winter when the hair was thick and long. Four Horns had heard that those were the kind of skins the white men wanted. He also said they prized beaver pelts, which they got in abundance from the western tribes. Slow didn't know why the skin of the beaver should be worth anything. Beaver were small, and it would take dozens of skins to make a decent robe for sleeping—hundreds to make a lodge. And the skin was not thick or strong like buffalo hide, so it was hard to imagine anyone wanting to give something of value for so fragile a thing as a beaver pelt.

They traveled for six days, camping at night and setting up the lodges, but not unpacking their belongings. Only the food and the things needed to prepare it were taken from the travois. Even though the countryside was beautiful, and they were going someplace he had never been before, Slow found the trip boring. Every day was the same: wake up, wash, eat, and help pack, then start walking. At night, they did everything in reverse, slept, and started all over again the next day when the sun came up.

But just when it seemed the trip would never end, the scouts came back with news that the fort was not far, half a day more. And when they came over the last rise, Slow was stunned by the scene. There, looking nothing like what he had pictured, was the famous fort. But the fort itself was nothing compared to what surrounded it. Hundreds of lodges, not all of them Lakota, were arranged in a dozen circles or more. After they rested on the hill-top, Sitting Bull took Slow a little way down and sat in the grass. He pointed out the Crow camp, and the Arikara, and the Cheyenne. There were Hohe lodges, Flathead lodges, and Arapaho lodges, too. More tribes of Indians than he had ever heard of could be found here.

Slow wondered how his father could tell one
from another. "Every people has its own style, its
own designs. You can tell the Crow lodges by the
way they paint them. You can tell the Hunkpapa
from the Arapaho the same way. You can even tell
the Oglala from the Miniconjou, if you know what
to look for."

"Won't we have trouble with the Crows?" Slow
asked.

Sitting Bull laughed and clapped him on the
shoulder. "No. At the fort, there is always a truce.
The white men want the skins and we want what
they have to trade, so we forget about our enemies
for a few days. That doesn't mean that we should
turn our backs to them, only that we don't have to
kill them when we meet them. They might even
have some things to trade for what we have."

"I don't understand."

Sitting Bull didn't laugh this time. It was a hard
thing to explain. He wasn't even sure he understood it himself, but he knew that that was the way
it had been since he was a boy, and probably long
before that.

Then Sitting Bull told Slow about the dentalium
shells, gathered by coastal tribes from the bottom of
the Great Water and transported all the way across
the western mountains. "Have you ever seen the
Great Water, Father?" Slow asked.

Sitting Bull shook his head. "No, I haven't."

"How do you know it's there?"

"You can't believe only in things you see with
your eyes, Slow. Some things you never see, but
you believe in them because you see them with

your heart. Or the eye in here." He tapped his head.
"When you get older, you will make a vision quest
and you will see things you have never seen before.
You might see things that no man has ever seen.
But that won't mean that these things weren't there
all along, waiting for the right time to make themselves known to you. And it is the same with these
shells and the Great Water."

Sitting Bull reached up and removed the choker
of dentalium he wore around his neck and dropped
it over his son's head. It was too large for the boy
and hung down over his chest a little. Slow ran his
fingers over the smooth shells, cool even in the
sunlight, and looked down at his chest where the
dentalium glittered white as snow.

He was about to ask another question, but Black
Moon shouted the command to start down to the
fort, and the *akicitas*, the warriors who were in
charge of the march, were busy getting everyone
moving again. The Hunkpapa wanted to make a
good showing as they arrived at the campground. It
would not do to straggle in like some rag-tag bunch
of fugitives. It was important to carry yourself well,
especially since you were under the scrutiny of
warriors who were your enemies and might try to
kill you the next time they saw you. It was important to show them that you were strong and proud.

Once on the flatland, they quickened their pace
and headed for an open space near the circle of
Oglala lodges. It was late afternoon by the time
they had set up their own tipis, and the first order
of business was a feast to show how well the
Hunkpapa were doing. They invited warriors they

knew from the other Lakota circles, and some
Cheyennes, too, who had long been friends in the
war against the Crow and the Pawnee.

Slow watched the welter of color as Indians mingled. Some Crows and Arikara visited during the
celebration, and, as usual, warriors on both sides
took the opportunity to ask for missing friends.
More often than not, the enemies knew one another
by name and reputation, and it was not uncommon
to talk over old battles, double-checking on out-
landish claims of battle exploits.

Occasionally an enemy warrior was asked to
show a scar from a wound allegedly inflicted by
one of the Lakotas, and sometimes a Lakota warrior was asked to do the same. In the absence of
written records, the plains warriors were very concerned that their oral histories be accurate, and
that no man claim credit for a thing he had not
done.

The celebrating went on long into the night, and
Slow was too tired to stay awake until it ended.
When he awoke early the next morning, the adults
were already preparing for their trip to the fort,
where the traders would be waiting for them. Slow
shadowed Sitting Bull, determined not to be left
behind.

Approaching the fort's high palisade, Slow
looked at the hills beyond for a moment, trying to
measure the size of the place. It was the largest
structure of any kind he had ever seen. As they
drew close to Fort Laramie, the place the whites
called Fort William, he saw why the warriors dis-
paraged the stockade walls. The vertical timbers

had been exposed to many years of weathering and truly looked like they were close to falling down.

Entering the gate, skipping behind Sitting Bull's travois, he looked up at the blockhouse directly over the opening in the wall and saw a strange black eye staring back at him. He moved to the side a little and saw that it was a long metal tube, like a Crow musket Sitting Bull had once taken in battle, only longer and very much larger. It looked as if it could swallow him whole.

Once inside, he stared in awe at a single pole standing in the middle. A strange cloth he had never seen before fluttered in the breeze, making a snapping sound that he could hear even over the hum of conversation as other Indians argued with the traders. Sitting Bull was directed to a line of Indians and told to wait. There were three ahead of him, and Slow climbed onto the travois to rest while they waited for the traders to finish their business with two Crow warriors and a Hohe.

The Crows had a stack of buffalo robes which the traders dumped on the ground and pawed through, one making strange noises, another scraping a stick on a white skin so thin Slow could see through it. When the trader had looked at all twelve skins, he said something in broken Crow, which made the two warriors laugh. They looked at Sitting Bull and smiled, then back at the white man, who repeated what he had said.

The Crows shook their heads, as if saying that they disagreed with the white man, who then said another thing in the same broken Crow. This time the two Crows nodded their heads. The trader walked away, returning with two muskets and a leather bag. Another man followed behind him, a round thing like a piece of tree trunk on his shoulder. The round thing was set on the ground, and the white man handed the two muskets to his customers, then tossed the leather bag into the air. One of the Crows snatched it and pulled open the drawstring. He stuck his hand inside the bag and pulled out a fistful of dull gray spheres, which Slow recognized as musket balls.

The second Crow broke open the end of the piece of tree, and Slow saw that it was hollow, filled with shiny black powder. The Crows seemed satisfied now. One of them picked up the hollow log filled with the black powder while the other shouldered both muskets and tied the bag of musket balls to his belt. The two Crows grinned at Sitting Bull then, who watched them angrily until they had walked out of the fort.

The next customer, the Hohe, had only two skins to trade. Both were excellent robes, and he seemed to know just what he wanted for them. The trader made a sign of some kind, and the Hohe nodded. The trader picked up a clay pot and poured some liquid that looked like water from a jug into it, keeping his fingers inside. Then he took a second pot and poured more of the liquid into it. The Hohe took the first pot and drank it off in what looked like one long swallow. The second mug was emptied just as quickly, and the Hohe belched, dropping the mug and starting to walk away, his legs not working all that well anymore.

Now it was Sitting Bull's turn. The trader's Lakota was no better than his Crow, but it didn't take long for Sitting Bull to explain what he wanted. Slow climbed down from the travois and the trader slit the rawhide holding the buffalo robes in place. Once more, the skins were dumped to the ground and pawed over. When the count was finished, all eight skins were tossed onto the pile of skins the Crows had traded, and once more the man walked away, coming back with another musket and another leather bag. This time, he had a second bag, made of thick cloth, and when Sitting Bull looked inside, Slow saw the same black powder the Crows had carried away in the hollow log.

Sitting Bull seemed satisfied as he lifted Slow to the back of the horse and handed him the musket, then took the horse's bridle and headed back out through the gate.

Once they were outside, Slow asked, "Why did the Hohe trade his skins for water, while you and the Crows got guns, bullets, and powder for yours?"

Sitting Bull shook his head. "It is a long story. I will tell you later."

Chapter 4

Missouri River Valley
1841

SLOW SQUATTED BEHIND A scrub oak, craning his neck to look up at the sheer rock wall towering over his head. He was leaning back so far he felt dizzy, as if he were going to lose his balance at any moment and fall flat on his back. The bow felt heavy in his hands, the strain of holding it ready was making his shoulders ache. But the swallows nesting in the rock wall were not concerned with how Slow felt. They came and went when they chose, flitting out of the niches in the sheer rock face so suddenly that they were gone almost before he saw them.

It was a small bow, and he sometimes wished that he had a better one, one with more power, but his father insisted that he was not ready for a man's bow. "When the time comes," Sitting Bull always told him, "I will know, and so will you. And then you will have a warrior's bow. Learn to shoot well with the bow you have."

So for now, all he had was a boy's bow, and
instead of elk and deer and buffalo, he shot at birds
and rabbits and prairie dogs. He could dream of
hunting the larger animals, but dreams were no
longer good enough. Even shooting at small birds
took skill, but it was not the same as tracking a deer
and bringing it down with one well-placed arrow.
This was not really hunting. But he trusted Sitting
Bull, and he would have to be content to practice,
to hone his skill.

Above him, the birds tumbled like leaves in the
wind for a foot or so after they launched themselves
into the air, black shapes fluttering wildly for a split
second before gaining their balance and swooping
off and away. He had been spending every morning
here for a week, bow in hand, blunt-tipped arrows
rattling in his quiver every time he moved. After
three days he thought the noise of the arrows
against the stiff buffalo hide of the quiver might be
giving him away, so he filched a piece of blue trade
cloth from Her Holy Door's meager supply and
stuffed it into the quiver to keep them quiet.

But so far the silence hadn't helped. The birds
were so quick and their flight so unpredictable. He
sighted along the arrow, thinking that waiting for
the perfect moment was like trying to predict
where lightning would strike a week before the
storm clouds came. It couldn't be done. It was
beyond medicine, it was even beyond luck. It was,
he was beginning to think, not going to happen at
all, ever.

Now and again, out of sheer frustration, he
would let loose with an arrow even though the

bird was already gone. It felt good to release the
tension in his arms and back, hear the hum of the
bowstring, and watch the arrow climb toward the
top of the cliff, where it would hang suspended
for a moment, then tilt over, slow as a falling tree
for a short eternity, then turn its nose down and
slowly gather speed as the earth reclaimed it. The
blunt-nosed arrow would land within a few feet
of him, sometimes intact, sometimes, when it hit
a rock, slitting the tip and rendering itself useless. But arrows could be had by the hundreds, so
it was a small price to pay to rid himself of the
accumulated frustration.

His mind was drifting, and he tried to bring it
back to the task at hand. Squinting to focus his
eyes, he saw another swallow tumble from the cliff,
and almost by instinct, he let loose. The bowstring
snapped and the arrow flew, sailing within an inch
or two of the oblivious bird. Slow kicked the dirt in
frustration and sat down with his back against the
stunted oak. Taking a deep breath, he watched the
clouds for a few minutes. He saw an eagle far off,
circling, then dropping like a stone. Even from this
great distance, he could see the magnificent bird's
legs extended, the talons curled like the inflexible
fingers of an old woman. The bird disappeared
behind a cottonwood as it plummeted to earth.

A moment later it reappeared, the talons now
dug deeply into its squirming prey—a prairie dog,
from the look of it. Imagining the piercing agony of
those talons, he shuddered. He wondered what it
would feel like to be as small as that prairie dog
and have a huge bird fall from the sky and seize

him in the blink of an eye. But he couldn't imagine it, or didn't really want to, so he shook himself free of the secondhand terror and climbed to his feet again.

Once more he stood looking up, the bowstring at his shoulder, the arrow drawn almost to its tip. This time he was going to wait, no matter how long it took, and let the bird find stable flight before he launched his arrow. Maybe that would make a difference. At least it was worth a try.

When the next swallow darted away from the red rock, he followed it, let it right itself, then let the bowstring loose. The arrow wobbled once, then slammed into the swallow. The bird seemed to stagger in the air, one wing no longer working properly, and off balance, moving backward like a Heyoka clown, it fluttered to the ground. A moment later, the arrow clattered to earth on some rocks, rattling like a gourd, and Slow raced for the downed bird.

He found it right away, still not certain what had happened. The long, arcing wings were still fully extended, but one clearly had been broken and lacked the graceful sweep of the other, the smooth curve of its leading edge now an odd angle. As Slow approached, the bird fluttered and hopped away, taking refuge in the brush. Setting his bow on the ground, Slow dropped to his knees and crept toward the cowering swallow, his right arm extended in a gesture meant to soothe the frightened bird, lull it into staying where it was until the open hand could get close enough to seize it.

The bird cheeped, then squawked, its beady eyes

darting this way and that as the hand drew closer. Backed into a corner now, it seemed to realize it was trapped. Slow leaned forward, cooing to the swallow to quiet it, and with one last dart of his hand, he closed the bird in his fingers, trying not to squeeze too hard. As he lifted the bird, a hand grasped his own shoulder and squeezed tightly. Startled, he dropped the swallow and turned, remembering his fear of the eagle's talons, jerking to pull himself free of the grasping fingers.

Sitting Bull shook his head as Slow straightened up. "A wise warrior never leaves his bow," he said, handing the weapon to his son.

"I was trying to get the bird."

"And if I was a Pawnee instead of your father? What would happen then?"

"I . . . I would have . . . I would have heard you, then," Slow stammered.

Sitting Bull shook his head and squeezed the boy's shoulder again. "You didn't hear me."

"But I would have heard a Pawnee," Slow insisted. "I know I would have."

"Does a Pawnee have hooves and snort when he walks? Does he have a rattle in his tail and shake it to let you know that he is coming?"

"No, but . . ." Slow looked at the ground now. For a moment, he saw the toes of his moccasins, and those of his father's. It seemed that he would never be big enough to know everything he needed to know, or to take care of himself when he made a mistake. He scraped one toe on the ground, watching the grass bend, then straighten again, then at the groove he had made in the soil. He wanted to look at his father, but couldn't force himself to lift his gaze.

Sitting Bull waited for a long moment, then lifted Slow's chin. Letting go, but holding his son's eyes with his own, he drew a finger under his chin all the way across his larynx. "You would not have heard a Pawnee, and he would have cut your throat before you knew he was there."

Slow knew that his father was right. He felt silly, but did not try to defend himself any longer. There was no defense and he knew it. He had made a mistake. He had committed the unpardonable sin of leaving his weapon while out on his own. It didn't matter that he was not far from the village. And it didn't matter, either, that the small bow would not have saved him from a Pawnee. He had to learn to do the small things well before he could do the big things.

"I was watching you," Sitting Bull said, letting his stern expression relax a bit.

"How long?"

The man shrugged his shoulders. "Not long. But long enough to see you hit the swallow. It was a good shot."

"I wish I could shoot at something besides little birds and prairie dogs."

"That is why I have come for you. The buffalo are not far, and I think maybe it is time for you to learn how to hunt them. You are old enough now."

Slow felt his face splitting into a broad smile. This was the moment he had been waiting for since he had gotten his first bow. Thinking about the weapon in his hand, though, his face fell. "I don't have a bow that is powerful enough to bring down a buffalo."

"Yes," Sitting Bull said, smiling himself now, "you do. Come on, we are already late."

With that, he turned and started walking away from the cliff. Slow had to run to keep up with his father's longer strides. They were heading for the cottonwoods where Slow had seen the eagle snare its prey an hour before. A tiny creek wound across the valley floor, clumps of trees marking its passage, thickest where the stream widened out into pools. Tethered to one of the trees, he saw his father's hunting pony, and next to it, his own gray.

When they reached the horses, Sitting Bull removed a package from the rear of his horse. Wrapped in buckskin, it was long and cylindrical, nearly five inches in diameter. Sitting Bull started to hand the package to his son, lifting it away from the boy's eager grasp once, then again, to tease him a little. Slow jumped, and when he got his fingers on the buckskin, Sitting Bull lowered it, let Slow cradle it for a moment in his arms, then said, "Go on, open it."

Slow sat on the ground, the cylinder in his lap, and tore at the thongs holding the buckskin closed. The knots were tight and gave him trouble. Finally, no longer able to control his impatience, he grabbed a small knife from a sheath on his belt and sliced through the four thongs, each of them parting with a sharp snap as the taut leather gave way. When all four thongs had been cut, Slow looked at the package, ran his fingers over the indentations in the buckskin where the thongs had pinched it, then opened the roll.

The bow he uncovered was beautiful. Smooth ash on the inner curve, the bark left on the outer face. The bow had been carefully crafted, polished almost to a gloss where the bark had been removed. A band of leather, three inches or so wide, marked the grip, and a pair of small eagle feathers fluttered from either tip. Already strung, it had been painted with bands of bright color and the stylized figures of two birds, either eagles or thunderbirds, he wasn't sure.

Looking up at Sitting Bull, he said, "It's perfect. It's the best bow I've ever seen."

Sitting Bull nodded. "Black Owl Flying made it for me. He knows how to make the best bows. His bows never break if they are taken care of. He can look at a tree and find where the bow is hidden, then cut away everything that is not the bow. It could not be longer or shorter. It is the only bow in that tree, and you should treat it with respect. Treat it with all the care that went into its making, and it will never fail you."

Slow plucked the sinew string, heard the pure hum of it, almost like the note of a flute. As it vibrated for a split second, it was a blur in the middle, and when it came to rest, there was perfect silence.

Slow got to his feet. Sitting Bull handed him a hunting arrow, its iron tip black from the fire, its razor edges shining in the morning sun. The boy looked around for a fitting target for his first shot, and when none presented itself, he aimed high, toward the sun, drawing the bow as deeply as he could. It was powerful, too powerful for his ten-year-old shoulders, and he struggled to get the arrow back to the head. He had to stop with a good eight inches of shaft still separating bow and arrowhead, and his arms were shaking. He forced them to be still. Sighting along the shaft of the brand-new arrow, he let go of the string, feeling a sharp sting where it slapped against his wrist. Lowering the bow, he watched the long, graceful arc of the arrow's flight as it cleared the cotton-woods and disappeared behind the crowns of the trees.

Looking at Sitting Bull, he licked his lips. "Thank you, Father," he said.

"Get on your pony, son. It's time for you to learn to hunt the buffalo."

Chapter 5 ===

Missouri River Valley
1841

EVEN BEFORE SLOW AND HIS FATHER reached the last ridge, beyond which the herd was grazing, he could hear the buffalo. The grunts of the bulls sounded like the earth itself moving. Dust rose over the ridgeline, filling the air with a faint beige pall as the animals moved restlessly, churning the earth and tearing at the grass.

Father and son rode cautiously, not wanting to spook the animals. Sitting Bull wanted Slow to learn the intricacies of the hunt, on which the life of the Hunkpapa depended. The best way to learn was by doing, but he was not about to send his son into the hunt without a little preparation. A buffalo herd could be dangerous. The bulls were ornery, and they were a lot quicker than their ungainly appearance suggested. The horns, worn by both bulls and cows, were vicious weapons, and an enraged buffalo was afraid of nothing.

Sitting Bull had seen more than one friend killed
by the huge beasts. He had seen, too, a horse
gored by a charging bull, its entrails pulled loose,
the frightened pony running, stepping on its own
intestines, pulling itself apart until it fell dead in
its tracks.

They reached the crest of the ridge and Sitting
Bull dismounted, telling Slow to do the same.
Their mounts and packhorses took the opportunity
to graze a bit. Far below, the herd stretched
halfway up either side of the ridges that formed a
long, vee-shaped valley. Slow gasped, watching the
numberless animals, many of them wandering aim-
lessly. Some of the buffalo were on the ground,
squirming on their backs, using loose dirt to rid
themselves of parasites. Slow saw a pair of huge
bulls square off, lowering their heads and pawing
at the grass before running together with a clash of
horns.

Calves drifted in their mothers' wakes, their tails
lashing the air, looking almost ludicrous, their
already bulky bodies held up by spindly legs. All
along the opposite ridge, Slow saw other
Hunkpapas watching the herd, trying to gauge its
temperament and making last-minute preparations.
The Lakota had been hunting buffalo for generations, but it was not something they did casually.
They depended on the animals for just about everything, and a mistake could send the herd rumbling
away before they had killed enough to meet their
immediate needs. And it was in the haste to make
up for their mistakes that hunters got hurt, or sometimes killed.

To guard against overanxiousness, *akicitas*, warriors chosen this time especially to police the hunt, made sure that everyone stayed in line. They would surround the herd, and timing was crucial. If anyone broke cover too soon, it could stampede the animals before all the hunters were in place. Such a man would have to answer to the *akicitas*, and his punishment could be severe.

Sitting Bull pointed out a cow and her calf on the fringes of the herd. "You should take a calf first, Jumping Badger. If all goes well, then maybe next time you can go after a cow."

The boy nodded, never taking his eyes off the two buffalo. Dropping to one knee, Sitting Bull continued. "Come in from behind, so the calf doesn't see you, and approach from the right side. If you can get your pony almost even, you will have a clear shot. Draw your bow fully, and aim for the shoulder. If you hit it right, you will get the heart or the lungs. But make sure you have control of your pony, and make sure you don't get between the calf and the cow. The cow will try to protect her calf, and if you are busy watching the calf, you cannot watch the cow. That is a sure way to get yourself in trouble."

Again, Slow nodded. He thought about asking a few questions, but knew that Sitting Bull had already thought through what he wanted to say, and he would have missed nothing that Slow needed to know. Interrupting with questions would just waste time and distract his father. He was too anxious to join the hunt, barely able to restrain himself as it was.

Sitting Bull continued, "The bulls are the most dangerous. They are almost as fast as your pony, and they can change direction quickly. If a bull spots you and decides to charge, don't think that you can bring him down. You are not ready for that, and before you realize it, it will be too late. He will be on you. Never drift into the middle of the herd, because you can't watch every direction at one time. If the calf you are after heads toward the middle of the herd, let it go and find another. As long as you keep to the outside edge, there will always be another target for you."

Two huge bulls had lowered their heads, and once again the thunderous crack of their collision reverberated through the valley. It was rutting season, and the bulls were competing for female attention. Other bulls were pairing off, and more duels began. But the buffalo seemed to have short attention spans, and the fights ended almost as soon as they began. Two or three rushes seemed to settle matters, and one bull or another would amble off, its tail flicking at flies, none the worse for wear, while the victor turned his attention back to the business of grazing.

"Are you ready?" Sitting Bull asked.

Slow was anxious to get started, but he wasn't sure he was ready. His father sensed the uncertainty. "No one is ready the first time, Slow," he said. "A wise man knows when he should be cautious. It is only natural that you hesitate, but you cannot hesitate forever. I would not send you down there if I did not think you were ready. Understand?"

Slow nodded. He was pleased that his father had confidence in him, and it bolstered his determination. "I am ready," he said. But his voice sounded less certain than his words.

Sitting Bull knew that he could not wait much longer for fear Slow would lose his nerve. Besides, there was his obligation to the others to be considered, and one man's son was nothing when measured against the general welfare. He said, "Let's get on our horses. We have to circle around the valley and get to the other side, where the others are waiting for us." Without waiting for an answer, he moved to his horse and swung aboard, reining in while he waited for Slow to mount his gray pony.

When the boy was mounted, Sitting Bull nudged his horse back downhill a few yards, staying below the ridgeline. It would reduce the chances of spooking the buffalo. The packhorses trailed behind him in a single line. It took fifteen minutes to reach the east end of the ridge. Crossing the narrow mouth of the valley, the buffalo well west of them now and out of sight, Slow was beginning to feel a new surge of confidence. By the time they had climbed to the opposite ridge and reached the end of the line of impatient hunters, Slow was convinced that he would take his first buffalo that day.

Sitting Bull picketed his packhorses, then mounted up again. He reached over to ruffle his son's hair, then nodded, and the hunt leader gave the signal to begin. Unlike a war party, where the point was to terrify the enemy with war cries, the hunters moved quietly, spreading out behind the herd and hoping to get right on top of it before the alarm began to circulate among the grazing animals.

But soon the approaching horses were too obvious for the buffalo to miss, and the herd began to move. At first the animals just milled around, raising their heads to pick up the scent of the intruders. They broke into uncertain trots, some in one direction, some in another. But as the Hunkpapa got closer, the nearest animals began to run. Soon a surge spread through the herd from one side to the other, and they were all in flight, heading west, down the length of the long, narrow valley.

Sitting Bull hung back, wanting to keep an eye on Slow without the boy realizing he was being watched. If things went well, he wouldn't interfere, but he would be close enough to help if Slow ran into trouble.

He watched as his son skirted the rear fringe of the herd, moving parallel to a handful of cows and calves. Slow held his bow with arrow notched but undrawn as he tried to maneuver his gray pony alongside a fat calf. He clutched two more arrows against the curve of the bow, ready for quick release, just as his father had shown him so many times. The calf kept changing direction on him, sometimes moving away from its mother and the rest of the herd, sometimes drifting into a clump of other calves. It might have been easier to pick another target, but Slow had his heart set on his first choice. Ahead, he could see the first few kills—dark, immobile mounds in the surging brown sea.

The buffalo parted to get past the fallen animals,

then reconverged. As the last of the herd passed the first few victims of the hunt, the carcasses remained in the trampled grass like great brown boulders. But Slow was too busy tracking his prey to pay much attention to the success of the other hunters.

He moved in closer, gaining confidence with every stride of his pony. The calf turned once to look at him, then veered away, and Slow kicked his heels into the pony's flanks for an extra burst of speed. He was just ten yards behind the calf now and closing in fast. Once more the calf veered, drifting to the right and cutting across his path. The gray responded, changing direction so horse and rider were once more behind the right flank of the terrified calf.

Slow drew his arrow now, squeezing the gray between his legs to hang on. He tried to aim, but the bounding pony made it difficult for him to hold to his target. The bowstring hummed and the arrow grazed the calf's back, the iron arrowhead plowing a shallow furrow in the flesh and leaving a bright red line to mark its passage.

Slow shook his fist in anger before notching another arrow from those in his hand. Adjusting it, he drew it back almost to the head, his frustration giving him strength. Before letting the arrow fly, he had to change direction yet again as the calf veered to avoid a fallen bull. The calf flew by on the bull's left, Slow on its right. He passed close enough to see three arrows buried to their fletching in the buffalo's shoulder, blood seeping from around the shafts.

Once past the bull, he adjusted his angle on the calf again and drew the arrow back full, letting fly while the pony was in mid-stride. This time he had better luck and the arrow found its mark. It must have struck bone, because it penetrated only a few inches and flapped loosely as the calf galloped on. Again closing the gap, another arrow strung and drawn, he shot for the third time. This time he saw his arrow bury itself to the feathers. The calf stumbled but did not go down, simply changing direction as it regained its stride.

But the calf seemed slower now, as if the arrow had found something vital. Its lips were bloody, and it snorted bloody foam as it turned to look at its tormentor. Another arrow ready, Slow drew close, aimed, and cut loose. Once more, the arrow buried itself completely in the calf's side. This time it stumbled, lost its feet, and fell to its knees, skidding several feet, its hind legs trying desperately to keep it moving forward.

Slow looked ahead, saw that he was not that far from another calf, and left his first animal to breathe its last as he kicked the gray into a full gallop. There was no danger of losing his calf to another hunter, because the markings on his arrows would identify it unmistakably as his.

Sitting Bull, confident that his son was in control of things, turned his attention to the hunt. He plunged into the herd's rear guard, singled out a fat cow, and quickly brought her down with three arrows placed so closely their shafts touched. Leaving his first kill, he moved on for another. There was always another winter to prepare for, and the upcoming one already had all the signs of being a cold and snowy one, even this early in the summer. It was time to start gathering supplies to get the family through the worst of the cold weather, when game would be hard to come by. And the later in winter you hunted, the thinner your prey, as the deer, elk, and buffalo used their fat to supplement their own more meager winter food supply.

By the time the herd disappeared to the west, Sitting Bull had brought down two cows and a bull. Slow was less fortunate. He had the one calf, but had not managed to get another. He sat there on the gray, surveying the valley, now deathly quiet, the thunder of thousands of buffalo hooves just a fading memory. The air was thick with dust, and the smell of blood gave it a sweet scent.

Several of the fallen buffalo were still alive, some trying to get to their feet, others panting and groaning as they lay on their sides, no longer having the strength to move. Already the hunters were moving among the dead and wounded animals, looking for their own prey and, as soon as they found it, setting to work with their knives.

There were many ways to butcher a buffalo, and the choice depended on what use would be made of the hides. If they were intended for robes, they would be cut one way, if they were to be fashioned into tipi siding, they were cut another.

Slow looked for Sitting Bull, finally spotting him a few hundred yards away, already busy with his first buffalo carcass. Nudging his pony into motion, he picked his way through the carcasses, feeling that something had changed, that he was not the same Jumping Badger he had been two hours ago.

Several of the hunters looked up from their work as he passed, and they waved to him and greeted him not in the way they would the children, but in the way they would one another. They were looking at him in a new way, which just reinforced his feeling that something had changed. He wondered, if he were to see his reflection in one of the white man's looking glasses, would he recognize himself, or was what he felt inside also apparent on the outside?

When he reached Sitting Bull, he slipped from the gray and squatted down beside his father. He had never butchered a buffalo, and he watched in fascination as his father removed the hide, leaving a bit of fat on the inside of the skin. When the hide had been removed, the real business of butchering began, and Sitting Bull looked up without slowing his work. "Get the packhorses," he said. "We'll do your calf as soon as I am finished with this cow."

Slow, somewhat deflated at being sent to do a chore, walked back to his gray and headed for the ridge. Well, he thought, maybe he doesn't see it, but I *am* different now.

Chapter 6 ═══════════════

Yellowstone River Valley
1845

SLOW SLIPPED OUT OF THE TIPI and walked into the center of the camp. He was fourteen now, tired of being considered a boy, but it was not easy to prove himself, to earn the respect of the warriors. Sometimes he would sit and listen to them, their tales of bravery, of battles against the Crows and the Hohe, and he grew envious. When, he wondered, would he have the chance to tell his own stories?

Sitting there, just outside the reach of the firelight, it was as if he didn't even exist. The warriors paid him no more attention than they paid the stray dogs that wandered from tipi to tipi, looking for a handout. It didn't seem right, somehow. It had been four years since he had killed his first buffalo. He did his share of work in the village. He was ready for the warpath, and no one could tell him otherwise. His mother, of course, would try to keep him a boy as long as she could. But she couldn't succeed forever.

Nearly every week, he raised the issue with Sitting Bull, but the answer was always the same. "Not yet," Sitting Bull would tell him. "You are too young for the warpath."

Sometimes at night he would hear Sitting Bull and Her Holy Door talking about him. Sitting Bull would tell her that Slow wanted to go on the warpath, and Her Holy Door would whisper sharply, "What did you tell him?" Sitting Bull would say that he had tried to discourage the boy by telling him that he was too young. "Well, he *is* too young," Her Holy Door would say. Sitting Bull would not answer, and Slow wondered whether that meant his father agreed with his mother, or that he disagreed but did not want to argue about it. They had had such a conversation the night before, but Slow was not discouraged.

He saw a few warriors sitting in a tight circle, talking among themselves. As he crept closer, their voices exploded in laughter. He tried to hear what they were saying, but the words were muffled. He moved even closer and sat on the grass, just close enough now to hear what was being said.

Good-Voiced Elk, a well-known warrior, was speaking. He was restless, and he didn't care who knew it. It had been months since the last war party, and he was tired of waiting for someone else to take the initiative. Sitting with a few friends, he suggested that it was time to pay a visit to the Crows. "We have left them alone too long. If we wait much longer, they will think that we are no longer here, or that we are like a bunch of old women. And then they will give us more trouble than we need. Better to remind them on our terms."

The other warriors nodded their heads. What Good-Voiced Elk said was true. It was not a good thing to let your enemy think you had forgotten about him, because it was a short step from there to contempt.

The Lakota had not had an easy time creating a niche for themselves on the plains. It was not that long ago that the Lakota were strangers, invaders, fighting desperately for a place to live. The Ojibwa had been armed with the white man's guns and there had been no choice but to flee ahead of them, leaving behind the Lakota lands in the forests of northern Minnesota.

The old men were always telling stories about that time, when the Ojibwa swooped down on them and destroyed their villages, killing women and children and old men. The bitterness lingered, passed down from generation to generation. And when they had at last been driven from their homeland, the Lakota had determined that it would not happen to them again. This time, they would be the invaders, they would take the land they needed to live, and if that meant war, then so be it.

Once they learned to use horses, the Lakota became the most powerful nation on the plains. Unlike some of the tribes already living on the plains, they had not been skilled on horseback. They couldn't ride like the Comanche or the Crows. But it hadn't taken them long to master the art.

The warriors all knew the old stories, handed down from father to son, grandfather to grandson. None of them was anxious to go back to the old days, when they had to worry about their enemies. It was better to be on top, to have the very name of your people strike fear in the hearts of your enemies, who were everywhere. That was the way it always had been, and that was the way it always would be. You had to fight to protect what was yours.

"I think," Good-Voiced Elk said, pushing his advantage, "that we should go on the warpath. We could use some new horses."

Short Bull nodded. "Do you want to lead the war party?" he asked.

"I will lead," Good-Voiced Elk agreed. "We should find ten or twenty men who want to go, and we will leave tomorrow or the day after."

"Sitting Bull will want to go. And I think I know two more men who might want to come along," Short Bull said. "I'll ask them tomorrow morning."

Gray Eagle looked up from the arrow he was making. "I think I might know a couple of men, too," he said.

Listening to them, Slow was getting excited. This might be his chance. He was anxious for his first coup, and going on a war party with his father, even if Sitting Bull was not going to be leading it, was more than he could have hoped for.

"Then it's agreed," Good-Voiced Elk said. "Tomorrow night we will smoke the war pipe. We will leave the day after tomorrow. We don't want too many men, because I want to move fast." He watched his friends get to their feet and disappear in the darkness. Sitting there alone, he listened to the crackle of the fire and, off in the distance, the howl of a wolf out on the plains.

Slow backed away quietly, watching the great warrior and wondering what was going through his mind. A war party was no casual undertaking. It was a great thing, an important thing, and a dangerous thing. Slow knew that some of the men he had just been secretly observing might not come back. They had all lost friends and family members on war parties. Just a few months ago, Slow's own uncle, Four Horns, had been left for dead on the plains. Four Horns had come back that time, but there was no guarantee that he would be so lucky the next time. The tribesmen did not take a war party lightly. No one would make you go. That wasn't the way the Lakota Sioux did things. Each warrior made up his own mind. And it was no shame to change your mind. Slow remembered once when his own father had returned home no more than an hour after a war party had left. Sitting Bull was a holy man, more attuned to the ways of the earth than most warriors, and more sensitive to the hidden meanings that surrounded them. A blade of grass, an eagle feather, the paw print of a bear—these were all messages from *Wakantanka*, and you ignored them at your peril. That morning, Sitting Bull had seen an eagle in the sky, not black or brown like most eagles, but all white, and he knew it was a sign. It would be bad medicine to go into battle that day. So Sitting Bull had returned home, not with his tail between his legs, but with his head held high.

Sitting now in the shadows, watching the broad back of Good-Voiced Elk, Slow thought about approaching the warrior, asking if he could go along on the war party. But he knew what Good-Voiced Elk would do. He would tell Slow to ask his father, and Slow already knew what Sitting Bull would say.

He could hear his mother, too, pleading with Sitting Bull not to take their son on so dangerous a mission. Slow's sisters, Good Feather and Twin Woman, would chime in too. No, if he were going to get the opportunity to count his first coup, he would have to keep his intentions to himself. If he rode out to join the war party, they would not send him back. So he would have to find out where they planned to rendezvous and make his own preparations in secret.

If he kept his ears open, he would hear Sitting Bull discuss the war party. He wouldn't be able to ask questions, because his father would see right through him. He would just sit quietly, listening for the tiniest clue.

The next day the camp would hum with news of the impending raid. There would be no celebration, because everyone in the village knew only too well that there might be nothing to celebrate. More than one war party Slow could remember had returned home with dead and wounded draped over their ponies. The village had been filled with wailing, the death song filling the air day and night as the dead were mourned and laid to rest on their burial scaffolds. He could still see the relatives, wearing old clothes, sometimes with their faces painted or smeared with mud to symbolize their loss.

But he listened and missed no opportunity to eavesdrop on Good-Voiced Elk, Short Bull, and the others. It was hard to hide his excitement, especially when Good-Voiced Elk had come to Sitting Bull's tipi to ask him to join the war party. Sitting Bull had said nothing, promising only that he would let Good-Voiced Elk know his decision as soon as he had made it. Sitting Bull's sharp glance at Slow had brought a knowing nod from Good-Voiced Elk, and he had said no more.

By sunset the next day, Slow knew all he needed to know. He made his own preparations, all the while feeling a little foolish. He had a bow, but his arrows were a boy's arrows, not those of a man. When they hunted, his father gave him hunting arrows, but they were inappropriate for Crows or Assiniboin. And he could not ask his father for war arrows. He would have to hope that *Wakantanka* would provide.

The night before the war party left, Slow could barely sleep. He kept tossing on his buffalo robes. Every sound drifting through the village took on demonic shape in the darkness. The hoot of an owl came from a Crow throat; the muffled thud of pony hooves outside the tipi was the first hint of an Assiniboin war party preparing to thunder down on the sleeping camp.

Every noise brought his hand to his bow, which was tucked under the edge of his sleeping robes.

His fingers would curl around the polished ash, and he could feel the cold sweat of his palms making the smooth wood slippery to the touch. Sometimes he would get to his feet, bow in hand, and tiptoe toward the entrance. All around him he could hear the breathing of his sleeping family, the resonant snore of his father, the sleeping sighs of his sisters, the whisper of his mother's breath.

With his hand on the tipi flap, he would suddenly feel silly and back away, lying down again, trying to forget what he was about to do. By tomorrow night, he thought, or the next night, all of this would be no more than an amusing story, one he would someday tell around a campfire, or to his own son, trying to make him understand why he was too young for the warpath. But that was little comfort now. At the moment, his muscles twitched like snakes beneath his skin, his throat was dry, and every nerve tingled.

By morning he was exhausted, but he forced himself to get up and go to the river for a bath. It was still gray when he stepped into the water. He could see the village horses grazing on the hillside, dark shadows in the dim light. He went out into the cold current, watching the bustle of activity beginning. He could tell which warriors were going with the war party, as one by one they came out of their tipis, made their ponies ready, gathered their weapons, and rode off.

As soon as he saw Sitting Bull leave, Slow waded out of the river and sprinted to his tipi. He gathered his bow and the war paint he planned to wear and, doing his best not to attract attention to himself, left the lodge and climbed onto the back of his gray pony. When he reached the rendezvous point, the warriors had assembled. Some were already streaked with war paint, while others stood by their mounts, decorating the ponies with bold splashes of brilliant color and daubing their own faces with bands of red and yellow and blue.

One of the warriors spotted Slow and tapped Sitting Bull on the shoulder. Slow's father turned around. His face, already painted, was barely recognizable behind the streaks of bright color. His eyes widened when he saw Slow, and he backed up a step, as if the boy were a frightening apparition. "What are you doing here?" he asked when he had regained his composure.

"I am going on the war party."

Sitting Bill shook his head. "No, I don't think so. You aren't old enough yet."

"If I wait for you to tell me I am old enough, I will *never* be old enough. I have already killed buffalo. I know how to hunt, and I know how to shoot accurately with the bow and with the rifle."

"That's not the point . . . your mother would never forgive me if anything happened to you."

Slow shook his head. "It is not up to my mother. And anyway, she would too forgive you. She knows that she can't keep me in the tipi forever. I have left the cradleboard behind. I don't want to be treated like a baby anymore."

"But you have no experience."

"How am I supposed to get experience if I always stay at home?"

Sitting Bull knew the boy was right, but he still

didn't want to agree. He held up his hand. "Wait a minute. Let me think about this." He moved away, Good-Voiced Elk following him.

Slow watched the two men conferring. The other warriors were all grinning at him, some pointing then whispering jokes and laughing, but Slow didn't take offense. He knew what they were thinking, and he knew that someday, when he was like them and some fresh-faced boy wanted to come along, he would have the same reaction. He would laugh and he would tease. But he knew, too, that in the end he would accept the newcomer, because there was no other way. He only hoped Sitting Bull saw things the same way.

It didn't take long for him to find out. Sitting Bull moved toward him, took the bow from his hand, and emptied the quiver of blunt-tipped arrows onto the grass. "These will not do for making war," he said.

Then he walked back to his mount and took a coup stick, its bright beadwork glittering as he twirled it once and looked along its length to make sure it was straight. Satisfied, he handed it to the boy.

Slow took the coup stick, trying to conceal his delight. The warriors muttered their approval as he hefted the coup stick high overhead. "It is a good day to die," he said.

"Not yet," Sitting Bull said. "You have to put on your war paint. And hurry, because it is already late."

Chapter 7 ===========

**Yellowstone River Valley
1845**

A WAR PARTY WAS NOT QUITE as exciting as Slow had
thought. They had been riding for two days
already, and so far there had not been a single
trace of Crows. And he had all the dirty work to
do. At night, he had to tend to the horses. During
the day, he rode near the rear of the line, as befitted his status as the youngest. He was beginning to
wonder whether it might not have been better to
have waited for Sitting Bull to tell him when the
time was right. But when he thought about it, he
realized that even then, he would have been
assigned the same chores. Better to get it over with
now, he decided. Some things just couldn't be
avoided.

The warriors teased him constantly. They
seemed to have a bottomless bag of tricks to play
on him, and they were adept enough in their practical joking that he even fell for the same trick more

than once. They never seemed to tire of calling out that the Crows were coming, and every single time Slow would lash his gray pony, clapping his heels against its sides to get it moving, only to hear the explosion of laughter all around him. The warriors knew he was eager, and they were making the most of it.

But it was not malicious, and Slow knew that he would have to bear it with good grace if he expected to be taken on another war party anytime soon. He had known he would have to work hard, but he had not expected to be bored. When they camped for the night at the end of the second day's ride, Slow tended the horses then moved to the campfire to sit next to Sitting Bull.

His father was a great warrior, and it made Slow proud to sit beside him and the other warriors, men whose names were known not just among the Hunkpapa, but among all the Lakota—the Oglala and the Miniconjou, the Sans Arcs and the Brule, the Two Kettles and the Blackfeet Sioux—all knew of Sitting Bull, celebrated not just for his bravery, but for his accomplishments as a holy man and a healer, as well. And now, sitting by his side, the black night pressing in from every direction, the sounds of the vast, empty plains drifting toward them on the night breeze, father and son each realized that their relationship was changing, changing in some profound way that each intuitively understood, changing in a way that could never be reversed.

Slow was truly growing up. He was no longer a boy, and not quite yet a man, but that would change tomorrow, or the day after, and both of them knew it. Slow was eager, but Sitting Bull felt resigned, almost sad. He had spent his life trying to keep Slow safe, but soon—sooner than he wanted to admit—it would no longer be up to him. Slow would have to fend for himself, and that would be even more difficult than it had been twenty winters before, when Sitting Bull had himself been just a boy.

Sitting Bull draped an arm around Slow's shoulders. "So, what do you think?" he asked.

"About what?"

Sitting Bull shrugged his shoulders. "This. Being on the warpath . . ."

"I don't know what you mean."

"Is it what you thought it would be?"

Slow paused a moment to think, then shook his head. "No. It's boring. I thought it would be different. I thought it would be exciting."

Sitting Bull laughed. "If we find the Crows we are looking for, it will not be boring. That much I can tell you."

"When will we find them?"

"I don't know. I don't even know if we *will* find them. Sometimes we ride for days, and if it weren't for our own reflections in the water, we would see no one at all. Sometimes we find more than we were looking for. Those are the worst times, the times when we lose a friend or a relative."

"The Crows are nothing to be afraid of."

"Yes, they are. All enemies are to be feared. A man who does not fear his enemy is a fool. The warrior does what he has to do even though he is afraid."

"Still, I am not afraid."

"That is good. Right now, there is nothing to be afraid of. Perhaps tomorrow it will be different."

"Do you think we will find the Crows tomorrow?"

"Maybe."

"What if we don't?"

"Then we will find them the next day . . . or the day after that."

"I hope so."

"The horses are all taken care of?" Sitting Bull asked.

Slow nodded. "Yes. But tonight I don't have to stand guard. It is Small Eagle's turn."

"Maybe you should get some sleep, son. Tomorrow will be a long day, just like today and yesterday. Every day is the same on the warpath. And if we do find the Crows, you will need your rest."

Slow was reluctant. He wanted to stay by Sitting Bull's side, but he knew his father was right. He was not used to the rigors of the warpath. He was accustomed to sleeping when he was tired and rising when he felt like it. The warpath was a special place, and one had to think of others. If he was tired, he might be careless, and if he was careless, he might get someone hurt, maybe even killed, and he did not want that on his conscience.

He walked away from the fire and lay down on the ground. He had his brand-new coup stick by his side, and he curled his fingers around the leather grip. It was beginning to look like the only Crows he would see would be in his dreams, and he might as well go armed.

He woke up later, the fire long since out. He thought he had heard a noise, but as he lay there, straining his ears, he began to think he had dreamed it. Trying to keep his eyes open was more than he could bear, and a few minutes later, he was asleep again.

Sitting Bull woke him early, shaking him by the shoulder. He sat up slowly, rubbed the sleep from his eyes, and reached for the dried buffalo meat Sitting Bull proferred. He chewed the meat slowly, aware of his aching muscles but trying his best to ignore them.

The sun was already warm on his skin, and as he looked around the camp, he realized that he was the last one to awaken. He felt embarrassed, but Sitting Bull didn't mention it. No sooner had he swallowed the last of the dried meat than Sitting Bull called to him to mount his pony. It was time to move on.

The scouts were already out, and the war party rode along slowly, letting their horses reserve their energy. If they encountered Crows, they would need all of it and more. So far from home, possibly outnumbered, perhaps heavily, they would have to be prepared to run for their lives. And if they found Crows and there were not too many, then the ponies would need their strength for the chase and the ensuing battle. It was a delicate balance, and there was always the chance that the difference between life and death would depend on the sturdy ponies beneath them.

The sun was almost overhead when the scouts appeared on a ridge ahead. Good-Voiced Elk rode out to meet them, and the rest of the war party waited anxiously to find out what he had learned. When he returned, he told the warriors that there was a Crow war party ahead, nearly forty strong. Two to one was not such bad odds, and it was decided to move ahead and set a trap for them.

On the far side of the hill, there was a long, narrow valley. A creek wound its way through the bottom, and it was likely the Crows would be looking to water their ponies. The Lakota would arrange themselves along the ridge on one side of the valley, and when the Crows dismounted, they would charge.

It was as good a plan as any, and Slow felt his heart begin to hammer in his chest. He hoped his medicine was strong, and that all would go well. The ridge was studded with clumps of brush, and the Lakota warriors broke up into small groups, using the brush for cover so they would not have to dismount. They wanted to be ready to charge at a moment's notice.

The gray pony sensed Slow's nervousness and kept tossing its stiff mane and pawing the ground with its hooves. The boy leaned forward to pat it on the neck and whisper in its ear, trying to calm it. He kept one eye on the mouth of the valley, holding his breath and waiting for his first glimpse of the enemy.

It wasn't long before the first Crow appeared, moving cautiously, swiveling his head to examine the ridge, looking for any hint of trouble. Slow licked his lips and took a deep breath. For a moment, he could swear the Crow was looking right at him. It looked almost as if the Crow's eyes were staring right through him.

But the enemy warrior soon shifted his gaze. When he was satisfied there was no one about, he turned and called over his shoulder, then nudged his horse toward some cottonwoods along the creek. Several more Crows soon appeared, followed by another bunch, and finally the entire Crow war party had made its entrance.

Slow was watching Sitting Bull, waiting for some sign that it was time to move, but it didn't come. Sitting Bull, like the other warriors, was waiting for Good-Voiced Elk to make the decision. It was his war party, and even though Lakota warriors fought as individuals, it was just common courtesy to let the leader give the signal.

"Hurry up," Slow whispered. The gray was getting more skittish by the moment, and Slow himself was ready to burst. Finally, when he could stand it no more, he kicked the gray and charged into the open, shouting at the top of his lungs. He had jumped the gun, but there was nothing to be done about it now.

Far below, the Crows heard his solitary shriek. They watched for several seconds. But the sudden ripple of war cries along the ridge, followed by the explosive appearance of nearly two dozen Lakota warriors, galvanized them.

The Crows scattered, some sprinting back the way they had come, some standing their ground as the Lakota charged downhill. Slow's gray was fast, and its burden was light, so he was far out in front. He turned once to see where the others were, realized that they were far behind him, but didn't pull up. Instead, he urged the gray to go even faster. Again he shouted, the war cry making his throat raw. It sounded shrill and tiny to his own ears, and for a second he wondered whether the Crows would laugh at him.

He brandished his coup stick overhead, kicking the gray pony again and again, using a leather quirt to wring every last bit of speed from the charging pony. One Crow warrior dismounted. He was armed with a bow, and Slow saw him notch an arrow as he moved away from his mount. Slow closed in on him so fast that he never had time to aim. Reaching out with the coup stick, Slow rapped the Crow on the shoulder and shouted, "This one is mine! I have struck the enemy!" The gray slammed into the dismounted warrior, knocking him backward as the arrow sailed harmlessly away. Everything seemed to be moving in slow motion now. The hum of the bowstring seemed to last forever. The whoosh of air from the Crow's lungs sounded like floodwater at spring thaw.

Slow turned to look over his shoulder and saw other Lakota closing in on the prostrate Crow. The enemy warrior was trying to get to his feet, but three Lakota leaped from their horses in unison, swarmed over the Crow, and battered him senseless with war clubs.

The howling of the Lakota filled the valley, and the rest of the Crows turned their horses and started to run as the Lakota thundered after them. Here and there, the sharp crack of an old rifle punctuated the incessant war cries of the attackers, and clouds of gray-white smoke from the gunpowder drifted just above the tall grass. As Slow turned his pony to follow, he caught its pungent scent in his flared nostrils.

His heart was still pounding heavily, and he looked at his chest for a moment as if expecting the organ to burst through his skin. He patted his chest once with an open palm, then spread his fingers. He could feel his heart hammering, but he wasn't afraid. Not now. He was elated, and he let out another high-pitched whoop.

The Crows never stopped. The momentum of the Lakota was irresistible, and for more than thirty miles, the two groups thundered across the plains. Now and then, the Crows would turn to launch a dozen arrows, fire a few bullets, and shake their fists. The Lakota easily dodged the arrows, fired at such long range, and the marksmanship of the Crows suffered because they were on horseback.

It was late afternoon before the weary Lakota finally allowed their enemies to retreat in peace. They pulled up and watched the Crows vanish over the next ridge, leaving only a cloud of dust to mark their passage.

Slow, soaked with sweat and grinning from ear to ear, was swept from his horse by Sitting Bull, who squeezed him in his arms for a moment, then held him at arm's length. "That was a very foolish

thing to do," he said. Then he smiled. He raised a
hand overhead and cut loose with one final tri-
umphant war cry. The other Lakota warriors gathered around father and son. Sitting Bull
announced, "Today my son, Jumping Badger, has
counted his first coup." He reached up to pull an
eagle feather from his hair and placed it on Slow's
head, tying it in place with strands of his son's
coal-black hair.

Chapter 8 ═══════════

**Yellowstone River Valley
1845**

ALL THE WAY HOME, Slow kept thinking about
what he had accomplished. That Sitting Bull had
scolded him, called him a foolish boy, said he
was reckless and that he could have gotten himself wounded or killed, did little to dampen his
enthusiasm.

He knew he should have been more careful, but
he also knew that Sitting Bull wasn't really angry
with him. His father was proud, and late at night,
he listened while Sitting Bull told the story of his
coup, each time refining it, adjusting the details,
stopping occasionally to listen to the other warriors
add what they had seen. It seemed almost as if
Sitting Bull were practicing for something, trying to
get the story just right, leaving nothing out but
adding nothing that was not true.

During the day, though, nothing had changed.
Slow still had the responsibilities of a boy.

Sometimes, especially when the others were resting and he had to tend to the horses, or stand guard on a distant hilltop with one of the other young men, he would grow resentful. It didn't seem right, somehow, that he should still be treated like a stripling. He was a warrior now, and everyone knew it. Or at least everyone in the war party knew it.

But customs had an imperative of their own, and being the youngest warrior in the war party, he had the duties that went with his status. The weight of hundreds of years of tradition was threatening to squash him flat, squeeze all the joy out of his wonderful achievement. He was almost numb with boredom, his eyes drooping from exhaustion, his joints sore from lack of proper rest.

He consoled himself with the thought that there would be other war parties, and he would not always be the tail of the buffalo. One day—and he knew it wouldn't be long—he would be the horns; he would call warriors to follow him instead of sneaking away from camp like a puppy to follow someone else. He would be the one to light the war pipe, the one to raise it to *Wakantanka*, the first to smoke it. It wasn't much comfort, but for the time being, it was all he had.

By the time the camp's tipis finally came into view, Slow felt as if his arms were made of lead. His whole body seemed too heavy to manage, and he wondered if he would ever again have the strength to climb onto the back of his pony. All he wanted now was to curl up in the buffalo robes and go to sleep. If he slept for a week, that would be all right with him. The entire war party, anxious to see their families, began to push their mounts a little harder now, reaching for one last burst of energy.

There would be a celebration, because they had been successful. They had killed five of the hated Crows, and they had lost none of their own men. They had a few new horses—just a handful—pitiful profit, it seemed, to show for so long and hard a week. But Slow knew that that was the way it went. Sometimes you came home empty-handed. Sometimes, too, someone didn't come home at all. Those were always the worst times, when the families sang death songs until you thought your heart would split open like a gourd.

Slow had heard the terrible wailing of a heartbroken mother more than once in his short life, and it never failed to tear at his gut like sharp claws. At such times, he would bury himself like a baby in the buffalo robes, cover his ears with his palms, and sing to himself—anything to drown out the mournful howl. But it never worked. Always he could hear the sound, even through the flesh and bones covering his ears. Once, not so long ago, the mourners had been his own relatives. His mother's brother had been killed by Pawnee raiders.

This time, at least, he knew he would be able to sleep; all the Lakota warriors were returning safely. When the returning war party reached the edge of the village, people gathered around, the wives and mothers standing on tiptoe, their anxious faces bobbing like corks on a sea of buckskin as they

searched the mounted warriors for a glimpse of
their husbands and sons. The children milled
around the women, jumping up to see a father or a
brother.

The old men were more restrained, standing on
the outer edge of the circle. They had seen enough
of war to know that bad news would find you sooner than you wanted. A man could afford to wait
because he couldn't really hide from it. And after
all, it wasn't as if not knowing changed things for
the dead man. He was still dead, and that was permanent. And what was a few minutes when you
measured it against forever?

For Slow, though, the homecoming was more
complicated. The headlong charge against the
Crows would seem like nothing compared to his
mother's anger. The Lakota never struck their children, but that didn't mean they didn't get angry.
And Her Holy Door would certainly be angry. She
would shriek at him until his ears burned, and then
she would turn her back. The cold shoulder would
freeze him then, and his teeth would chatter as if
he were stranded in a blizzard without a robe to
protect him.

At first, Sitting Bull would try to calm Her Holy
Door down, but sooner or later he would fail. Slow
knew that, too. And then his father would just
stand aside and let the tantrum run its course. He
would tell Slow then that it was better than having
Her Holy Door mad at both of them. For Sitting
Bull, maybe. But for Slow, it would be like having
the weight of the world on his own still slender
shoulders. And for a time, he would feel like an

orphan. For a time, he might even wish he were, because anything would be better than having to endure his mother's wrath. But sooner or later she would forgive him. She would understand, even through all the scolding, that he had done what he was born and bred to do. And when she had given voice to her own anxiety, changing it first into rage and then into complaint, she would hug him. And the thought of her arms around him was almost enough to steel him for the onslaught. Almost, but not quite, because Her Holy Door could be formidable when she was angry, worse than any Crow.

The warriors, as was their custom, started to circle the camp, boasting of their exploits, and the women and children were forced to back away to make room for the horses. Slow, watching from the back of his gray, realized that Sitting Bull had not joined the victory celebration. Instead, he dismounted and lifted Slow from his pony. Slow was sure he was in for it now. Sitting Bull dragged him toward his lodge and hauled him inside. Her Holy Door tried to come in, but Sitting Bull shouted for her to stay outside.

Slow began to stammer that he was sorry, but Sitting Bull waved off the explanation, sweeping him up in a bear hug, nearly crushing his lungs in the process. Then he moved into the shadows at the edge of the tipi and reappeared with a small pot. Without a word, he began to daub black paint all over Slow, starting at his forehead and working his way down until the boy was covered from head to foot in the black paint of victory.

Still saying nothing, Sitting Bull dragged Slow back into the open. Once more lifting the boy in his arms, he clapped him down on the back of a fine bay stallion, Sitting Bull's favorite horse. "He's yours now, son," Sitting Bull said, his voice shaking a bit as he stepped back to examine the young warrior on his new warhorse.

Then, in a loud voice, Sitting Bull called out to the camp at large. The strong voice seemed to echo from the hills behind the camp, and everyone stopped what they were doing and began to move toward Sitting Bull's tipi. Taking the bay by the bridle, Sitting Bull moved toward the center of the camp.

When he reached the middle of the circle of tipis, he raised his voice again. "My son has struck his first enemy!" he announced. "He is no longer to be called Jumping Badger or Slow. Instead, I give him the name *Tatanka Iyotanka*. And from this day forward I will be known as Jumping Bull."

Slow gasped. His father had given up his own name, surrendering it to his son. He was now to be known as Sitting Bull. The boy remembered the story of how his father had come by the name, the visit from the big medicine buffalo, and he felt a lump in his throat. This was no ordinary name. This name was special. Not only had it been his father's, but it had come from *Wakantanka*. It would be a burden as well as an honor to carry such a name. It meant that great things were expected of him . . . perhaps even greater things than those of which he dreamed. And it meant, too, that things would change for his father. Jumping

Bull had been the second name given by the medicine buffalo, representing the second stage of life, and he wondered for a moment whether it meant that his father was moving through some sort of invisible barrier and, if so, whether he had been the cause of it.

His father was not finished yet. He handed the newly christened Sitting Bull a brand-new lance, one that had never been into battle, one that he had fashioned with his own hands. The bright iron blade glittered like a shooting star as it was waved overhead, and when his father finally placed it in his hands, he traced the perfect symmetry of the polished wood with trembling fingers.

Already the warriors were shouting out, telling the rest of the village about his dash against the Crows, how he had struck the enemy with his coup stick, and how he had shown the nerve of a great warrior.

The young Sitting Bull felt his head swimming. The women were crowding in around him now, singing of his triumph, their shrill wailing sending chills down his spine. He spotted Blue Eagle and Little Calf, two of his closest friends, pressing in among the women, trying to get to the front of the circle surrounding him now. The two boys stood there slack-jawed, their eyes big as the full moon. They were in awe of him now, stunned into immobility by the news. Later, they would remind each other that they had known him when, but for the moment, all they could do was gape.

Jumping Bull had slipped away, but Sitting Bull had not noticed. Now his father was back, once more pushing through the crowd and calling attention to another gift. When he reached the side of the big bay, he handed the gift to Sitting Bull without a word.

Sitting Bull stared at it, turning it this way and that to let the light catch the brilliant colors. It was a shield, brand-new, like the lance never used in battle. Like all Lakota shields, it was a circle of wood covered with tough hide. At the four cardinal points, a tuft of eagle feathers fluttered in the hot breeze, one each representing North, East, South, and West. The center of the circle contained an image that had come to his father in a vision. Some said it was a bird, perhaps an eagle, while others said it was a man. Still others argued that it was both—a birdman. But Sitting Bull knew that it had been painted on the thick buffalo hide by a holy man, and that it was powerful medicine. The bright red, dark blue, and deep green paints seemed to glow with an inner fire as they reflected sunlight back into the sky.

Raising the shield high overhead, Sitting Bull uttered a war cry, and unlike the dry squawk of a few days before, this time his voice was full and rich—not as powerful as his father's, but no longer the reedy squeak of a boy. It was a man's voice, and a man's war cry. He nudged the bay into a walk and circled the camp, waving to friends, and reveling in the friendly slaps of the warriors. This would be a day he would never forget.

When he had completed his circuit of the village, he dismounted in front of Jumping Bull and solemnly embraced him, as if meeting him for the

first time. He heard the catch in his father's voice
and patted his shoulder. As he started to back
away, he caught sight of his mother, standing a few
feet behind Jumping Bull. Her face seemed composed of warring halves, one emotion after another
passing across her features. Pride was there, certainly, but fear, too. She knew what this day meant,
knew what might happen to him. She had lost him,
now. The ghostly sorrow of some future day when
he might not come home seemed to suffuse her features for a moment, until her joy at his victory
gained control. She gave him a smile, at first pale
and weak, just a flicker. But when he stepped
around Jumping Bull and wrapped her in his arms,
she beamed with pleasure.

He was no longer her little boy, but had become
what she had always known he could be, and
hoped he would be—a proud Lakota warrior. And
there was no point in trying to pretend that it could
be otherwise. She lay her head on his shoulder and
stroked his back, her sturdy fingers digging into the
flesh along his spine. Her breath was hot and came
in short gasps then she backed away to hold him at
arms length, tears streaking her dark skin. She
sniffed once, chewed her lower lip, then slowly
shook her head up and down.

She approved, he knew that. But it seemed that
she had not until that very moment. "There is a lot
to do," she said. "There will be a victory celebration, and you will be at its center, son. I'd better get
ready." She nodded once, as if the suggestion had
come from him, then turned away. Only then did
she reach up to wipe away the dampness from her

cheeks. A moment later, she vanished into the milling throng, and Sitting Bull turned once more to the admiring well-wishers.

His first victory dance, he thought—that was something to look forward to. He had seen them before, of course, but since he had never struck an enemy in battle, he had not been allowed to participate with the warriors. Tonight, for the first time, he would join them as they danced and told the whole village of his accomplishment. His legs felt like jelly, and he wondered whether they would hold him.

But the warriors swept him away, and he forgot about his concern in the frenzy of the moment.

Chapter 9 ═══════

**Musselshell River
1846**

SLOW HAD NO TROUBLE getting used to his new name. Being called Sitting Bull, the name of his father, was a great honor. This was not just because his father was a great warrior and a holy man, but because the buffalo itself was so important to the Lakota, and it meant that he would one day be important, too, if he was true to the spirit of the buffalo and of the Lakota traditions.

The upright eagle feather he wore in his hair each day reminded him that he had garnered his first coup. The feather's upright position reminded him, and everyone who saw him, that not only had he struck the enemy, he had struck the enemy first.

Only the first four strikes earned a warrior a coup, and each was symbolized by the angle of the feather. Upright meant first coup, while the other three were represented by the feather's direction and deviation from the vertical. He knew that there

would be more coups and more eagle feathers to
come, but the first one is always special. It was a
watershed in a warrior's life, a kind of transition
from boy to man that every Lakota male dreamed of
from the moment he was old enough to understand
the way his people lived.

The newly named Sitting Bull saw his coup
feather every time he bent over a stream to drink,
every time he rode along the edge of the river and
saw his reflection in the shimmering surface of the
current. It was a constant reminder, not just of
what he had done, but of what was expected of
him. He was a warrior now, and that meant that
great responsibilities lay squarely on his shoulders.

It was all well and good to play a boy's game of
hoop and javelin, shoot blunt arrows at birds, run
footraces with the other boys—those had only been
preparation, games intended to teach him what he
needed to know to be a warrior. Now that it had
come to pass, he was able to look back at those
things of his youth and see how much more they
meant than he had realized. Now his life, and the
lives of his family and friends, might be at stake
every time he drew a bow. His skill with the lance
might bring down a buffalo when his family was
hungry, or save the life of a friend on the warpath
against the Crows or the Hohe. And his great speed
might save his own skin one day if his horse were
killed or wounded in battle. Or it might enable him
to come to the aid of a beleaguered or wounded
friend.

Jumping Bull had tried to explain these things to
him ever since he had been old enough to listen.

He had thought he understood, but he had only been fooling himself. Now, though, it had all become clear. It seemed to him that for years he had been looking into a muddy pool, where things moved, barely seen, through the murky water, a glimpse here and a hint there, and because these hints and glimpses were all he saw, he had thought they were all there was to be seen. But he had been patient, as his father had counseled him. He had waited, and now the mud had settled, the water was pure as crystal, and he saw everything so much more clearly.

Jumping Bull understood that his son had changed, had reached an important point in his life. He understood that it was tempting for Sitting Bull to think that he was finished growing, finished learning. The boy had always been inquisitive, and he had treasured those walks in the hills, those long hours watching the birds and the rabbits and the buffalo. He was proud of Sitting Bull, but not so proud that he shared the boy's temptation to think that growing and learning were finished.

Just as his legs would thicken, his shoulders broaden, his arms grow more powerful, so too would Sitting Bull's mind grow more penetrating, his patience deeper, his understanding sharper. That would come in time, as long as he was willing and open to knowledge. Jumping Bull knew that it would be more difficult to teach his son now, but more important than ever. As it was, he would be a fine warrior, but that wasn't enough. There was so much out on the plains, so much in the sky that a man ought to know if he were going to lead his people and keep them safe from harm. And these were things that no man ever learned completely, no matter how long he lived or how closely he studied the world around him. The important thing was not to think you knew it all, but to keep on learning. Jumping Bull wondered whether he was equal to the task of showing his son these truths.

Each time a war party went out against the Crows or the Hohe or the Flatheads and Sitting Bull went along, there was a chance that he would not come back. Jumping Bull knew this, but he did not dwell on it. He could not allow his concern for his son's safety to stifle the boy. If Sitting Bull were going to be a great warrior, he would have to take risks, learn how to handle himself in unimaginable situations, think on his feet, and let his courage protect him. That is not an easy thing for a father to watch. Sometimes when Sitting Bull went on a warpath, Jumping Bull stayed home. It was better, he thought, to let the boy become his own man, rather than a looking-glass reflection of his father.

Also, there was the danger that Sitting Bull might worry more about what his father thought than what the enemy was doing. That was the surest way to get killed. In battle, you had to think only about your adversary. It was fine to take risks to demonstrate your courage. Jumping Bull, like every other Lakota warrior, had done that. Sitting Bull would do it, too. But he had to keep his attention on the enemy, not on his friends or family. If you rode against the Crows while looking over your shoulder to see whether your friends were impressed, they would not be impressed for long.

A year after his first coup, Sitting Bull's band was camped on the Musselshell River, north of the Yellowstone, at the western fringes of Lakota territory. The hunting was good, and the camp was busy. But the presence of the buffalo herds meant that other Indians could be in the area, and the camp leaders, Jumping Bull among them, took care to send scouts in every direction. The best defense against a surprise raid was not to be surprised at all.

Every day, scouts in twos and threes went out, to report on the movements of the buffalo herds and to watch for signs of an enemy presence. In the second week, the scouts came back with the news that unknown Indians were lurking in the area—probably scouts for a larger band nearby. They were watching the Lakota camp, and there was the chance that they had already sent word of their presence back to the main band and now simply wanted to make certain that the Lakota village stayed put.

Jumping Bull dispatched fifteen men to investigate. Sitting Bull went along. They rode up into the hills, where the scouts had seen the spies. When the war party reached the point where the spies had been seen, Sitting Bull dismounted, along with his uncle, Four Horns. Already adept at reading sign, Sitting Bull was anxious to sharpen his skills. He talked to anyone and everyone about interpreting the least evidence, from bent grass to snapped twigs, and Four Horns was one of the best there was at reading sign.

A moccasin print would tell more, maybe even the tribe the spies belonged to, because every tribe had its own technique for constructing footwear. Four Horns found some broken twigs and a patch of grass that had been closely cropped, perhaps by waiting ponies. There were horse apples at the edges of the grazed patch, and they were fresh. Four Horns used a stick to gauge how long they'd been there, inserting it a couple of inches then withdrawing it to assess the moisture, and announced that they were no more than an hour old.

The anxious Hunkpapa looked at the hills around them, as if they already felt eyes on them. Four Horns found some pony tracks, the slightest of impressions in the damp grass and, on a wet patch of earth, a clear print. "That way," he said, pointing to the west. "Flatheads, I think."

The warriors waited for Four Horns and Sitting Bull to remount, then moved off in the direction Four Horns had indicated. They rode cautiously now, not knowing for certain how many of the enemy there were. The signs indicated two ponies, but if they had ridden off to get allies, there was no way to estimate how many there might be.

Up one hill and down the far side, they were able to track the two mounts. Skirting the edge of a creek, Four Horns found where the Flathead ponies had crossed. The Lakota followed, two men making the crossing first to make sure no one was waiting in ambush on the far side of the stream. When they gave the all clear, the rest of the band followed.

It was getting warm, and the dew on the grass was drying quickly. This would make it harder to follow the pony tracks. The Lakota kicked their mounts into a trot. Four Horns was in the lead, keeping one eye on the ground and the other peeled for the enemy. Sitting Bull rode beside his uncle, checking the terrain ahead, looking for possible ambush sites. As they neared a ravine, cutting diagonally across their path, he called his uncle's attention to it.

"That would be a good place to hide and wait for us," he said.

Four Horns nodded. "It would be. But remember, we don't know if they know we are here."

"Shouldn't we prepare for the possibility? Act as if they had seen us? If they were watching the camp, they might have seen us ride out. They may have either run away or gone to get their brothers."

Four Horns thought for a moment, then agreed. "I think maybe we should do as you say." He told the other warriors to move cautiously and stay back from the ravine, just in case. They rode parallel to it for a few hundred yards, watching carefully, looking for some sign that the enemy lay in wait. Anything could give them away—a careless peek, the tip of a feather, a startled bird or rabbit.

If one of the enemy was careless and did not pinch the nostrils of his horse, it might whinny when it scented the Hunkpapa ponies. That is all it would take to give them away. It was up to the Hunkpapa to notice the little things that might take away the advantage of surprise.

Sometimes just moving slowly was all it took, because one of the warriors lying in wait might get impatient and break cover. Four Horns remembered only too well how Sitting Bull had done that very thing against the Crows the year before. His nephew had charged down toward the Crows before they were safely contained in the trap so painstakingly laid. That was not a crime, but was simply the kind of thing that young warriors did because they had not learned patience.

The Lakota sat their mounts for a few minutes, watching the ravine. Suddenly, twenty Flatheads burst up and out of it, charging in a tight group toward the waiting Lakota. There was a slight advantage in numbers for the Flatheads, but four to three were good odds. The Lakota stood their ground, launching a volley of arrows from their bows and balls from their two muskets.

The Flatheads skidded to a halt and spread out in a skirmish line, staying on their ponies for a moment, then, when the line was in place, dismounting. They were quick to fire, and the Lakota were forced to back up a bit.

Sitting Bull announced that he wanted to do the daring line, a gallop from one end of an enemy line to the other, deliberately exposing himself to fire. Four Horns tried to dissuade him. For a moment, he tried to imagine what it would be like to ride back to the village with his nephew's lifeless body draped over his pony. How would he tell Jumping Bull what had happened?

But when Sitting Bull insisted, Four Horns agreed. "Just be careful. Don't get too close."

Sitting Bull might not have even heard the final warning, because he kicked his pony into a spurt of speed to reach one end of the Flathead line, then charged forward to get close enough for the daring line. Without breaking stride, the gray wheeled left, and Four Horns watched as the boy kicked his heels and snapped his leather quirt, the pony seeming to glide over the ground.

The Flatheads took the dare and concentrated their attention on the solitary horse and rider. They had several guns, and Four Horns watched the puffs of smoke blossom from the musket muzzles, then heard the sharp crack of the report. He saw clots of dirt kicked up by the bullets all around the bay's hooves. Arrows arced through the air in what seemed an endless rain, but Sitting Bull dodged them expertly, using the bay's body to protect himself, twisting and turning in the saddle as arrows came close.

At the far end of the line, he was still on the bay and raised his hand triumphantly, riding back toward his uncle at a full gallop. Once more, the Flatheads tried to cut him down, but the increased range made it still more difficult.

Four Horns smiled at him. "I see you were hit," he said.

Sitting Bull looked down at his foot, where fresh blood glistened in the sunlight. "It is a small wound," he said. "I don't even feel it."

"You will later," Four Horns warned.

The young warrior smiled. "I think so, but right now I think we should chase those Flatheads back where they came from."

Four Horns agreed, and the Lakota closed on the Flathead line. The two Lakota with muskets concentrated their attention on the Flathead riflemen, trying to even out the disparity as best they could.

The Flatheads dropped back under the fury of the Lakota assault, slowly edging back toward the ravine. Already, three Lakota had been wounded, and two Flatheads lay in the dirt, their ponies waiting patiently beside the motionless warriors.

Pressing the attack still harder, the Lakota forced the Flatheads back into the ravine. Sitting Bull wanted to charge down after them, but Four Horns called him back. "They have the advantage down there," he said. "We will be easy targets as we try to descend, and they will pick us off one by one. Let them go. They will not be back."

"But . . ."

Four Horns shook his head. "No. Let them go. A warrior has to know when he has fought enough. Besides, you have been wounded. We have to find you a red feather worthy of such bravery."

Chapter 10 ═══════════

**Yellowstone River Valley
1849**

SITTING BULL LAY ON HIGH GROUND. Far below, the
Crow camp was silent. It was a small band, so
small that not even the dogs had been brought
along. Beyond the handful of tipis, a small herd of
horses grazed peacefully. It was near sundown, and
the Crows were already preparing for a night's rest.
A few women sat in a circle, some of them working
on clothing while the others prepared food for the
evening meal.

As near as Sitting Bull could tell, there were no
more than a couple of dozen warriors with the
small band. Their horses numbered around fifty,
and two or three dozen more were picketed outside
the tipis, close at hand in the event the band was
attacked.

The Hunkpapa war party was small, just eighteen men, counting himself, under the leadership of One-Horned Elk. They were slightly

outnumbered, but unlike the Crows they were not encumbered with family and possessions. It ought to be relatively easy to steal some horses, and the chances of serious pursuit were slight. Backing away from the ridge, Sitting Bull could barely suppress his excitement. At eighteen, the warpath was still glamorous, and he raced down the hill to vault onto his horse, anxious to inform the rest of his band that he had found some horses.

He walked his horse for the first half mile, not wanting to risk being overheard. By the time he reached the war party, they had already camped for the night, but Sitting Bull's news seemed to galvanize them. Gray Horse thought they should wait until morning, but Wolf Killer argued that the Crow were probably looking for a buffalo herd and might be likely to move on at first light. It was better, he argued, that they strike now, when the Crows would not be expecting it.

Wolf Killer's view prevailed, and One-Horned Elk nodded his approval. It took less than a half hour to make ready. The warriors were already painted for the warpath, and they went through their ritual preparations quickly, some of them making sure their war charms and medicine bundles were in place, others checking their weapons, invoking the aid of *Wakantanka*, or walking off to be by themselves for a few minutes, perhaps to pray or to reflect on what might happen if they were killed or wounded.

Finally they were all ready. Sitting Bull was mounted on his warhorse, flicking the bridle nervously. He made sure once more that his lariat was coiled carefully, and tucked it more securely into his breechclout. If he were knocked off his horse, the lariat would play out as the horse moved away, giving him a chance to grab the woven rawhide rope and regain control. A man on foot, even one as swift as Sitting Bull, was at a severe disadvantage in combat against a mounted enemy. Often warriors were killed when they were unhorsed and surrounded by a swarm of enemy warriors on horseback.

Satisfied that his lariat was ready, he moved toward One-Horned Elk and waited impatiently beside him.

One-Horned Elk looked at him with a slight smile. "You look like you are not sure you want to go," he teased.

"I want to go," Sitting Bull assured him, trying not to sound too eager. He knew that some warriors were reluctant to ride in battle beside a young man who might panic, or who might be so reckless as to endanger others as well as himself. The Lakota made it a practice to rescue their wounded and retrieve the bodies of their casualties whenever possible. A reckless man might get himself killed or wounded so close to the enemy line that it meant another warrior would have to expose himself to danger in order to try to recover the foolhardy victim.

But One-Horned Elk had ridden beside Jumping Bull for years, and he knew Sitting Bull had been well trained, and that despite his youth, the young man had a good head on his shoulders. Still, it

didn't hurt to tease him a little to help him relax.
Going into battle tense and nervous was like fighting with one hand tied behind your back.

When the other Hunkpapa were ready, One-
Horned Elk gave the sign, telling Sitting Bull to
lead the way since he had found the Crow camp.
They rode at a trot, allowing time for the Crow get
settled for the night. Their plan was to swoop
down on the enemy, drive off their horses, and
make their getaway immediately, leaving the Crow
to flounder around in the dark. There would be
some moonlight, but not enough to be of real bene-
fit to the pursuers.

When they reached the last hill before the Crow
camp, Sitting Bull raised his hand to halt the war
party for last-minute instructions. As usual, the
plan called for the posting of some warriors on the
ridge above the enemy camp, while others moved
down to drive off the horses. Busy with the
rustling, it was not possible to keep an eye on the
sleeping enemy. That job would be handled by the
reserves on the hilltop, who would sound the
alarm in the event of discovery and charge down to
delay pursuit while the horses were driven off.

When One-Horned Elk had chosen those he
wanted to wait on the hill with him, they spread
out in a single line. The others positioned themselves to come in on the Crows from the far side,
where the horses were. The herd would be driven
right through the camp to create confusion and to
pick up some of the mounts picketed outside the
tipis. They would never try this if the Crow camp
was larger, but it seemed like a reasonable risk

and would make the victory stories more colorful. It would also give the raiders a chance to count coup on the befuddled defenders as they came out of their tipis to see what was happening. And if the Crow were ready for a good fight, so much the better.

Sitting Bull went with the assault force. Fanning out, they formed a shallow half circle around the Crow herd and started to push the animals, quietly at first, then with yips and shouts as the horses drew closer to the small group of lodges.

The animals bolted, scattering among the Crow lodges as the sleepy warriors spilled out into the open. Several of them were knocked to the ground as the horses rushed past, the Hunkpapas right behind them. Several of the Lakota leaned over to grab picket ropes staking warhorses to the ground, slashing them with a flick of their knives. The startled ponies rushed after the rest of the Crow herd as soon as they realized they had been cut loose.

Gunfire erupted now as the Crow men started to recover from their surprise. Hearing the gunshots and not able to see clearly what was happening, the Lakota contingent on the hilltop charged down toward the Crow lodges. Sweeping through the tiny camp, they gave vent to war cries and fired arrows in every direction, taking care only to avoid their comrades.

Several of the Crows were knocked to the ground by the new assault, and three of them were killed outright. The rest of the warriors scattered, women and children running after them into the darkness toward the river. On a return sweep, the

Lakota stopped long enough to count coup on the three fallen Crows and to take trophies. Two scalps were taken, a hand was severed, and in the ultimate indignity, the genitals of one naked Crow were carted off. One of the Hunkpapa, in a grandstand play, charged toward the retreating Crows and snatched up a woman, catching her just before she was about to plunge into the river. The warrior draped her, kicking and screaming, across his pony and rode off into the dark.

The Crow were too scattered now to mount an effective counterattack, and several of their best war ponies had been driven off with the rest of the herd, so the Hunkpapa knew they were safe from pursuit. Only a foolhardy Crow would dare chase a heavily armed band of Lakota in Lakota territory, and even then, not until sunrise. By then, the Hunkpapa planned to be miles away from the Crow camp.

After an hour of hard riding, they stopped just long enough to rest the horses. The woman was then bound hand and foot and secured to one of the stolen ponies. Her captor, Short Elk, rigged a lariat around the pony's neck and looped it around his left hand for the rest of the ride.

The next day they posted sentries and rested for a few hours, letting the captured horses graze and watering their own mounts before turning them out to join the others. It was still a long way to the Hunkpapa village, and they wanted to make the rest of the trip in one leg. Sitting Bull watched the woman, who seemed to have gotten used to the idea of her captivity. She made no trouble and was not molested by any of the warriors. It was Lakota custom to either adopt captives into the tribe or release them in exchange for ransom. Sitting Bull presumed that Short Elk would take the woman into his lodge, since his current wife was well along in her third pregnancy and he had had no luck finding another Lakota woman who would have him.

Late the next afternoon, the shrieking members of the victorious war party rode into camp, circling among the lodges and boasting of their accomplishments. The stolen horses were parceled out among family and friends, after the warriors had picked one or two apiece to keep for themselves. The trophies were put on display and caused a sensation, especially so the severed genitals. These were subjected to disparaging evaluation by the older women, causing the younger women to titter among themselves.

The boys too young to have been on war parties of their own seemed especially interested in the scalps, and they approached with some trepidation, prepared to run should the absent Crow owners suddenly materialize under the disheveled and bloody hair.

Sitting Bull, as was the custom, had sung his own praises, then retired from center stage to let the more experienced warriors have the spotlight. During the animated retelling of events, one of the young women noticed the Crow prisoner and started to whisper to a neighbor in the crowd. Before long, ripples of conversation had spread, and it began to look as if the women were more interested in the Crow woman than in the achievements of their own men.

Sitting Bull was curious and watched the phenomenon with some bafflement. He moved closer, intending to ask what was going on, but before he had a chance the women broke away from the crowd and rushed toward the Crow prisoner. They knocked Short Elk aside and swept the Crow woman from her pony, dragging her toward the edge of the village.

Sitting Bull could no longer restrain himself and moved into the crowd. He was surrounded by other warriors, most of whom wore the same baffled expression. Short Elk was jumping up and down, trying to make himself heard. He was aptly named, being no taller than most of the women, so he was having some difficulty getting their attention.

"What's happening?" Sitting Bull asked One-Horned Elk.

"They say they know the Crow woman. They say she is loose, that she has no morals."

"How do they know that?"

"Blue Eagle Woman told them. Remember two years ago she was taken by the Crows? They held her for nearly a month before we were able to get her back. She says the Crow woman went from lodge to lodge, sleeping with every Crow who would have her. The women think she will do the same thing here, if Short Elk is allowed to keep her."

"But what business is it of theirs? If Short Elk wants to keep her, it is up to him."

"They won't give him the chance," One-Horned Elk said. "Watch."

The woman was swept away now, beyond the edge of the camp. The chattering Hunkpapa women dragged her by the hair, kicking and clawing at their legs as she tried to break free. Near the river, they hauled her upright and proceeded to lash the prisoner to a cottonwood.

The women fanned out then and disappeared into the brush along the riverbank. They reappeared with their arms full of dry branches. Sitting Bull couldn't figure out what they were intending to do until one of them ran back to the camp, returning with a burning brand. Now he knew they were planning to burn her alive.

Chewing on his lower lip, he tried to decide what he should do. It was not his right to interfere. Lakota society didn't work that way, and anyway, he was too young for anyone to pay attention to. If he had been older, with more coups, more authority, perhaps he could have reasoned with them. But he knew he didn't have enough of either, so he didn't try.

Instead, he paced back and forth, more and more upset at what was about to happen. The Crow woman seemed to understand now, too, and she started screaming insults at the Lakota women, spitting at any of them who came within range. The woman with the brand waited nearby while her allies yelled insults. Once, she feinted with the torch, sweeping it in under the Crow woman's nose and singeing her hair in the process. The stink of burning hair reached all the way to where Sitting

Bull was standing, and it nearly turned his stomach. He had killed his share of Crows, but that was in battle. That was different somehow. This wasn't right. He knew it, but didn't know how to prevent it from happening. Once, he thought to cry out to the women to stop, but his voice caught in his throat.

He continued to pace as he saw the torch tossed on the heap of bone-dry branches. The flames jumped and sparks drifted upward on the current of heated air. The Crow woman screamed as the flames began to lick at her legs. The smell of singed buckskin filled the air as the fire started to burn her dress.

Sitting Bull could stand it no longer. He took his bow from his shoulder and fitted an arrow to the string. Without a second's hesitation, he drew the bow full, until the arrowhead nicked his knuckle, and let it fly. He was noted for his marksmanship, and his skill served him and the Crow woman well. The arrow pierced her heart, killing her instantly.

The women fell silent, turning to see where the arrow had come from. Sitting Bull stared at them, daring them to say something, but the women, cowed and ashamed now, could not look at him, They stared at the ground and one by one slunk away. The flames climbed higher as Sitting Bull turned his back and walked up into the hills. He had to get away, to be alone, to think about what he had witnessed, to try to understand it. But he knew he could not.

Chapter 11 ═══════════

**Yellowstone River Valley
1851**

SITTING BULL WAS GAINING greater prominence almost daily. Every time a war party went against the Crows or the Assiniboin or the Arikara, he went along. And there was hardly a time when he came back without another coup.

His prominence as a warrior was now matched by his increasing reputation as a composer and singer of songs. His studies with Four Horns and Black Moon continued to deepen his awareness of the great mysteries that surrounded the Lakota on every side.

If anything, as a young warrior of twenty he was even more fascinated by nature and its complexities than he had been as a boy of five. He never missed an opportunity to watch the world around him. Nothing escaped his attention—not a single leaf floating on a current of air, not an ant stumbling its lonely way through the grass, not the solitary howl of a wolf at midnight. The more he knew, the more he wanted to learn.

His insatiable curiosity left him little spare time. And there were occasions when it seemed that he was every bit as much the object of curiosity for others as the world was for him. As a renowned warrior, he was considered a good catch by the young Hunkpapa women of marriageable age. As a member of an influential family that included chiefs and holy men as well as great warriors, his desirability was considerably enhanced. Everyone knew that he was destined for great things. He was famous throughout the Lakota nation for being the fastest runner anyone had ever seen, and he never missed an opportunity to demonstrate his great speed . . . especially when someone was willing to bet a horse or a buffalo robe.

And those footraces, in which only Crawler could come close to catching him, were run under the admiring gaze of the young women of the village. More than once, after leaving an opponent in the dust, he would stand at the finish line with the young women gathered around, congratulating him.

As busy as he was, he had not failed to notice that one young woman seemed more than fleetingly interested in him, and he was flattered by her attention. Light Hair was considered a real prize, and more than one suitor for her hand had been sent packing. It was not that the marriage gifts the warriors offered were insufficient, either. No amount of bartering between the would-be husband and her family made any difference. Light Hair knew what she wanted, and what she wanted was Sitting Bull.

He was beginning to think that maybe he wanted Light Hair, too. Like the other young men, he would occasionally wrap himself in a blanket, leaving little but his eyes exposed, and pull a prospect under the blanket for a few minutes of conversation. Light Hair knew that he was special and hoped that he would realize that she was his for the asking. But she was not going to compromise her reputation to win him, either. Lakota courting customs were clearly defined, and one flouted them at great risk. As the daughter of a chief, Light Hair was not prepared to take that risk, because it was not just her own reputation that would be tarnished, but that of her family as well.

She had been watching Sitting Bull for more than six months before he finally invited her under his blanket. They stood there talking quietly, Sitting Bull clearly nervous and not saying much. She didn't want to seem pushy, but neither did she want to waste an opportunity that, for all she knew, might not come again any time soon.

"Maybe we could take a walk," she suggested.

Sitting Bull seemed baffled by the suggestion. "A walk? Why?"

"Maybe your tongue will loosen if there are not so many people watching us so closely," she said.

Sitting Bull conceded the truth of her observation with an embarrassed smile. "I can sing better than I can speak," he explained.

"I never noticed," she said. "You didn't seem to

have any trouble talking to Pretty Door a few days ago."

"She is easy to talk to."

Light Hair bristled. "And I'm not?" she demanded, making as if to pull the blanket aside and leave him standing there.

"No, no, I don't mean that you're not easy to talk to. I just meant that . . ."

"Well, what *did* you mean?" She had the hook set now, and she was not about to cut him loose easily. He would have to fight to spit it out.

"I, uh . . . I just meant that it's easy to talk when it doesn't matter."

"Is that supposed to mean that talking to me matters more? Or does it mean that the less it matters, the less you say?"

Once more, Sitting Bull squirmed uncomfortably. It was not going nearly as well as he had hoped. And Light Hair was not doing anything to make it easier for him.

She tapped him on the chest. "You are such a fast runner, but right now you don't seem fast at all. You seem like you have turned to stone."

Sitting Bull just bobbed his head. This woman was worse than any Crow war party. She made him feel like a five-year-old again. And for a moment, he wished he were. It was a lot easier to get a girl's attention by chasing her with a dead fish or pulling on her braid than it was to be standing there alone together, the whole world shut out by the blanket.

Light Hair was beginning to think that she had pushed him too hard, and decided to make it up to him. "I was just playing," she said. "Trying to make you less sure of yourself."

"You managed that quite well," Sitting Bull acknowledged.

"Maybe we will do this again, when you have more to say," she suggested.

Again, all he could do was nod his head. When she pulled away from the blanket, it was left dangling from one shoulder, and he felt suddenly naked. He saw that the other courting couples were watching him, and he turned away, wrapping the blanket around himself again, and stalked off to Jumping Bull's lodge where no one could see how flustered he was.

When he went inside, Her Holy Door glanced up, then went back to her quillwork. But she was not going to let the opportunity to instruct him pass unremarked. "You should have done that a long time ago," she said.

He looked at his mother curiously. "Done what, made a fool of myself in front of the whole village?"

"You didn't make a fool of yourself—or no more so than anyone else, anyway. Your father was no more accomplished at courting than you seem to be, but we managed to find each other. If Light Hair is meant for you, it will work out. At least now she knows you are interested."

Sitting Bull walked over to sit beside his mother. "You think so?" he asked.

She nodded. "I know so."

"Do you think she is a good match for me?"

"That is not for me to decide."

"But what do you think?"

"I think she comes from a good family. She is pretty, she is strong, and she will keep you in line. From where I sit, you could do a lot worse than Light Hair."

"Then I will have her."

His mother laughed. "It is not that easy. The question is not whether you will have her, but whether she will have you. She knows what she wants, and if she wants you, *then* you will have her. You are not the only young man in the village who has an eye on her."

"Who else?" he asked, sitting a little taller. "Who else?"

Her Holy Door shrugged. "I don't know all their names. But if you want her, you had better let her know it . . . and soon. She won't wait forever for you to find your nerve."

Sitting Bull took the warning to heart, and six weeks later he and Light Hair were married. To celebrate the wedding, they went off alone on a hunting trip. It was a strange experience for Sitting Bull. He had spent twenty years in Jumping Bull's lodge. He had hunted for his family and for those in the village who could not provide for themselves. Now he was standing on another threshold. He had taken the step, but realized it was going to be a while before he understood its full implications.

Getting away by themselves was a good way to begin. He had his own lodge now, with Light Hair there to share it with him. Someday there would be children, and he could do for them what Jumping

Bull had done for him. His new life was going to take some getting used to.

On the second day away from the main village, they encountered a small herd of buffalo, and Sitting Bull brought two down. He and Light Hair butchered the animals together, and it seemed like a perfect beginning to what they both hoped would be a lasting thing. Jumping Bull and Her Holy Door had been together for more winters than Sitting Bull had been alive, and the match seemed ideal. He could only hope that his own would be as successful.

Two days later, while moving their lodge, they spooked some deer, and Sitting Bull again turned hunter, dropping a big buck this time. Once more they butchered their kill, and it was obvious they were already beginning to work well together. Sitting there on a hill that night overlooking their lodge, they talked about what it would be like to grow old together. Sitting Bull was finding it harder to ignore the reality of age now that Jumping Bull and Four Horns were getting on in years.

As a young man you took your elders for granted in some ways. It wasn't that you didn't respect them for what they had accomplished or what they knew. Lakota culture was based on reverence for the old, for their contributions in the past, and their ability to continue to contribute in the future. If you thought about it all, and as the descendent of holy men and medicine men Sitting Bull thought about it more than most, you realized that your elders had made everything possible. It wasn't a long leap from there to understanding that by fulfilling your responsibilities now, you were continuing that tradition, making it possible for those who would come after you to experience the same things you had experienced.

But there was another way in which you never thought of the old as anything but old. It was as if they had always been there, the wrinkled skin never smooth, the gray hair never blue-black, shining in the sunlight, the flesh on the arms thick with muscle, corded with tendon, instead of slack and soft, the way it looked now. It was hard to think that the same thing would happen to your own body, assuming you lived long enough for aging to take its normal course.

It was easier sometimes not to think about such things. It was easier to lie back in the grass, knowing that your lodge was warm and dry, that you had food, and that everything you needed was out there, if only you had the strength to get it.

Wrapping his arms around Light Hair, he tried not to think at all. It was better to savor the moment, thinking only about the two of them, being young forever and then one day simply vanishing from the face of the earth. There would be no slack skin, gray hair, or aching joints. They would be there one day and gone the next.

They watched the stars and whispered, enjoying the smell of the flowers surrounding them in the dark and the scent of crushed grass beneath them. High above, the stars were cold white points against a blue-black sky, you knew there were things you did not understand and could not control. But as long as they stayed where they were and you stayed where you were, it didn't matter.

They slept on the hill that night, not intending to, just dozing off peacefully in each other's arms.

The next day they moved their lodge again. It was already beginning to be old hat, as if it were a thing they had always done, but somehow it was exciting and new, too.

That evening, camped along a creek, the lodge up against some cottonwoods, Light Hair made some broth from the deer. She used a horn spoon to skim some of the fat from the boiling liquid. Sitting Bull was sitting across from her, watching everything she did as if it were something no one had ever done before. He saw her freeze and he tensed, instinctively realizing that something was wrong.

Reflected in the slick grease in the spoon, Light Hair could see a cottonwood limb through the smoke hole at the top of the lodge. In the center was the face of a Crow warrior, staring down at her. She whispered to Sitting Bull, "Don't look up, don't even move."

Without waiting for an explanation, he reached for his bow and quiver, sliding an arrow out with his fingertips.

"What is it?" he whispered.

"There is a Crow looking down at us from the top of the lodge." He started to move, but she hissed, "Stay there; don't let on that we know he's there."

Sitting Bull notched the arrow and in one swift movement drew it full and let it fly through the smoke hole. They heard a thud and Sitting Bull ran for the entrance, already notching a second arrow.

Outside, on the grass under the trees, he found smears of blood. He knew he'd hit the Crow, but did not know how badly. Nor did he know whether the Crow was alone or had been scouting for a larger party.

They broke the lodge down and packed hurriedly, deciding that it would be best to return to the main village. If there were Crows in the area, they could not afford to be out alone.

As they headed home, Light Hair complained that their time alone had been too short, but Sitting Bull reached over to pat her on the thigh. "We have all the time in the world, winter after winter, stretching out ahead of us until we are both too old to remember this time."

Chapter 12

**Little Missouri River
1856**

IT WAS JUNE, THE TIME THE LAKOTA called the moon of the chokecherries, and Sitting Bull was coming to the end of a long preparation. He had wanted for as long as he could remember to become *wichasa wakan*, a holy man, like his father and his uncle Four Horns. But this was not a thing one willed. It took long preparation, intensive study with one who already was *wichasa wakan*, and dedication. He had prepared, studying with his father and his uncle and with Black Moon, and he was ready.

But there was one final step to be taken. One could not become a holy man without having danced the sun dance, and this too took preparation. In the fall of 1855, he had told Black Moon that he wanted to dance at the next sun dance, and the holy man had nodded. "It is time," he agreed. So once more Sitting Bull had begun to prepare himself for an ordeal that was a centerpiece of the Lakota religion.

Sitting Bull had undergone his vision quest, which was personal, but the sun dance was larger than any one warrior. It was tribal, in a way doing for the whole people what the vision quest accomplished for the individual. Only courageous warriors danced, and even some of them were not equal to the excruciating ordeal—especially if they chose one of the four most difficult dances of the six forms. Sitting Bull, as was his wont, intended to dance the most challenging of all.

When they camped on the Little Missouri in early June, the preparation began in earnest. This was a special time, a time when things were not as they usually were. As a *heyoka*, Sitting Bull was used to things being strange. After all, the *heyoka* sometimes did things backwards, crying when they were happy, laughing when they were sad. And to be *heyoka*, you were already marked as someone special. Only one who had had a vision of the thunderbird could become *heyoka*, and this Sitting Bull had done.

Now he was ready for the most demanding challenge he had yet faced. The sun dance was complicated, and the rules were rigid. As the most important and sacred ritual in Lakota religion, it was the most narrowly circumscribed and carefully observed. No one dared to change anything, or deviate in any way from the prescribed rules.

The first four days of the sun dance were given over to general celebration. Even though dancers might be dancing for personal reasons—

in fulfillment of a vow, in a request for something only the gods could deliver, perhaps in thanks for a favor granted or supplication for a life spared—the celebration was general. More than any other single aspect of Lakota life, even the buffalo hunt, it united all the people in one single undertaking. After the four days of celebration, those designated for the dance were separated from the rest of the people for more instruction. They stayed in a sacred lodge with the shamans who had been instructing them. One holy man had overall responsibility for the entire dance and the twelve days of ritual, and in 1856, the honor fell to Black Moon.

When the dancers had been given their last-minute instructions, once more isolated themselves for a vision, and purified themselves in the sweat lodge, they were ready.

A hunter was dispatched to look for the centerpiece, a forked cottonwood tree that would represent an enemy at first and then, for a period of four days, would be the very center of the Lakota universe. The tree had to conform to precise specifications. Once it was found it was marked, and only chaste women were allowed to participate in its felling. It was a special honor to be chosen as the one to deliver the last few blows of the ax, the ones that actually brought the cottonwood down.

Then part of the bark was peeled back, baring the wood to a point just below the fork. Some of the branches were stripped and the fallen tree was carried to the center of the dance lodge, which was not like other lodges. The warriors who carried it

used sticks, because only shamans were allowed to
touch so sacred a thing. The tree was painted four
different colors—red, blue, green, and yellow—representing each of the four winds—west, north, east,
and south. Medicine bundles containing tobacco,
an arrow for successful hunting, and other items of
significance were attached, and the pole was
tipped into a hole already prepared for it and
raised upright.

Also attached to it were thick thongs which
would be used in the dance. For the form Sitting
Bull had chosen, four pairs of parallel incisions
had to be made, two each in his chest and back,
and wooden skewers inserted under the flaps of
skin and muscle. Thongs were then attached to the
skewers. Another part of the sacrifice in Sitting
Bull's chosen form was the offering of pieces of
flesh. To make this offering, an awl was used to
raise small bits of flesh, which were then severed
with a sharp knife. Men could offer anywhere from
twenty to two hundred pieces, and Sitting Bull
chose one hundred to be taken from his arms.

As the incisions were made and the pieces of
flesh sliced away, the blood that continually
seeped from the ritual wounds was wiped away
with sweet grass. When he was finally prepared,
the next step was to hang suspended from the
thongs, which were weighted on the other end
by buffalo skulls. As he dangled there, staring at
the sun through the open roof of the lodge, he
continued to bleed.

Again and again, he cried out in supplication to
the unseen. "Give good health to my people. Bring

the buffalo to feed my people." Endless variations on the same theme, a prayer uttered over and over. Hanging there suspended, the skewers tearing at the muscle, he heard words from his past, saw things that he had forgotten.

He remembered the time the yellowhammer had awakened him from a careless nap to find a grizzly bear standing over him. He remembered how he had frozen, lying there as if dead, his eyes open, staring up at the huge bear, its claws dangling over him. Even now he could smell the stink of the bear and feel the drip of saliva from its gaping jaws. His memory of the bear's breathing beat like a drum in his ears, mingling with the drums from the ceremonial musicians, a steady pulse that seemed to reach back in time beyond him, beyond Jumping Bull, beyond his grandfather—reaching back all the way to the time when the first Lakota stood alone on a hilltop looking out over the sacred land of the Paha Sapa.

It was a rhythm older than life, more insistent than a beating heart. He felt his own heart hammer against his chest. The sun seemed to grow larger and larger, as if it were descending on the lodge, threatening to incinerate him. The whole sky turned brilliant yellow, then white as the blue was swallowed by the expanding sun. He felt the trickle of blood over his chest and back, smelled the sweetness of it mingling with the salty sourness of the sweat that soaked his hair and ran into the cuts, stinging like a thousand bees.

He was a boy again, chasing the buffalo for the first time. The pounding drums, the beating of his blood, became the thunder of a thousand hooves. He could see the calf he had killed on his first hunt, watched as it turned, saw it look at him, and saw the sun reflected in the calf's eye. This time it was the eye that grew large, and then the sun within it, and once more whiteness swallowed the world, leaving him in a blank, empty space where there was nothing but his pain to fill it.

He spun then like a top . . . or perhaps it was the world spinning around him. His feet, legs, and abdomen seemed to have disappeared, his body ending at the incisions in his chest. There was only the sun and the pain until, as if by a miracle, just when he thought he could stand it no longer, his feet touched the ground and he felt arms surround him. He breathed in and out, each deep inhalation sending stabs of pain though his chest and back. Slowly his vision returned. He was lowered to the sage leaves in the shade, and for a while he could rest, until it was time to be suspended once more. Closing his eyes, he felt a serenity wash over him. Away from the searing heat for a few moments, he was able to see clearly, to think clearly, to consider what he had seen in his visions. They were *wakan* and he would talk them over with Black Moon or Four Horns, with someone who would help him to understand what they meant.

Then it was time to resume. Once more he was suspended, and once more the sun became his universe. This time, the whiteness contained a point of color, far off across the universe, and he stared at it, watching it grow slowly larger, as if something were moving slowly, deliberately toward him from the other side of the world.

He beckoned to it, crying out, begging it to approach him, but before it reached him, it winked out, like a closing eye, and the whiteness was total once more. He had a vision of a buffalo, the largest buffalo anyone had ever seen, and the animal spoke to him, calling him by his first name. "Jumping Badger," it said. "Jumping Badger."

He wanted to ask the buffalo questions, remembering the visitation of the medicine buffalo to his father. He wanted to know, he wanted to understand, he wanted to ask a thousand questions, but the buffalo simply repeated his name over and over again, then turned and walked into the sun, its great shadow swirling like water in a pool, surrounding it, then swallowing it up and shrinking away to the size of bead and then vanishing altogether.

Again the salt trickled into his wounds and the skewers tore at his flesh, and once more he was lowered to the ground for a rest.

When he was hauled into the air again, the music was faster, the drums beating louder, and he counted the drumbeats one by one, then two by two, then three by three as the rhythm changed, the drummers adding accents, grouping their beats in clusters. It seemed to him then that his heart echoed the drumming, skipping beats where there was silence, pounding harder where the drummers struck the skin covers of their instruments with extra force. Smoke seemed to well up out of the earth now, surrounding him in its foggy pall.

Where there had been nothing but the infinite expanse of white, as if he walked on the surface of the sun itself, tiny as a bug, alone, now there was a world of gray. Shapes appeared in the misty distance like shadows.

The fog rippled and swirled, tantalizing him as it seemed about to dissipate, revealing the things that moved in its deepest heart, then rushing toward him in great banks, like fog off the river in cold weather, taking the secrets away and leaving him empty, a great, yearning void in his mind, a place where he sensed something was missing, something *Wakantanka* wanted him to know, but would not tell him—something he had to discover for himself.

He tilted his head back, stretching until he thought his spine would snap like a brittle stick, and opened his mouth. He felt a great rush go out of him, thought that he had screamed, but he heard nothing.

Then the fog began to twist like a great funnel, swirling, turning darker and darker, until it became a tornado. Far off in the distance he heard an incessant roar that became a howl, then seemed to whistle. It came toward him, then backed off, as if it were alive, and uncertain of him. He could hear the drums only distantly now, the great roaring coming back like sudden thunder.

His lips were dry, his throat parched. He rubbed the tip of his tongue against the dry skin, tasting the salt caked on his chin. He watched the swirling darkness now and once more it was full of shadows, things that moved, that shimmered as if they

were made of water, changing shape likes trees on
the horizon in summer heat. He reached out as if to
touch them, but the movement of his arm sent
knifelike pain through his chest and back, and he
howled in agony as his arm fell limply to his side.
He was spinning now, or thought he was, twirling
like the dark apparitions before him, but no matter
how fast he whirled, the shimmering black thing
was always in front of him, as if the universe itself
were spinning, and he with it.

For a moment it was silent. Even the drums in
the lodge seemed to have quieted. Then a whisper,
like wind far off, hissing as if through brittle leaves,
and he heard a flute, the drums began again, the
flute soaring above them, its solitary wail echoing
in his ears as if he and it were in some dark cave
full of swirling murk. The whisper grew louder
again, like the howling of a tornado, it rose in
pitch, coming closer and closer, but nothing he saw
seemed to change. It was as if something he could
not see was bearing down on him, faster and faster,
coming closer, and he wanted to see, tried to force
his eyes to show him this thing that would not be
seen. And then a voice, deep and resonant, called
him by name as the buffalo had. But this time he
was called Sitting Bull. He felt the world trembling
with the power of the great voice.

He cried out again, his own voice frail and tiny
beside the deep thunder of the thing he could not
see. Again and again he called out, until his throat
grew raw, and finally the thunder spoke to him
again, "*Wakantanka* will give you what you ask
for. *Wakantanka* will grant your wish."

He tried again to raise his arm, to reach out to the heart of the darkness that surrounded him, but he could not. He cried out again, but the thunder had gone. His own voice died away, tiny, feeble, like the sound of a pebble falling off a cliff. Silence surrounded him. He felt a fire in his chest as one of the skewers in his flesh tore free.

The added weight ripped the other skewer in his chest loose, and he felt a snap as his weight shifted and he tilted forward. The strain of his weight was too much for the skewers in his back and they ripped free too. As he fell, it seemed to him that he would never land, as if he were falling through a tunnel with no bottom, where there was no light. He was spinning faster and faster, his head and feet twirling like the seed of a maple tree spiraling in the wind. His world went black.

Chapter 13

Missouri River Valley
1856

THE TRICKLE OF WHITES into Indian territory that began in the 1840s was now threatening to become a flood. The Hunkpapas stayed as far to the north as they could, trying to limit their contact with the white settlers. Keeping to themselves, they wanted only to live as they had always lived. But that was becoming harder and harder to do.

The buffalo herds were thinning because the white hunters were slaughtering them for their skins, leaving the carcasses to rot in the sun. The Lakota depended on the herds, deriving most of their sustenance from the great beasts. The meat was their main source of food, the hides were used for making the walls of their tipis and for robes, the horns were used in ceremonial headdresses—even the bones found use.

More and more often, especially to the south, hunting parties would ride for days and days with-

out finding a herd. As often as not, they would ride
into a valley only to find it covered with bones,
picked clean by scavengers, the huge rib cages
empty of everything but the weeds growing up
through them.

Worse than finding the bones was stumbling
on a recent kill, the meat rotting in the sun, filling a valley with its stink. The putrescent carcasses gleamed in the sun under a skin of
writhing maggots. Buzzards hopped from carcass
to carcass, their great wings fanning the air, ugly
naked heads bobbing as they tore at the rotting
meat with beak and talon. Interrupted, the huge
birds would squawk and beat the air to chase off
intruders.

Because they were the furthest north of the
Lakota groups, the Hunkpapa were the most insulated from the white incursions. They heard about
them from the Oglala, whose hunting grounds were
directly in the path of the white settlers. But wiser
heads among the Hunkpapas were concerned about
other intruders. The United States Army had been
building forts all across Lakota land. There had
been a great council at one of the forts in 1851.
Many of the Lakota chiefs had been present and
some had even touched pen to treaty paper, but no
Hunkpapa had signed. Still, to those chiefs who
thought about it, the presence of the white soldiers
could only mean trouble.

The white soldier chiefs and the commissioners had said the forts were necessary, because
the army was there to protect the white settlers
from the Indians, and the Indians from the white

settlers. But no one among the Lakota could remember a time in the five winters since the treaty paper was signed at Fort Laramie that the soldiers had punished a white man for anything. There were plenty of times when Indians had been punished for things they had not done. It seemed that the treaty worked only one way, and the Hunkpapas were glad they had not signed. Many among them were beginning to think that, whether they had signed or not, they had been compromised by the treaty.

News traveled slowly among the plains Indians. A band of hunters from the Brule would come across a band from the Miniconjou and they would exchange information. When the Miniconjou hunters encountered an Oglala war party, they would pass on what they had learned from the Brule, and learn something new from the Oglala. So word traveled, but slowly, like water seeping through sand. If the news was important, someone would ride from one village to another to pass along the information. It was only at the great summer gatherings for the sun dance that most of the Lakota were in one place. And even then, some bands did not make an appearance.

The council of the Hunkpapas, led by the chiefs Four Horns and Bear's Rib, wanted nothing to do with the white men, settlers or soldiers. They wanted only to be left alone. But some of the Hunkpapas knew that was not to be, Sitting Bull among them. He hoped he was wrong. It was better to ignore the whites whenever possible, saving your worries for the Crows and the Arikara and the Pawnee. The white men claimed they were only interested in a safe route to the great ocean to the west, and as long as they just passed through, it might be possible to get along peacefully.

Even that slim hope didn't last long. It was only the year before that a white officer named Grattan had attacked a peaceful village and killed many people in an argument over an emaciated cow. Everyone knew that the cow was worthless, but that didn't seem to matter to Grattan, and when a Brule chief named Conquering Bear had refused to surrender a Miniconjou warrior for the theft of the cow, Grattan had attacked the camp. He didn't seem to understand that Conquering Bear had no authority to surrender a man who did not want to be surrendered. Not only was the warrior a member of a different band, but no Lakota chief had that kind of authority, even over warriors in his own band. Lakota warriors made up their own minds, went where they wanted to go and did what they wanted to do.

Grattan had paid a high price for his ignorance. He and his entire command of thirty men had been killed in the fight. Then the white men started to call it a massacre and sent more soldiers to punish the Lakota, who had done nothing more than defend themselves from an unprovoked attack. General Harney was sent to punish the Lakota for defending themselves, and this time it *was* a massacre, with more than a hundred peaceful Brule Lakota killed—most of them women and children.

To some of the Hunkpapas, all of that seemed a long way away, but Sitting Bull knew better. Just twenty-five years old, he had wisdom beyond his years. He understood that the white men were not going to go away, that if anything went away it would be the buffalo. For the time being, though, there didn't seem to be anything that could be done about it. It was best to pursue the old ways, until *Wakantanka* showed the Lakota what to do. White Buffalo Woman had come to them once before; perhaps she would come again, this time bearing the key to a puzzle that most Lakota warriors dismissed as a petty annoyance.

But the problem was never very far from Sitting Bull's mind. When he hunted, there was plenty of time to think, and even on the warpath, there were moments when he found himself thinking of the white man instead of the Crows. But life had to go on, and he did his best to concentrate on those things he could control.

In the fall of 1856, after the summer hunt, it was apparent that the Hunkpapa needed more horses, and there was only one place to get them—from the Crows. A war party of nearly a hundred warriors assembled and headed west, along the Yellowstone River, into the heart of Crow country.

For five days, they sent scouts out in every direction, hoping to spot a Crow village. And for five days, the scouts came back disappointed. The country was so vast that it sometimes took as much luck as skill to find the enemy. The Lakota could follow a trail as well as anyone on the plains, but before you could follow it, you had to find it.

Like most of the plains tribes, the Crow established their villages in river bottoms, where there would be plenty of water for drinking, cooking, bathing, and the livestock. The Yellowstone wound through hills and mountains, like a snake in its death throes, and the Hunkpapas' patience was wearing thin as they followed its riverbank. On the morning of the sixth day, the war party turned to a medicine man for counsel, and after communing with the spirits, he announced that they would find a Crow village within one day.

With renewed hope, the leaders of the war party sent out scouts for the sixth time. The rest of the raiding party continued in a leisurely way along the river, waiting for the scouts to return. It was late in the afternoon before the scouts appeared on the crest of a ridge off to the left and waved their bows excitedly overhead before charging downhill with their news. They had found a village not far away, and the excited warriors began to prepare for the attack.

It was well after sundown before all the men had painted themselves and their war ponies and assembled their weapons. Many of the warriors had medicine rituals they had to perform before each battle, and this delayed their departure still further.

The ride to the Crow village took nearly three hours, and the final approach had to be cautious. There would be sentries posted, particularly around the large herd of horses, and the dogs that were a fixture of every village might give them away before they got close.

Sitting Bull was one of the planners of the raid, and once the layout of the village became apparent, it was decided to try to cut the Crow herd in half and move off without a battle, if possible. They had come for horses, not blood, and if they could get away without having to loose an arrow, that would make the raid all the more successful.

It was delicate work, moving in and out among the horses. Now and then, the bark of a dog would cause the Hunkpapas to freeze in their tracks, and every man gripped his bow or rifle a little more tightly, holding his breath, hoping they had not been discovered. After an hour, the herd had been cut in two, and the most difficult part was about to begin.

Sitting Bull posted a handful of men between the village and the stolen horses who would give the alarm in the event of discovery. The rest of the warriors nudged the horses into motion. It was tricky getting them to move without stampeding. The thunder of hooves would have awakened the village, but if they were too careful, the escape would take until well past sunrise, when discovery would be inevitable.

Wisely, twenty-five or thirty of the warriors had been left behind, lining the ridge above and behind the village, ready to charge at the first outcry, and the stolen horses were being pushed in their direction. Once the horses were herded over the ridge, the pickets rejoined the main party and the Hunkpapa started to drive the stolen animals at a gallop. The sky was already turning gray, and it would not be long before the village awakened. In no time at all, the theft would be discovered.

Pursuit was certain, and they wanted to put as much distance as they could between themselves and the Crow village. The farther they managed to get before the inevitable counterattack, the more likely they were to make off with at least some of the stolen animals. But the herd slowed them considerably. The Crows would not take long to catch up to them. Once that happened, a group of men could be sent on with the herd while the rest of the war party held off the pursuit.

It was less than an hour after sunrise when the first war cries from the Crows drifted toward them on the wind. Sitting Bull dropped toward the rear of the herd in time to see the first few Crows break over a ridge about two miles behind. As he watched, several more warriors followed, then still more. He gave the alarm and hastily organized the defense of the Hunkpapa retreat.

The best warriors were at the rear of the Hunkpapa line, while the youngest and least experienced were charged with handling the stolen herd. Choosing high ground, the Hunkpapas formed a line the full length of a long ridge and waved their bows and arrows, daring the Crows to attack them. For several long minutes, the Crows charged on ahead, until they reached the crest of the next ridge.

Deterred by the large war party arrayed before

them, the Crows stopped to consider the best tactics, while the Hunkpapas continued to taunt them, hurling insults not just at the warriors across the valley from them, but at Crows several generations back, as well. More than one of the Hunkpapas dismounted to turn his back and raise his breechclout for the ultimate insult, but the Crow were being cautious. They knew only too well how fierce the Lakota were, and it would not be wise to rush headlong into a battle with so large a war party.

Three Crows, either as provocation or out of impatience, separated from the main band and started down the hill, their horses moving easily through the tall grass. They hurled their own insults at the Hunkpapa, daring them to come down and fight. One of the trio broke away from his companions and dashed among the advancing Hunkpapas, his long warbonnet trailing behind him like a comet's tail. He struck one Hunkpapa with his bow, then counted coup on a second before one of the Lakotas grabbed the tail of the warbonnet and yanked it from his head.

The second of the trio charged into the fray and killed one of the Hunkpapa warriors before being driven off, and Sitting Bull, angered by the loss of the warrior, challenged the third Crow to combat. He rode straight for the last of the three Crows, who was armed with an old musket.

Sitting Bull carried his shield. The sturdy buffalo-hide covering of the shield could deflect arrows well enough, but it was useless against bullets. Sitting Bull had his own gun, an old muzzle-loader, and dismounted because he was still not used to firing from horseback. Charging ahead on foot, running full tilt, he saw the Crow drop to one knee and aim the musket. Sitting Bull in turn dropped down to hide behind his shield as the Crow fired. The musket ball passed through the shield and was deflected by its wooden frame, then pierced Sitting Bull's foot at the toes and passed all the way through along the length of the sole and out the back of his foot.

Ignoring the pain, he got to his feet and, knowing that it would take time to reload the musket, limped toward the Crow, who was desperately trying to pour powder into his flintlock's muzzle. Sitting Bull closed in on him as he stuffed a patch and ball into the muzzle and yanked the ramrod loose. Sitting Bull took aim with his own gun and fired, catching the Crow in the shoulder and knocking him to the ground. Leaving his gun in the grass, he limped the last few yards and drew his knife, plunging it into the Crow, who was trying valiantly to get to his feet.

Sitting Bull hadn't known it, but his adversary was an influential chief. He realized the man's importance only when he glanced toward the rest of the Crows. They had seemed on the verge of charging, but had now broken up into small groups, as if uncertain what to do. In another moment, with one final war cry, they turned tail and disappeared over the ridge and were gone.

Sitting Bull limped back to his horse and climbed onto its back, trying to ignore the pain in his foot. Like his father and grandfather, he was a healer, and he knew the wound needed looking after. He had some herbs for a temporary poultice, but the foot needed the ministrations of a more experienced medicine man. The pain was excruciating, but it was a small price to pay for the fine horses they had acquired. He would deal with the consequences of the wound when he had the luxury of time. Now it was time to get home.

Chapter 14

**Yellowstone River Basin
1857**

THE HUNT HAD BEEN GOOD. The buffalo had been plentiful, and the stores of meat were more generous than they had been in many winters. The women were working feverishly on the hides, tanning them, adding decorative quillwork, and painting them. The parfleche bags were full of pemmican because the late summer harvest of berries had been heavy.

But the warriors were restless. Sitting in the lodges in front of the fire made a man lazy. You could spend the time making arrows, but what good were arrows if you didn't use them? Even making a bow, which took more time, was not enough to fill the long winter. With the hunt behind them, and the long, sluggish winter days not that far off, it seemed like a good time to send a war party against the Hohe.

One night, sitting around the fire in the Strong

Heart Society lodge, Stands-at-the-Mouth-of-the-River raised the issue, his listeners attentive. "We have not gone on the warpath against the Hohe in a long time," he said. "If we leave them alone indefinitely, they will no longer fear us at all. Already they are coming into our hunting grounds and taking buffalo."

There was a chorus of assenting "Hows!", and Stands-at-the-Mouth looked at his comrades with a slight smile. "I think maybe we should remind the Hohe that we are here, and that Lakota land is for Lakotas, not for Hohes."

Again the chorus agreed. The Hohe, also called Assiniboin, were fairly closely related to the Lakota. Their language was quite similar to Lakota, and it did not take much for a Hohe to understand a Lakota—or vice versa. There were legends about the relationship, some suggesting that the two peoples had once been one, but if that was so, it was long ago now, and made no difference. They were enemies now, and enemies had to be kept at a distance, no matter how close they once might have been.

Stands-at-the-Mouth took the long deerskin bag he had been cradling across his knees and unlaced the rawhide thong holding the flap closed. Pulling it away, he extracted an elaborate pipe, its mouthpiece carved, its shaft painted in bright colors. Tilting the long deerskin bag, he dumped a smaller leather pouch in his lap, opened it, and pulled out a few pinches of tobacco. As the *blotahunka*, or war leader, it was his responsibility to prepare the war pipe and oversee its ritual circulation among those warriors who wished to join the war party.

After carefully packing the bowl of the pipe, tamping the tobacco with a fingertip, adding another pinch and pressing in into the bowl, he returned the pouch to the deerskin bag, then leaned forward toward the fire. He found a suitable twig, a bright-yellow flame at its end, and touched the flame to the bowl, sucking once, then again, then a third time. Each time, the flame all but disappeared as it was drawn down into the bowl of the pipe. Rich smoke started to swirl around Stands-at-the-Mouth as he puffed until he was sure the pipe was lit. Tossing the twig back into the fire, he raised the pipe overhead, then brought it down toward the earth. He completed the ritual offering by pointing the pipe to the four points of the compass. Then he said, "I think we should leave in two days. Those who want to join me should smoke the war pipe."

He handed the pipe to his neighbor on the right, who raised it overhead, took a puff, and passed it on. Slowly, the pipe made its way around the circle of the Strong Hearts. Not all of them smoked, but most did. The Strong Heart Society claimed some of the most respected warriors in the entire Lakota nation as members. Not only the Hunkpapas, but the Oglala, the Sans Arcs, the Miniconjou, and the other divisions of the Lakota had several warrior societies. The Kit Foxes, the Crow Owners, and the Plain Lance Owners were as respected as the Strong Hearts, and many of the finest warriors belonged to more than one. These societies provided the policing that had to be done, and they were quite necessary because a society as democratic as the Lakota was always perilously balanced on the fine line between individual autonomy and total anarchy.

It was an honor to be asked to belong to any of the societies, but being a member of the Strong Hearts was a special challenge. Each man wore a special sash into battle, identifying him as a Strong Heart, and when fighting on foot, the custom required him to wear a picket line which he would stake to the earth as the battle began, knowing that he was not to remove it or sever it until the battle was won. And then, only his friends or relatives could pull up the stake.

Membership was not accorded lightly. And the courage of the warriors who were members of the society was well known not just among the Lakota, but among their enemies as well. Occasionally, the mere sight of a picketed Strong Heart was enough to break off an engagement as the enemy warriors realized what they were up against and thought better of the warpath on that particular day.

Sitting Bull was a member, and he wore his sash proudly. When the war pipe reached him, he puffed without hesitation. Light Hair was expecting their first child and he was restless, feeling as if his days on the warpath might be curtailed once the baby arrived. His foot was still troubling him, even now after more than a year. His speed was gone, and he still walked with a limp that he was beginning to think might be permanent. Like many men facing fatherhood for the first time, he was scared, and felt the need to assert himself in some way that would allow him to control a life that suddenly threatened to be beyond his ability to influence it.

The pipe made the rounds, and when it had come full circle, Stands-at-the-Mouth was well pleased. He had a war party comprised of some of the most outstanding of all Hunkpapa warriors. Sitting Bull by this time was widely known among all the Lakota not just as a warrior but as a composer of songs and a skillful medicine man. He exemplified the four cardinal virtues among his people—courage, fortitude, generosity, and wisdom. There wasn't a man in the tribe who did not consider it an honor to take the warpath with him, and some highly regarded warriors had been known to withdraw from a war party upon learning that Sitting Bull would not be along.

Going against the Hohe was a special undertaking; perhaps because the two tribes were so closely related, they reserved their most intense enmity for each other, much as family members upon having a falling out seem to hate each other more than anyone else ever could. For whatever the reason, a war party going against them was likely to be well attended.

On the morning of the second day after the smoking of the war pipe, already painted for the warpath, the warriors assembled and Stands-at-the-Mouth, as the war leader, led them away from camp and headed north toward Assiniboin country.

It was another two days before they found the Hohe, and when they did, the small enemy raiding party was taken by surprise. The Hohe ran for their lives, driving their mounts into and across a shallow lake. The water slowed their escape and allowed the Hunkpapa to catch up to them.

For a while, the water was whipped up by the floundering horses of both sides, and then by the churning arms and legs of warriors from both war parties as the attack broke down into hand-to-hand combat.

Sitting Bull drew close to his first coup in the middle of the shallow water, reaching out with his bow and rapping a fleeing Assiniboin smartly across the shoulder. The sharp crack of the polished ash on taut skin sounded like a pistol shot, and Sitting Bull saw the red welt raised by the blow as the Hohe leaped from his pony and swam for the far shore.

Turning his attention to another coup, Sitting Bull pushed his mount on through the deepest part of the lake and into the shallow water on the far side. There, another Assiniboin who had chosen to swim, leading his pony across, was struggling to remount as the horse tried to keep its feet and haul itself up and out of the water.

Once more, Sitting Bull raised his bow and smacked the enemy warrior on the shoulder. Before he could do anything more, a rifle ball struck his horse in the neck, shattering its spine and killing the horse instantly. The horse had been a great favorite, and its death infuriated Sitting Bull, who waded out of the lake looking for someone to punish for the loss.

Ahead of him, he could see the rest of the Hohe raiding party heading into some dense timber and disappearing. He looked around for a horse he could use, but by the time he found one, the Assiniboin had vanished into the forest. Chasing them further would be dangerous, and in any case, since they were just a raiding party, there was little to be gained. It was more important to remind them of the Lakota's presence and strength, and that had been accomplished. It would have been nice to have found a village and stolen some horses, but any nearby village would be alerted now to the Hunkpapa warriors and would be ready for them.

He heard shouting and turned to see what it was all about. He spotted Swift Cloud and two other warriors closing in on a young Assiniboin boy, no more than twelve or thirteen years old. The Hohe had a bow with an arrow notched. He was forced to back up as the three Hunkpapa warriors pressed him. He knew that as soon as he shot the arrow, he'd be left defenseless. Even if he found his mark, the other Hunkpapa would be on him before he could notch another.

The boy backed down a slight hill, into a shallow depression beside the lake, then started up the other side. The Hunkpapa widened their circle around him slightly, spreading out so that he could not watch all three of them at one time.

By now, the rest of the Hunkpapa had returned

to the edge of the lake and were watching the small drama unfolding. They had seen things like this before, some of them a hundred times. There was little or no room in a warrior's heart for boy who would be a warrior himself one day, and who would someday then have a Lakota boy at his own mercy. The only way to prevent that from happening was to kill him now, while the opportunity presented itself.

The Hunkpapa were mocking the boy, cheering their comrades on, and whistling. The Hohe, perhaps despairing that he could do anything to save his life, finally launched his arrow, or tried to, but he lost his grip. The arrow fluttered a few feet, wobbling, and fell to the ground.

The Hunkpapa laughed uproariously now. "The boy is a great marksman," Swift Cloud said. "Perhaps I should run for my horse before he shoots again. He will surely get me if I give him a second chance."

"You won't get far," Gray Eagle said. "This Hohe can shoot an arrow into the heart of the sun, if he chooses." That brought another roar of laughter.

The boy was still backing up, glaring fiercely at his taunters. But there was something about his expression, perhaps the fact that it was softened too much by his tender age, that made it seem sad instead of warlike. His eyes darted from corner to corner and back as he tried to fit another arrow to his bowstring. Swift Cloud feinted toward him, then fell back in mock terror as the boy almost involuntarily pointed the arrow at him.

Another feint from Gray Eagle made the boy lose
his balance for a moment, tripping backward over
the lip of the depression. His eyes found Sitting
Bull now, and he must have sensed something,
because his expression changed. He looked squarely at Sitting Bull for a moment, then ran toward
him. The move took Swift Cloud and the others by
surprise, and he got through unmolested. He threw
his arms around Sitting Bull and cried out, "Older
brother, help me!"

Once more, the warriors laughed. Swift Cloud
grabbed him by the arm and pulled him away, but
not without difficulty. The boy was wiry, and he
was clinging to Sitting Bull with all his might.
When he finally pried the boy loose, Swift Cloud
drew his knife as he twisted one of the Hohe's arms
up behind his back in a hammerlock.

The boy winced but did not cry out, instead
reaching out to Sitting Bull with his free hand and
saying again, "Older brother, help me . . ."

Sitting Bull walked toward him and took the
extended hand, then told Swift Cloud to let go of
the boy's pinioned arm.

Swift Cloud looked as if he had been asked to
drink the lake behind him, or some other equally
impossible thing, and held onto the boy's hand.
"Why should I let him go?"

The other warriors muttered, partly because it
was so unusual a request that Sitting Bull had
made. Interfering with Swift Cloud's right to do
as he saw fit with his captive was bold, even
impertinent. Also, it sounded as if Swift Cloud
were prepared to fight to have his way, and that

was something no one wanted to see. The Hunkpapa had enough trouble with their enemies. Fighting among themselves was disruptive and pointless.

Once more, Sitting Bull said, "Let him go."

And this time, he got help. Circling Hawk said, "Yes, let him go."

"Why?" Swift Cloud demanded to know. "Why should I let him go? He is a Hohe. He is our enemy and I have captured him."

"It was a brave thing he did, fighting you like that. Standing up to all of you with just a boy's bow. He called me 'older brother,' and I have answered him. He is my younger brother now. I will adopt him into my family."

Swift Cloud seemed stunned by the announcement. His eyes closed partway and his brow furrowed, as if he were having great difficulty understanding what had just been said to him. He looked almost as if it had been spoken in some strange tongue that he had never heard before. But this time he let go of the boy's hand, and once more the Hohe wrapped his arms around Sitting Bull and looked up at him as if he could not quite believe his good fortune.

More and more of the Hunkpapa were assenting to what Sitting Bull proposed, and the tide was running against Swift Cloud now. He looked toward Stands-at-the-Mouth for a moment, reached out his hand, hesitated, then patted the boy on the shoulder and nodded his head.

"It is a good thing Sitting Bull has done," he said. "It is a good thing."

By the time they returned to the village, the warriors were teasing the boy as if he had been
Hunkpapa born and raised. Even Swift Cloud
seemed to have taken a shine to the boy and rode
alongside him, chatting as if they were old friends.
As they rode into camp, Sitting Bull took the boy's
bridle in his hand and circled the village, singing
of the great victory against the Hohe, and telling
everyone how he had found a little brother whom
he planned to adopt.

Chapter 15

**Rainy Butte, Cannonball River Valley
1859**

SUMMER DAYS WERE SPECIAL. The sun dance was still some weeks away, and the weather was warm, the chill of the winter finally baked out of the land. The oppressive heat of late summer on the great plains had still not closed its grip on the Hunkpapa territory.

The children were free to come and go as they pleased. The women took advantage of the warm afternoons to catch up on their work and their gossip, sitting in small groups while they worked on clothing for the next winter. The young men, wrapped to their eyes in blankets, watched the girls, sometimes pulling one into the blanket for a few minutes of conversation. The warriors spent some of their time replenishing their supply of arrows, working on a new bow, or, when time permitted, gambling on footraces, horse races, and just about anything else that could possibly support a wager.

But despite the tranquility of the weather, Jumping Bull was in agony. No longer a young man, he had been having trouble with his teeth, and today he felt as if someone had built a fire in his jawbone. It hurt when he lay still, and when he tried to move it hurt even more. Nothing had succeeded in relieving his pain, not a poultice, not an herbal broth, not a chant from any of the half-dozen medicine men he had summoned to his lodge for relief.

Even when two boys ran into camp with the news that two Crows had been spotted nearby, he stayed in his tipi, trying to sleep, hoping that when he awoke the pain would be gone. A handful of warriors took a cursory ride around the village, looking for signs of the Crow interlopers, but they saw nothing more than a single moccasin print. It didn't seem like much to worry about. The *akicitas* were all made aware of the sighting, but even they seemed inclined to dismiss it as either the product of overactive imaginations or of mistaken identification. Surely the Crows would not be foolish enough to attack a Hunkpapa village so far from their own country.

That afternoon, despairing of getting any rest, Jumping Bull took a walk into the hills above the camp, looking for some new herb that might put an end to his suffering. But he saw nothing he hadn't seen before, and for that matter, nothing he hadn't chewed, soaked, or pasted on his aching jaw at least once in the last two days.

He was hoping that the pain would subside soon. They were planning to move the village in a day or so, and he was exhausted from lack of sleep. Moving the village was no easy thing, although it happened with great frequency. It required cooperation from everybody old enough to carry his own weight, and now, with every step rattling up through his aging skeleton to strike like a hammer blow to his jaw, he dreaded the thought.

But two days later, it was no better, and moving the village could no longer be delayed. The horses had cropped nearly all the grass, the water was muddied and sour, and a move upstream was more than desirable, it was necessary.

Rainy Butte towered in the distance, gleaming red and blue in the morning sun as the Hunkpapa started to pack their belongings. It wouldn't take long, but it would take sustained effort to get everything ready. It was controlled chaos as travois were hitched to the horses, the tipis disassembled and packed, the lodge poles used to carry still more, their tips dragging the ground, cutting twin grooves in the soft earth.

The summer heat was making the people a little sluggish. The children complained that it was too hot to move, that swimming in the Cannonball River made more sense. The adults thought the same but were too responsible to give in to the urge. But they didn't move as quickly as they usually did. Finally, everyone was ready and the horses started out, a couple of boys scampering along in the lead. The women and children moved in bunches in a ragged column and the warriors, as usual, brought up the rear, most of them walking, leading their horses, and joking with friends. The *akicitas*, as always, worried about security, but on this morning they were the only ones who did. They rode up and down beside the meandering column, urging everyone to move quickly and keep together. It was no easy task to police a Lakota village on the move. The women teased them and the children drove them crazy, darting out of line to follow a rabbit or pick a few flowers.

They hadn't gone more than a mile when a hillside above them suddenly swarmed with a band of Crows, all on horseback and commanding the high ground. The Hunkpapa warriors, taken completely by surprise, were disorganized, and it took them a moment to realize what was happening.

The Crows charged downhill, led by a man wearing a warbonnet, its long trail of eagle feathers aloft behind him. The bright colors of the Crow war paint and the glitter of morning sun on polished lancepoints, arrowheads, and the occasional firearm seemed to disorient the Hunkpapa even more as the Crow war party cut across the head of the line of march, separating a few of the boys from the main body.

The packhorses reared up, yanking their leads from careless fingers, and the women were forced to chase after the frightened animals. The Crows had surrounded the two boys in the lead now, and the Hunkpapa warriors were rushing to get on their ponies to mount a counterattack. The squeal of frightened children and the war whoops of the Crows made communication difficult. The older men tried to get the column organized, herding women and horses together into as tight a group as they could manage, while the young men moved against the Crow invaders.

One of the two boys had already been felled by a Crow. The war party outnumbered the Hunkpapa defenders, making reprisal an uphill battle at best. The Hunkpapas split into two groups and charged the Crows from two different directions. As a diversion, this might have been successful, but as a counterattack, it was not terribly effective.

However, the Crows did give ground under the furious assaults. As they retreated, the Hunkpapas gained confidence and the two smaller units recombined, now confronting the enemy as one unified force. Sitting Bull led the charge, giving an exultant whoop as the Crow began to break up into smaller bands, scattering in every direction.

One of the Crows, perhaps thinking that he had the upper hand or that he might delay the pursuit long enough to allow the rest of the war party to regain its momentum, charged out to challenge one of the Hunkpapas in battle. Swift Hawk accepted the challenge and charged him full tilt, knocking the Crow from his horse and flinging himself on the fallen man in a murderous fury.

The rest of the Crows, watching as four Hunkpapas in succession charged in to count coup on their beleaguered comrade, made a break for it, and the Lakota plunged on in hot pursuit. One of the trailing Crows had the misfortune of riding into an area dotted with gopher holes, and his pony stepped into one of them, breaking a leg and throwing his rider from the saddle. As with the first Crow, this one was swept up by an avenging tide.

Seeing the approaching Hunkpapas, he threw down his weapons and began to cry, but there was no mercy for him. If anything, his submission was taken as a negative factor, a sign of cowardice, and the Hunkpapas cut him down without a second glance.

While the rest of the Crow war party beat a hasty retreat, Sitting Bull and his half of the force chased after them at a full gallop. But as they had charged on past, one brave—or foolish—Crow warrior decided to stand and fight. He stayed on his pony, riding back and forth across the line of Lakota, his rifle braced across his thighs. Sitting Bull had left mostly younger men behind, merely as a precaution, while he took the more experienced men with him, trying to catch the retreating band of Crows.

The young Hunkpapa warriors seemed confused, uncertain what to do about the solitary Crow guard who had brought them to a temporary halt. Jumping Bull rode up, his gray-streaked hair looking almost white in the bright sun. He was too old for this kind of combat, but it galled him to see a single Crow warrior making a mockery of his people.

"If you won't take him, I will," he shouted to the young Lakotas, and pushed his horse toward the lone Crow. "For a long time, I have had a terrible toothache and wished I were dead. Now is my chance." Without another word, he kicked his horse again and rumbled toward the dismounting enemy warrior.

On the ground now, the Crow raised his rifle. Jumping Bull leaped from his own horse, notching an arrow as he hit the ground running. The Crow fired, hitting the old warrior in the shoulder and forcing him to lose his grip on the bow and arrow.

Jumping Bull didn't slow down. He charged ahead as the Crow tried to fire again but found his gun empty and instead drew his knife. Jumping Bull reached for his own knife as he closed in, but his sheath had slipped around to the small of his back. As he fumbled for the hilt, the Crow was on him, stabbing him above the collarbone.

The Crow stabbed again and again, holding Jumping Bull by his hair and grunting with every blow of the knife. The old man tried to defend himself, but the vicious swipe of the razor-sharp blade slashed him again and again, until his hands and wrists were slippery with blood and he could no longer ward off the attack. For some reason, not one of the other Hunkpapa warriors made an attempt to come to Jumping Bull's defense. They were frozen in place, some wringing their hands, others just staring dumbly, until Many Horses, a friend of Sitting Bull, rode up and saw what was happening.

He charged toward the grappling men, but before he could do anything to help, the Crow made one more vicious stab with the knife, driving the blade straight down and burying it deep in Jumping Bull's skull, snapping it off as the old man fell to the ground. In a flash, the Crow vaulted onto his pony and made his escape.

Many Horses pursued Sitting Bull, who was still chasing the fleeing Crows, and told him what had happened. "Jumping Bull has been killed," he shouted, waving his bow to get the chief's attention.

Sitting Bull rode back, leaving Many Horses in the dust. When he saw Jumping Bull spread-eagled on the ground, his hair soaked with blood, he looked at the sky for a moment, then at the other Hunkpapas, as if daring them to tell him how this had been allowed to happen, how none of them had had the courage to lift a finger to help an old man. One of the cowed warriors pointed toward the fleeing Crow who was responsible for the murder, and Sitting Bull wheeled his warhorse and galloped after him.

In his frenzy, he lashed at his horse with his quirt, and the big dun seemed to fly over the ground, eating up the distance between him and his quarry. The Crow apparently realized he was in trouble, and kept turning to look over his shoulder. Cry after cry welled up in Sitting Bull's chest, some of rage and some of grief, but to the Crow they were indistinguishable. He was running for his life, and he knew it.

Two miles later, Sitting Bull caught up to him and fired his musket, hitting the Crow on the shoulder and knocking him from his horse. The man tried to scramble away as Sitting Bull circled him once, then again, then a third time, still on his horse, daring the man to get up.

The Crow finally managed to stagger up, and Sitting Bull launched himself through the air, drawing his knife at the same instant. He snaked an arm around the killer's neck and sliced the blade once across the Crow's throat. Then something murderous and uncontrollable came over him.

He slashed and hacked at the Crow, who was already dead, as if he wanted to reduce him to an unrecognizable mass of ribboned flesh and slivered bone. Again and again and again, the knife rose and fell, and with every stab, Sitting Bull howled like an animal, venting his rage and his grief toward a blank and indifferent sky. He no longer looked at his victim, but craned his head up as if daring something in the sky to stop his murderous rage.

He felt a hand on his shoulder then and whirled to find himself staring at Many Horses's tear-streaked face.

"It's finished," Many Horses said. "The Crow is dead, Sitting Bull. It's finished."

Sitting Bull rode back to the scene of his father's death and dismounted. Her Holy Door was sitting in the grass with Jumping Bull's head in her lap, rocking back and forth and singing. Her voice was almost a croon, as if she were singing to a sleepy child, but as she saw Sitting Bull walking toward her, she lost control and the words of the death song became a mournful wail.

Her Holy Door raised her hands in the air, whether to show her son his father's blood or to berate *Wakantanka* for his father's death, Sitting Bull wasn't sure. The blood began to run down her wrists and forearms to her elbows, some dripping back into the clotted gray hair from which it had seeped. Sitting Bull knelt in the grass beside his mother, draped an arm around her shoulders, and rocked her like a baby while she sang. The words tore at his heart, and tears coursed down his cheeks. He saw teardrops land on his mother's bloody skin, leaving small lighter colored ponds in the horrible crimson.

When she was done with her chant, he closed his eyes and tilted his head back to sing his own death song, improvising the words as he went. The rest of the Hunkpapa gathered around the trio, closing in until there was not a break in their ranks, and when Sitting Bull was done, he looked for Many Horses, finding him standing on the inner edge of the circle.

"We will camp here," he said. Many Horses nodded and picked a handful of warriors to supervise.

Sitting Bull lifted his mother to her feet, then bent to pick up his father's body. He looked into the old man's face, the wrinkled skin that once had been as smooth as his own, the eyes closed now forever, and chewed at his lower lip. The moment he had known would come, and had hoped he would not live to see, had come at last.

It was time to prepare Jumping Bull for the burial scaffold.

Chapter 16

Missouri River Valley
1864

As SETTLEMENT CONTINUED IN THE COUNTRY east of the Missouri River, pressure on the eastern Sioux, the Dakota, grew intolerable. Reduced to reservations and dependent on the whim of a United States Congress that seemed to have no idea of the conditions on the reservations, they needed the annuities promised them in a series of treaties. But the treaties were honored only sporadically, and the Dakota grew desperate. A Santee Dakota chief, Inkpaduta, began to lead covert raids against the white settlements, and officials were unable to locate him.

In 1861, a hard winter had ravaged the Santee, who were waiting for the promised annuities, only to find they had been delayed by low water on the river routes to the Indian agency. While they waited, they were unable to hunt; and when the annuities finally arrived, they amounted to the princely sum of two dollars and fifty cents per person. When there was no food, the agency was forced to feed more than a thousand people for the entire winter. The following year the government, with questionable wisdom, decided to subtract the cost of that food from annuities due for the year 1862.

The Santee and the Sisseton people pressed the agency for fair treatment, but Congress was slow to act, and once again there were food shortages. In an aborted attempt to get the food they needed, a small band of warriors attacked the agency, intending to take the food they felt belonged to them. But a squad of soldiers, with the aid of a howitzer, was able to drive them off.

Once more, the Dakota were reduced to begging for their sustenance. One insensitive trader was overheard suggesting that the Indians should learn to eat grass. The remark enraged the younger men, but the chiefs were still trying to preserve the peace and restrained the hot-blooded young warriors. They knew their control was precarious, and they tried with little success to convince the government to respond to the needs of both the northern and southern Dakota.

On the way home from an unsuccessful hunt, four young warriors approached the settlement of Acton, Minnesota, and asked several whites for whiskey, which was refused them. They left angry, spoiling for a fight, and soon came upon a farm in an outlying area. Once more, they asked for whiskey, and again they were refused. The settler was accompanied by two friends, and the four young Dakota challenged them to a marksmanship contest.

The nervous settlers reluctantly agreed. After the first round of firing, the Dakota reloaded faster than the three settlers and turned their guns on their opponents. When the smoke had cleared, the three white men were dead, along with the wife and daughter of one of them.

The four warriors returned home, fully expecting punishment. Instead they were greeted like heroes. Many other young warriors wanted to rise up against the whites and take back their native land by force, since pleas and prayers had proven ineffective. Little Crow, a chief of the Santee, tried to persuade the young hotheads to be patient, but the warriors were in no mood for moderation. Already in a precarious position because of his advocacy of peace, Little Crow did his best, but when it became apparent that he was not going to prevail, he agreed to go along with the younger men.

On April 16, 1862, the uprising began. The agency post for the lower Santee was attacked. The trader who had made the insulting remarks was one of the first to die, and as he lay on the ground, the enraged warriors crammed his mouth full of grass—a message for the rest of the whites. But the main object of the raid was food, not punishment of the whites, and while the warriors were busy stripping the storehouse, several whites escaped from the agency and fled to Fort Ridgely, fifteen miles down the Minnesota River.

Captain John S. Marsh was the military commander of Fort Ridgely, and he immediately led a column of fifty men out of the fort, intent on taking back the agency and capturing the raiders. But as he crossed the Minnesota River, the Santee attacked, killing half of the soldiers. Marsh himself was wounded and drowned in the river crossing.

The news spread quickly, and apparently the discontent was so general that more and more Santee joined the uprising. Repeated raids destroyed the town of New Ulm, not far from the agency and the fort, and the Santee then turned their attention to Ridgely itself. Three times they attacked and three times they were driven off. The howitzers at the fort gave the defenders the advantage, but the Santee managed to inflict casualties and considerable damage. Before they were able to capture the fort, however, reinforcements under the command of Henry Sibley—who had been commissioned a colonel by Alexander Ramsey, the governor of Minnesota Territory—arrived and drove off the attackers.

Sibley, despite some serious blunders that cost him several dead and wounded, soon put an end to the rebellion. But the Santee were in no mood to submit meekly. Little Crow led a significant portion of the Santee nation westward out of Minnesota and onto the plains, where they soon set up camp with a band of Hunkpapas.

Of those who remained behind, nearly four hundred were convicted in hasty trials of crimes against the white settlers, and over three hundred of those were sentenced to be hanged. President

Lincoln reviewed the cases individually before the sentences could be carried out, however, and reduced the number of death sentences to thirty-eight. Thirsty for blood, the settlers pushed for the executions, and on December 26, all thirty-eight Indians were hanged on a massive scaffold. It was learned the next day that two of those hanged had been mistakenly executed, but the white settlers did not seem overly concerned about the error.

To the west, Sitting Bull's Hunkpapas, while welcoming the Santee, were now in a difficult position. Already pressed by troops from the southwest, they knew they would also now face military pressure from the east, as a punitive expedition was launched after the Santee fugitives. By the summer of 1863, the United States government had decided that the rebellious Santee had to be punished. That they were now allied with the Lakota to the west seemed not to matter. Two columns were dispatched, one under Sibley, now a general, and a second under General Alfred Sully. Sully began establishing more forts, this time in Lakota land, and this campaign marked the beginning of warfare between the Hunkpapa and the United States that would continue for the next fifteen years.

Sitting Bull, now the most prominent Hunkpapa war chief, had no choice but to fight to defend the hunting grounds. Already angry at the influx of settlers and miners along the Missouri, precipitated by the discovery of gold in the upper Missouri Valley, he had led several raids against small groups of white intruders. But those raids were a kind of warfare that the Lakota knew well, hit-and-run guerrilla tactics that worked against small groups of invaders. Sully and Sibley were leading heavily armed columns of well-trained soldiers, and the Hunkpapa were about to encounter a kind of warfare already visited on the Oglala and other more southern Lakota by General Harney in his punitive expedition after the Grattan affair.

In July of 1863, Sibley's column inflicted defeats on a mixed contingent of Hunkpapa, Santee, and Blackfeet Lakota—on the twenty-fourth at Big Mound, on the twenty-sixth at Dead Buffalo Lake, and again on the twenty-eighth at Stony Lake. In each battle, Sibley's overwhelming superiority in firepower drove the Indian forces further and further west. Hampered by the need to protect their families and to move all their worldly goods or lose them to the invading white army, Sitting Bull's forces were reduced to fighting a defensive campaign, delaying the advance of Sibley's column just long enough to allow the women and children to pack and move the camp.

At Dead Buffalo Lake, Sitting Bull garnered special honor, advancing on the column on horseback, ignoring the bullets flying all around him while he attacked a mule skinner, counted coup, and made his escape, driving a stolen army mule ahead of him. But it was a hollow triumph; the army pressed on, and the Sioux were driven relentlessly westward.

At all three battles, loss of supplies was the most serious damage inflicted. Many lodges, vast quantities of meat necessary for the coming winter, weapons, and household articles had to be abandoned. The meat was tossed into ravines, where the Hunkpapa hoped to retrieve it as soon as the fighting stopped. But each time the army discovered the abandoned food they burned it, along with everything else the soldiers could find.

After the battle at Stony Lake, Sibley turned back to Minnesota and the Sioux moved across to the west bank of the Missouri River. It was tempting to think that the worst was over. Looking for buffalo, the Sioux again crossed the Missouri. Sully, as Sitting Bull knew, was at Fort Pierre. Slowed by drought, he was presumed to have given up the field for the year, but that was a miscalculation. At Whitestone Hill, Sitting Bull and Sully locked horns once again, and the encounter cost the Sioux forces one hundred dead, one hundred and fifty-six taken prisoner, and once more huge losses of food and other supplies.

Once again the Sioux scattered, the Santee heading east and the Hunkpapas recrossing the Missouri yet again and heading north. They needed food, and the Ree might be willing to trade corn for buffalo hides. Sully broke off his pursuit and turned his attention to building another fort on the Missouri, raising Fort Sully near the meeting of the Missouri and the Cheyenne Rivers. The fort was fully garrisoned, and Sitting Bull now realized that the white soldiers had come to stay. The winter would allow him time to regroup, but he knew that when spring came, the soldiers would take the field again.

All winter long, Sitting Bull and the other Sioux chiefs made preparations for the coming campaign. At the same time, they sent messages by whatever means came to hand—traders, missionaries, friendly Indians—that Lakota lands were inviolate and that the white men did not belong. It was saber-rattling, but the chiefs were determined to back it up with force if necessary. However, Sully paid no attention.

In the spring of 1864, Sully led a column up the east bank of the Missouri. An advance unit stumbled into an ambush set by three warriors, and an engineer was killed. Sully's men caught the three warriors and beheaded them, setting the severed heads out on stakes on a hilltop. If there had been any doubt that Sully meant business, there could be no longer.

As word of the atrocity spread, the Sioux began to concentrate their forces near the Knife River. By mid-July, Sully had three thousand men in the field, and the Sioux had established nearly fifteen hundred lodges, quarters for several thousand warriors. When word reached the huge village of Sully's approach, the Sioux broke camp and moved northward to the edge of the Dakota badlands, establishing a camp nearly four miles long at Killdeer Mountain. They had chosen their position with an eye both to defense and escape, should it prove necessary. Sitting Bull and the other chiefs conferred on the best way to halt Sully's column. They were confident, and their sheer numbers seemed to give them an advantage they had lacked in previous confrontations with both Sibley and Sully.

When word reached them that Sully was coming, the warriors prepared for the battle in high spirits. Sitting Bull was accompanied by his uncle, Four Horns, and his nephew, White Bull. Instead of moving the camp, as they had before, they left it in place. Those who would not be involved in combat climbed the mountain to get a good overview of the battle, and the mountainside teemed with women, children, and old men.

The Sioux rode out from the village confident, almost cheerful. They had wanted a good fight, the chance to teach the white soldiers a lesson, and it looked like their chance had finally come. Five miles from the village, the two forces met, Sully at the head of twenty-two hundred men. He had left several hundred soldiers behind to protect a wagon train of immigrants and miners headed for the gold fields.

Sully's men had dismounted, because the land was not fit for cavalry tactics, and they spread out in a long skirmish line. There were other troops behind it, holding the horses and manning the long-range weaponry. The Sioux squared off, and the two lines stood facing one another, each waiting for the other to make the first move. One Lakota, Lone Dog, decided to test the waters. "I'm going to ride across their line," he said. "If they shoot at me, then we should shoot back."

He advanced on horseback, keeping a wary eye on the skirmish line, then crossed in front of it, waving a huge, ornate war club and shouting at the soldiers as he would at a band of Crows. Before

long, bullets were sailing all around him, kicking
up dust around the hooves of his war pony, and
whistling as they passed over his head. He made it
all the way to the far end of the skirmish line without being hit, then turned toward the Sioux line,
the troopers still trying to bring him down.

Lone Dog rode for cover, then reappeared almost
immediately, intending to dare the soldiers once
more. But by this time, the fight had gotten started.
The skirmish line began its advance. Armed with
better weapons, the soldiers pressed the Sioux
hard, driving them back slowly but surely. The
Sioux, used to individual combat, had no supreme
commander. They fought in their usual way, each
warrior—either alone or with a small group of
friends—advancing as he saw fit. But the disci-
plined white soldiers were controlled and deliber-
ate in their advance, easily overmatching any
thrust made by solitary warriors or the occasional
knot of charging Sioux.

For five miles, the Sioux were driven back, fighting every inch of the way but losing ground steadi-
ly. Sully's artillery had bursting shells and used
them to good effect, reserving them for concentrated groups of Sioux on horseback. The rapid fire
and long range of the soldiers' guns kept the Sioux
beyond their effective range, where bows and old
muskets could not reach the soldiers at all.

The warriors were forced now to take cover in
ravines and hollows and clumps of brush. Once
more, they were fighting not to conquer but to
delay. The women and children swarmed down
the mountainside now, rushing to break camp and

salvage as much of their possessions as they could, while the warriors tried to slow the advancing column.

The cover offered by the ravines concentrated the Sioux and made them easy prey to the artillery. Shells lobbed into the ravines were wreaking havoc all along the line. Whenever the Sioux tried to mount a counterattack, gathering fifty or a hundred warriors for an assault, a unit of the column would detach and army discipline enabled it to beat back the Sioux assault, often turning the tables and inflicting heavy casualties as the Sioux were forced to withdraw to high ground, where they were still within reach of the army rifles.

One crippled Lakota, a man who was unable to walk and barely had use of his arms, asked to be allowed to die in battle. His wish was granted, and Bear's Heart was lashed to a drag pulled by a horse. He advanced on the white soldiers, his feeble arms pulling helplessly at makeshift reins. He was unarmed and could not defend himself, let alone inflict damage on the soldiers. He was cut down by heavy fire and lay in the field, beyond help, while the battle raged on.

The column was close to the Indian settlement now, and the Sioux were desperate. As Sitting Bull and Four Horns tried to fend off a thrust toward the scurrying noncombatants, Four Horns was hit in the back. "I am shot," he called.

Sitting Bull rushed to his uncle's aid and grabbed the bridle of Four Horn's horse, while the older man hung on as best he could. Leading the horse to cover, Sitting Bull helped Four Horns from his mount and tried to remove the bullet, but it was buried too deeply, and there was no time to get at it. Dressing the wound, Sitting Bull saw the soldiers overrun the village. Most of the lodges were still standing, and hardly any of the supplies had been removed. It was the same as Dead Buffalo Lake and Stony Lake. The village was taken by the soldiers, and the women and children ran for their lives.

As Sitting Bull helped Four Horns back onto his horse for flight, the soldiers had already begun to torch the tipis, and thick black smoke was curling up into the cloudless sky.

Chapter 17 ══════

Missouri River Valley
1864

SITTING BULL LED FOUR HORNS to safety as the Sioux bands scattered, leaving Sully and his men in possession of the village . . . or what was left of it. For miles, Sitting Bull kept looking over his shoulder at the thickening black smoke as the Sioux lodges were reduced to cinders. He was worried about the loss of food. Then, too, with the buffalo harder and harder to find, lodges were going to be more difficult to replace. It took several skins for a single lodge, and there had been hundreds of lodges in the village, most of them abandoned to the enemy. How difficult it might be to hunt enough buffalo to replace them was something he could only imagine.

But he had more important things on his mind on this ride. Every glance at the dense black smoke reinforced the impression he had gained that a new way to fight had to be found. The white men did not fight like the Crows or the Hohe. They had tactics that the Hunkpapas had never encountered, and they fought for different reasons. They were not interested in glory. They did not care whether they managed to touch an enemy with a hand or something held in the hand, the only thing that really mattered to a Sioux warrior. As it was, the white soldiers seemed content to remain at a distance and fire their guns. Killing Sioux was all that mattered to them.

Intuitively, Sitting Bull understood that the gap between his culture and that of the white soldiers was enormous, and since the white soldiers were not going to cross over to his ways, he would have to find a way to convince the Sioux to adjust to the white man's way of making war. If he couldn't, then the Sioux would be pressed further and further west, something the Crows were unlikely to accept. And he knew that it would be increasingly difficult for the Sioux to get guns, because the white men would try to prevent their modern weapons from falling into Sioux hands. That would put the Lakota at a further disadvantage against the Crows and the other tribes to the west. But he knew that changing the habits of a lifetime would take a great deal of persuasion. Killdeer Mountain had convinced him, and he had to find a way to teach the others what he had learned.

On the long ride, he had plenty of time to mull it over. He also had more immediate concerns to attend to. Four Horns was in great pain, but managed to stay on his horse. "I can feel the bullet inside," he said.

"Can you ride?"

"Do I have a choice? We have to find the women and children. We can't leave them unprotected with the Long Knives on the warpath."

The wound had stopped bleeding, and Sitting Bull knew that the herbs he had applied would help it heal and prevent infection, but he wished he had been able to remove the bullet.

It was near nightfall by the time they found the fugitive Hunkpapas. It had not been as easy as usual to follow them, because there were so few travois, which normally gouged the earth and left a clear path for returning hunters and warriors to follow. The Hunkpapas had gone their own way, leaving the Santee to make their own choices. In the days following the Killdeer Mountain battle, the Sioux regrouped. They kept scouts out to watch for Sully's column while they tried to reestablish themselves, making new lodges and hunting almost around the clock to replace the pilfered food.

Camped on the western edge of the badlands, the Hunkpapa were joined by several other bands, including some Brule and Sans Arcs Sioux and even a contingent of Cheyenne. Sitting Bull knew that Sully would not leave on his own, but he wondered whether the Sioux could drive him away, outgunned and desperately in need of supplies as they were.

Night after night, he talked with the other chiefs, trying to make them see what he had seen at Killdeer Mountain. "They do not fight like we fight," he told them. "They keep coming, even when one of them is killed. Sometimes when one of our warriors is killed, we take time to mourn, maybe even stop fighting altogether, but the white soldiers never stop. It is like they don't care what happens to anyone. When a white soldier is killed the others keep on fighting. They walk right past him like he is not even there."

"If we have enough warriors, we can defeat them," Spotted Eagle, one of the Sans Arc chiefs, argued.

"How many is enough? You saw how many Long Knives there were. There were more of us, many more, and still they drove us away and burned our village."

"They have better guns. If we can get such guns, then we can defeat them."

"No, it is not just the guns, and not just the numbers. It is the *way* they fight. They have one leader and they all do what he tells them to do. We don't fight like that, so we sometimes get confused. It is then easy for them to push us back."

"We fight as we have always fought," Spotted Eagle insisted. "That is not our way to fight."

"I think maybe it should be. I think maybe the only way to defeat the Long Knives is to fight the way the Long Knives fight."

"Does Sitting Bull want to be the one great war leader like the one the Long Knives have? Is that why he tells us this?" another of the chiefs asked.

Sitting Bull shook his head. "No, I want only that we consider it, to see if it is something we can learn to do. If it is, then we will have to deal with the question of who should be the one leader."

Spotted Tail, the Brule chief, put in, "The Long Knives don't have just one chief, anyway. A long time ago, it was Harney. Now it is Sully and Sibley. They are told what to do by the Great Father in Washington. They told us that at Fort Laramie when many Lakota touched the pen to the peace paper. The Great Father is not even there when the Long Knives fight against the Sioux, so the Long Knives do what they want, just like the Lakota warriors."

Sitting Bull shook his head vigorously. "No. They are told when to stop and when to go. They stop when they are told to, and they go when they are told to. They fight when they are told to, and they fight until they are told to stop fighting."

"It is something to think about," the Brule conceded. "But I don't think it is something we can do. Besides, if we don't have the good guns the Long Knives have, it won't matter whether we fight like they do."

"It is the only chance we have," Sitting Bull insisted.

It went on like that for days. Sitting Bull was getting frustrated because he knew that he was not getting through to his allies. They were too used to the old ways. And Sitting Bull himself did not yet fully understand what it was he was asking them to do. But he feared that the Lakota would not learn until it was too late to do them any good.

While the Lakota grappled with their future, Sully's troops came again, and once more the Lakota were forced to run for their lives. They scattered, Sitting Bull and his Hunkpapas heading southeast, trailing a buffalo herd. But while on the hunt, word came that another wagon train of white settlers was coming, and the Lakota rallied to try and turn it back.

The train was accompanied by a contingent of troops under the command of Captain James Fisk, and the wary and war-weary Hunkpapas tracked it for several days, hoping to find an opportunity to attack. On September 2, the train was slowed, then halted altogether, by the difficult passage at Deep Creek. It was the opening the Hunkpapa had been waiting for.

Sitting Bull led a charge against some of the halted wagons, galloping headlong toward a mounted soldier, who quickly drew his revolver to ward off the war chief's assault. Sitting Bull, ignoring the wild gunfire, rode up to him and tried to wrestle the soldier from his horse. The soldier fired again, and this time the bullet struck Sitting Bull above the left hip, going clean through and passing out through the small of his back.

Swinging low over the side of his horse to shield himself from another gunshot, he backed away. White Bull had seen what was happening and went to his uncle's aid, accompanied by Little Assiniboin, Sitting Bull's adopted younger brother, and another warrior. They managed to lead him safely out of the battle, but he was done for the day.

The members of the wagon train fought their way along for three days until they found a place to make a stand. They used the wagons to defend themselves, arranging them in a circle and stripping sod to stack along the perimeter for additional protection.

In the Hunkpapa village was a white woman who had been taken prisoner by the Oglala several weeks before, then traded to a Hunkpapa warrior named Brings Plenty who had taken her as a wife. The Hunkpapa demanded that she write a note to the besieged immigrants, and the paper was then taken and staked on a hill in a forked stick where the white settlers could see it. The paper was used to open negotiations. The Hunkpapa planned to barter the woman, named Fanny Kelly, for supplies. But no one had bothered to consult with Brings Plenty on the matter.

The besieged immigrants had christened their fortifications Fort Dilts, in honor of one of the troopers slain in the first Sioux attack. Determined to resist, the white troopers dragged their feet in negotiations, offering just some coffee, sugar, and flour. But the Hunkpapas were insistent that they wanted four wagon loads of food in exchange for Fanny Kelly.

Sitting Bull was recovering from his wound and unable to take part in the first negotiations, which quickly broke off. The Hunkpapas withdrew when word reached them that reinforcements were coming to the aid of the immigrants, and it was decided that it would be prudent to move the Hunkpapa village before they arrived. That much, at least, had been learned from the Killdeer Mountain episode.

While he recuperated, Sitting Bull had plenty of time to observe Fanny Kelly. She was being treated well, and the women of the village all seemed to

like her. She was doing her share of the women's
work, apparently willingly. He realized that she
was far more submissive than the Hunkpapa
women, and wondered whether it was from fear or
just an aspect of her personality. It also made him
wonder if all white women were like Fanny Kelly.

Watching her, he realized how much he missed
Light Hair, who had died nearly seven years ago in
childbirth, leaving a son, who himself lived only
four years. The Lakota ways were hard and took
their toll on women and children, as well as the
warriors. He had taken other wives after Light Hair,
but she was irreplaceable, perhaps because their
only child had died and there was nothing left of
her except the memories. Nothing, not the new
wives, not the children they had given him, could
make up for her loss. She was special, not because
she had been the first, but because she had been
the best.

Light Hair had been cheerful and full of spirit.
She had argued with him when she thought he was
wrong, unlike Fanny Kelly, who never raised her
voice to Brings Plenty. Light Hair had laughed and
sung, too, even playing practical jokes on him, just
as he did on her—and on anyone else who came
within reach of his mischievous sense of humor.
But Fanny Kelly was not like that at all. She went
about her chores without protest, but without a
smile, and Sitting Bull knew she was desperately
unhappy.

Other warriors, impressed by her efforts, tried to
get Fanny away from Brings Plenty. They tried
everything from sweet talk to offering several horses

in exchange, but Brings Plenty was more than happy with her and turned away every offer. Now and then, Sitting Bull would sit with her while she worked, trying to teach her the rudiments of the Lakota language. But he was making little progress, and conversation was difficult. He wanted to know what she was thinking, but there was no way for him to ask and no way for her to tell him.

Soon, delegations of Indians from the agencies came, bearing gifts and trying to ransom the woman. But Brings Plenty was adamant. He would not part with her at any price. Each time one of the delegations was refused, the situation grew tense. There was the constant threat that they would try to remove the captive by force. Sitting Bull wanted to avert bloodshed at all cost and started trying to convince Brings Plenty that he should let the woman go.

But Lakota democracy was absolute, and Brings Plenty was free to do as he chose. Sitting Bull was faced with two options—he could try to persuade Brings Plenty to surrender Fanny Kelly, or he could take her by force and set her free. One seemed impossible and the other was unpalatable. It would force the warriors to take sides at a time when they could not afford internal dispute. They needed all their hostility for the Long Knives. The woman was becoming a distraction and represented the very real possibility of dividing the village.

One night he walked to Brings Plenty's lodge. Invited inside, he sat down and got right to the point. "You should feed the woman well, fatten her up. She is like a bundle of sticks."

"Why?" Brings Plenty demanded.

"Because we will have to send her back to the white men before long."

Brings Plenty shook his head. "No. I won't send her back. She belongs here and no one will take her without my approval."

Sitting Bull tried again a few days later but met with no success. Finally, in December, a band of Blackfoot Sioux arrived at the Hunkpapa camp. Their leader was Sitting Bull's boyhood friend and footracing opponent, Crawler, a huge man who had a fearsome reputation in battle. He was still a good friend to Sitting Bull and told the chief why he had come. "We are here to buy back the white woman," he said.

Sitting Bull realized that the time had come. He knew that Crawler would not go home a failure, and he did not want to have to fight his friend—especially over a bundle of sticks. "We will bring her back," he said. "But you must let me talk to Brings Plenty. I will convince him to let her go."

He sent for Brings Plenty. When the warrior arrived, Sitting Bull explained that Crawler had come for Fanny Kelly and would not leave without her. Crawler offered six horses in exchange for the woman's freedom, but Brings Plenty refused them and stalked back to his lodge.

Crawler shook his head. "I think we will have to take her by force," he said.

Sitting Bull asked for a few moments alone with Brings Plenty and walked to his lodge. Brings Plenty invited him in, but it was obvious that he was determined not to give in. Brings

Plenty was sitting on a buffalo robe on the far side of the fire pit. In the flickering light, Sitting Bull saw the reflection of a knife blade on the robe beside him.

Outside, the Blackfeet were milling around the entrance to the lodge. The Hunkpapa, angry that the Blackfeet would come into their camp and try to tell them what to do, joined them in an ugly mood. Sitting Bull stepped outside when he heard the angry muttering. He raised a hand, and both contingents fell silent.

"Friends," he said, "this woman is different from us. She walks a different path, not our path. You can see from her face that she is unhappy and homesick. It is not right that we should keep her here against her will. So I am going to send her back."

There was a subdued mutter among the Hunkpapas, but Sitting Bull was adamant. He told Crawler to go inside and bring Fanny Kelly outside. "And tell Brings Plenty I said so," he added. Then, in a low voice, he warned his friend that Brings Plenty had a knife at his side.

Crawler entered the lodge and found Brings Plenty and Fanny Kelly seated side by side across from the fire. It was a bitterly cold day, and Crawler leaned forward to warm his hands at the fire.

"I have come for this woman," he said.

"I don't want your horses," Brings Plenty insisted.

"Friend," Crawler said, "I think you should accept the offer."

"Friend," Brings Plenty countered, giving the

word a bit of an edge, "I think I will keep the captive. It is my right."

Crawler saw the knife glittering on the buffalo robe and tried once more. Again he was refused.

He moved still closer to the fire. Suddenly, he drew his revolver, grabbing Fanny Kelly by the shoulder and pulling her behind him. Keeping his revolver trained on Brings Plenty, he backed out of the lodge, where the Hunkpapa were fighting among themselves. But Sitting Bull had gathered the Strong Heart Society warriors and now took command. He had Fanny Kelly escorted to the council lodge, where the council selected several Hunkpapas to accompany the Blackfeet and their captive. It was decided to send a sizable contingent to the white man's fort, where they would be able to do some trading as well as demonstrate their goodwill by the return of the captive. To make certain there was no trouble, it was decided that Sitting Bull go as head of the Hunkpapa delegation.

The visit to the fort was uneventful. The Hunkpapas managed to trade for some much-needed powder and lead, but there were no new guns to be had. And Sitting Bull was no closer to forging the coalition he needed. The feud over Fanny Kelly had been disruptive, and it would take time for the divisions to heal.

Chapter 18 ═══════════

Missouri River Valley
1865

AT THE BEGINNING OF 1865, word started to filter northward to the Hunkpapa camps about a raid on the Cheyenne village of Two Kettles, whose chief was known to be favorably disposed to the white man. At Sand Creek, white soldiers under the command of Colonel John Chivington had destroyed the village without provocation. The casualties ran into the hundreds killed and still more wounded. Most of the dead were women and children, and the soldiers had mutilated the bodies of the women, taking trophies. One soldier was overheard to say that his trophy would make an ideal tobacco pouch, as he severed the breast of a young woman. Instead of scalps, the soldiers took the pubic patches of their female victims and dangled them on poles or hung them from their belts.

Fleeing survivors poured northward into Lakota territory, and word of the atrocities spread across the plains from village to village. The reaction among the Lakota was predictably mixed. For those chiefs who were already inclined to believe that a war against the Long Knives was unwinnable, the message of Sand Creek was clear—make the best peace you can, *now*. Young Bear's Rib, who had succeeded his father as leader of a band of Hunkpapa, was among those who felt that peace was imperative at any price. And he was not alone. Lone Horn, a Miniconjou war leader, was also drawn to the peace faction, as was the Hunkpapa chief Running Antelope.

These chiefs had originally resisted the white invasion, but they had come to believe that further resistance was futile, and that the longer the war against the Long Knives lasted, the harsher would be the terms of settlement.

Other chiefs were diametrically opposed to appeasement. Among the Oglala, Red Cloud was determined to drive the white soldiers from the Powder River country, now the last great source of buffalo. The herds had continued to dwindle under the assault of white hide-hunters and the mindless slaughter by settlers and soldiers passing through buffalo country, who killed hundreds of animals for sport, leaving the carcasses to rot in the sun.

Two army officers staged a contest to see who could kill the most buffalo in a single day. Taking only the buffalo's tongues as proof of their kills, together they dropped more than two hundred animals in one day's hunting.

But among the Oglala, there was another chief, more implacable even than Red Cloud, and that was Crazy Horse. His single-minded dedication to turning back the white flood would eventually bring Crazy Horse closer and closer to the one man who was as fiercely determined as he—Sitting Bull.

Because the Hunkpapa were among the most northern of the Lakota, they were in some ways the most insulated from the pressure of immigrants. The wagon trains along the newly opened Bozeman Trail passed to the south of Hunkpapa hunting grounds. But General Sully was adding more forts along the Missouri, probing deeper and deeper into Lakota territory, and leaving sizable garrisons behind. These forts became the focus of Sitting Bull's resentment, and he was resolved to burn them to the ground and send the white soldiers back where they had come from.

In addition to Fort Pierre and Fort Sully, in the coming years there were several more targets, including Forts Rice, Berthold, Union, Stevenson, and Buford. Some were little more than trading posts garrisoned with small contingents of troopers, and since the Lakota were increasingly dependent on the white traders for guns and ammunition, they were willing to tolerate their presence. But the military forts—Buford, Stevenson, and Sully—were an affront that Sitting Bull could not ignore.

To the west, the Oglala would eventually have military irritants of their own in Forts C. F. Smith, Reno, and Phil Kearny. Red Cloud, Man-Afraid-of-His-Horses, and Crazy Horse focused their attentions on these forts with the same implacable hatred Sitting Bull directed at those installations nearer to Hunkpapa country.

Of them all, Sitting Bull reserved the most intense hatred for Fort Rice, which had taken the place of Fort Sully as the principal military post along the Missouri, just a few miles above the mouth of the Cannonball River.

During the early spring of 1865, Sitting Bull organized several raids on Fort Rice. He had come to understand the significance of the post and was trying desperately to persuade other Hunkpapas of the need to eliminate it.

Around the council fire, he hammered away at the issue whenever the opportunity presented itself—and whenever he was not leading a war party against a supply train or a wagon train or a cavalry column searching for bands of "hostiles," as the bands under leaders who thought as he did were characterized. His primary sounding board was his uncle, Four Horns, probably the most respected of the Hunkpapa chiefs and one of the four shirt wearers, who were charged with directing the activities of the tribe.

One night in March, he raised the issue once more. "You all know that Sully will come again soon. The forts he built are getting stronger every day, while we fight among ourselves. If we wait too long, we will not be able to drive the Long Knives away. They say that the war between the white men will be over soon, and they will then have thousands of soldiers to send against us."

Four Horns nodded thoughtfully. "What you say, I have also heard. But I don't see why the white man would want this land. He wants only to build his railroad. The railroad is far to the south and does not bother us."

"But when they found gold, they bothered us," Sitting Bull reminded Four Horns. "Who can say they will not find gold in our country? Who can say they will not want to build a railroad here? All they do is lie. You know as well as I do that the promises they made to the Indians at Fort Laramie have all been broken. You heard from Inkpaduta and Little Crow how the promises made to the Santee were broken. You know, as I do, what happened to the Cheyenne at Sand Creek. And those were Indians who were friendly to the white man. What will they do to us, if we let them?"

"There is a difference between fighting to defend your country and your family, and looking for trouble," Four Horns argued. "If we take the warpath against the forts, the Long Knives will come looking for us. Now, they leave us alone."

"For how long, uncle? Why are they building forts if they plan on leaving us alone?"

Four Horns just puffed on his pipe. Sitting Bull knew it was because he did not have an answer, so he pressed his argument. "If Sully comes, it will not be because of a few puny raids against wagon trains. It will be because the white man wants this land, just like he wants the Powder River country. We have to do like Red Cloud and Crazy Horse. We have to fight while we still can."

"Red Cloud—" Four Horns began, shaking his head "—he is different. He wants to be the chief of all the Lakota, so he makes war to make the people stand behind him."

"Red Cloud is a great warrior, and he is doing what he has to do. Just as Crazy Horse is . . . and just as I am."

"What do you want to do, then?"

"I want to destroy Fort Rice. I want to push the Long Knives back to the east."

Four Horns nodded. Sitting Bull couldn't tell whether it was a gesture of agreement or resignation. His uncle knew that he would not easily be dissuaded and just might feel that going along with Sitting Bull's plans would give him some influence. But that was not a bad thing. Four Horns was a wise man, and his word carried great weight among the Hunkpapa. Of the four shirt-wearers, he was the most respected. If he agreed with Sitting Bull, no matter what his reasoning, it would be a great help.

"All right," Four Horns finally said. "We will attack the fort, but I don't think we will be able to destroy it. The Long Knives are very strong. Their guns are better than ours, and they have more of them."

"But this is *our* land; that is one thing they do not have. We are fighting for something that matters to us. They are not. They are paid soldiers who fight because that is their job. They cannot stand against us if we are all together."

"We will see," Four Horns said.

The other chiefs around the council fire, who had remained silent through the exchange, now nodded. "How!" they said, and Sitting Bull knew he had the support he needed, at least for a little while. How long would depend on what he was able to achieve against the Long Knives.

In the beginning of April, he led a war party against the fort. It was like the others, a high palisade of timbers, with blockhouses for lookouts and additional defense at the corners. Inside, some buildings, barely thrown together, were used for sleeping quarters and storage, as well as offices for the commanders. Built on flat land on the west bank of the river, the fort was surrounded on the other three sides by hills and ravines. Most of the ravines were wooded and offered excellent cover allowing for a covert approach.

Leading his band through one of the ravines, Sitting Bull found an ideal vantage point from which to observe activities at the fort. Watching from a clump of thick brush, he saw the herds of horses and cattle grazing on the grassy flats surrounding the fort and decided that one way to flush out the inhabitants would be to drive off the animals, but that was not going to be easy, because negotiating the ravines while driving the stolen stock would leave the war party dangerously exposed. The Long Knives could follow on high ground and easily pick off the warriors at long range if they were hampered by large numbers of horses and sluggish cattle.

While Sitting Bull watched, the gates opened and a small party of mounted men came out, leading several wagons. The warriors behind him were getting restless and the sight of the soldiers made them anxious to get started. But Sitting Bull restrained them, watching the wagons as they headed upriver and into the hills.

Ducking back into the ravine, he mounted and led his warriors northwestward, hoping to find the wagons out of sight from the fort. An hour later, two scouts hurried back to report that the Long Knives were cutting wood for their fires, and that there were twenty men—eight guards and twelve woodcutters, all armed with new rifles. If they could be overcome, the Hunkpapa could add the new weapons to their arsenal. The numbers were favorable for an attack.

When the war party crested a hill overlooking the work site, Sitting Bull crept forward to watch the woodcutters, busy with their long, two-man saws in a stand of cottonwoods. The guards did not seem particularly worried about attack, and the warriors fanned out, ready for the command to charge downhill.

When it came, the Hunkpapas let out a loud whoop and quirted their ponies over the ridge and down. The work party seemed to freeze in its tracks, and Sitting Bull saw the woodcutters run for their wagons, leaving their saws still stuck in the trees. He thought the soldiers were going to make a run for it, and he kicked his horse to wring a little more speed from it, but the woodcutters pulled rifles from the wagons and formed a ragged line on the far side of the wagons.

They opened fire almost immediately, and the bullets started to whistle all around the Hunkpapas as they pressed their assault. Blue Buffalo was hit and fell from his horse, bleeding heavily from a shoulder wound, and Standing Elk was hit in the forehead and killed outright.

The Hunkpapa turned to the north, launching arrows and firing their few weapons, but they were too far from the soldiers to have much effect. Pulling up just out of range, they raised their bows and rifles and shouted insults, but Sitting Bull knew that the Long Knives could not be provoked the way the Crows or the Hohe could. Instead of coming out to avenge a slandered relative or to prove the charge of cowardice was groundless, the soldiers, who did not understand the language, contented themselves with firing a few rounds in hopes of getting lucky.

Circling toward the riverbank, Sitting Bull led his men back into the fray, but the soldiers simply moved around their wagons, again interposing them between themselves and their enemies. Once more, the Hunkpapa charged straight ahead, this time driving their horses directly toward the wagons, only to be driven back again by the rapid fire from the breech-loading rifles, which were so much faster than the Hunkpapa muskets.

Two more warriors fell under the relentless onslaught. Sitting Bull managed to count coup on one of the woodcutters as he drove his warhorse through a gap in the wagons. He felt the heat of a bullet as it passed within a fraction of an inch of his left cheek. Two of the woodcutters had been hit with arrows, but were not wounded badly enough to stop firing.

When he reached the Hunkpapa line again, he called for his men to fall back. Warriors and soldiers exchanged fire at long range, but neither side incurred another injury. The Hunkpapa had already suffered losses—two men killed and three badly wounded.

Sitting Bull was somber on the way home. He had expected an easier time of it, but the Long Knives had fought well. They were supposed to be weak from having endured a long winter with poor rations, but there was no evidence of that. Some other way would have to be found to lay siege to the fort . . . but what?

Chapter 19 ═══════════

Missouri River Valley
1866

FOR SEVERAL MONTHS, SITTING BULL LED raids against Fort Rice and its defenders, but with indifferent success. Again and again, bands of Hunkpapa swept down on the work crews and the herds, driving off small groups of horses and cattle, but the defenders of the fort were efficient, their weaponry superior, and the Hunkpapa still too fragmented to overcome such difficulties.

Sitting Bull was getting frustrated, and more than once earned derision from other warriors when he withdrew early from a battle he had initiated. Again and again, he tried to convince the rest of the Lakota to join together, to try to achieve by sheer numbers what they could not do otherwise.

But more than anything else, it was Her Holy Door who was pulling him in another direction, who seemed to distract him. Worried about his safety, she never lost an opportunity to remind him that he was not just a warrior, but a son, husband, and father.

When he returned from yet another raid on Fort Rice, one which had netted him three horses but inflicted no damage on the Long Knives other than a good scare, she took him aside.

"You should be more careful," she said. "You know, with your father gone, if anything happens to you, there is no one else to care for your family."

"I care for them," he snapped. "I see that they have food, that their lodges are warm."

"But what if something happens to you? What happens to me if you are killed by the white soldiers? What happens to your wives, your children?"

"What would happen to you if I were killed by the Crows?" he snapped. Regretting his harshness, he tried to smooth things over immediately. "I am a warrior. A warrior makes war. If not, he is a failure. And a good warrior makes war on his enemies. Now the Long Knives are more dangerous to us than the Crows."

"But you are also a leader—a great leader—and a leader knows that there are some things more important than glory. You can't feed the village babies with scalps. Maybe Running Antelope is right. Maybe the best way is to make peace with the white man."

Sitting Bull snorted. "Make peace? You don't understand what you're saying. The white man makes peace with the Indian only when he has taken everything he wants. What kind of peace is that?"

Her Holy Door was quiet for a long time. In the protracted silence, the crackling of coals in the fire pit was the only sound in the lodge. From outside, he could hear the noise of children playing, calling to one another, squealing with delight over some prank or other. At another time, the sound would have given him pleasure. He might even have gone outside to join the children. That was a thing he missed now, and he wondered whether Her Holy Door was right. Somehow his life seemed empty, hollow as a gourd, a dried-up thing the wind would blow away. It was so hard trying to fight a war when the enemy wouldn't fight fairly. Or, if not fairly, at least in a way he could understand. He wished he could be as oblivious of the future as the children outside, but it was far too late for that.

In the lodge next door, two women who mattered to him were probably wondering why he was home so seldom. The children sometimes looked at him as if he were a stranger. He would come home from a raid on Fort Rice, and they would shrink into the shadows at the edge of the lodge, watching him as if trying to decide whether they knew him or not.

That was no way to live. But neither was moving to a reservation, riding up to the white man with your hand out, waiting for whatever meager ration he chose to give you—a handful of moldering corn, some rotten meat, or rancid butter. That was not the way a man should live. Why didn't the white men understand that? What was so wrong with living as the Hunkpapa had always lived? The country was vast; there was plenty of room for the white men elsewhere. They did not need Hunkpapa land. But they were greedy, they wanted it, and they were prepared to take it regardless of the cost.

He looked at his mother sadly, feeling as if all the cares of the village were resting on his shoulders, pressing him down until he was no thicker than a blade of grass.

While he tried to frame some sort of answer, something to meet his mother's concerns without compromising his own position too severely, Four Horns entered the lodge. He nodded to Sitting Bull and sat down across from his nephew.

"The white men have asked us to meet with messengers from the Great Father in Washington," he said.

Sitting Bull scowled. "You're not thinking that we should meet them, are you?"

Four Horns shook his head. "No, I'm not thinking that, but some chiefs are."

"Running Antelope," Sitting Bull said, not bothering to conceal his scorn.

Again, Four Horns nodded. "Yes, but not only him. There are others, too. And not just Bear's Rib."

Sitting Bull spat when he heard the name of the young chief. "Bear's Rib has been helping the Long Knives at Fort Rice. He is selling his land and his people for wagons full of white man food."

Four Horns took a deep breath and held it for what seemed an eternity. "There is much that we should think about before we decide what to do," he said.

"There is nothing to think about. I know that I

will not meet with anyone from the Great Father, not as long as the Long Knives are in Lakota lands. And he is not *my* father, anyway. He is nothing to me."

Four Horns smiled. "You have a way of putting things that does not allow one to misunderstand you," he said.

Sitting Bull laughed. "I suppose so. But this is too important a thing for me to be misunderstood."

"So, you won't go? Under any circumstances?"

Sitting Bull shook his head. "Never!"

"Then neither will I."

And when the peace commissioners came, bringing with them yet another packet full of paper promises, Running Antelope and Bear's Rib touched the pen. So did chiefs from the other Lakota tribes. They were promised annuities in exchange for leaving white travelers alone and for withdrawing from white travel routes, both existing and as established in the future. When Sitting Bull heard the last, he knew he had not made a mistake in refusing to attend the conference.

Encountering Running Antelope a few days after the conference ended, he asked, "And where will the whites travel in the future?"

Running Antelope looked at him blankly, and Sitting Bull repeated the question, this time with a preface. "You touched the pen to the white man's treaty paper. The paper said that Lakota would withdraw from white man travel places now and in the future. Where will they be in the future?"

Running Antelope still seemed not to comprehend the question.

Sitting Bull pressed again. "You don't know, do you?"

"No."

"But you won't go there, when the white man does? No matter where it is?"

"No."

"Suppose he comes here? Will you leave?"

"I . . ."

"Suppose he goes to *Paha Sapa*? Suppose he finds something there in the Black Hills that he wants? Will you let him have *Paha Sapa*?"

"No!"

"But the paper says you will. It says that you will withdraw from any place he wants to travel. It does not say that he won't travel to *Paha Sapa*, does it?"

Running Antelope had no answer. He licked his lips, and Sitting Bull watched him closely. The chief's eyes seemed to be focused anywhere but on Sitting Bull, and he soon made an excuse to leave. Sitting Bull let him go. There was no point in trying to change his mind, and even if he could, the treaty paper had already been signed, and there was nothing that Running Antelope could do about it now.

For the rest of the year, Sitting Bull continued to snipe at Fort Rice, but the defenses were stronger than ever. Aside from running off stock and an occasional ambush, there was no success to speak of. And now, the Long Knives were building another fort, one they called Fort Buford. It was even deeper in Lakota territory, not far from the mouth of the Yellowstone, and followed the same plan as Fort

Rice. It was the deepest permanent military intrusion into Hunkpapa territory, and Sitting Bull was determined that it had to be eliminated before it got fully entrenched.

While Sitting Bull turned his energies to ridding his land of Fort Buford, Red Cloud and Crazy Horse found they had to contend with three similar fortifications in Oglala territory in the Powder River valley—Forts Reno, Kearny, and C. F. Smith. Whether intended or not, the erection of these forts had a direct effect on Sitting Bull and the Hunkpapa, as well as the Oglala. Their presence meant that Sitting Bull could not count on help from the Oglalas, who were now busy with their own occupying army.

News from the Powder River was sketchy, but late in December the Hunkpapas were cheered by word that nearly a hundred Long Knives had been killed by Oglala warriors under Red Cloud and Crazy Horse. Sitting Bull learned of the attack on Captain Fetterman and his troopers firsthand from his nephew, White Bull, who was there at Fort Kearny during the battle.

As the winter settled in, Sitting Bull established a village ten miles up the Yellowstone, within easy striking distance of Fort Buford. His first assault enabled him to gain control of some outlying buildings, but when the soldiers rallied the following morning, the Hunkpapa were forced to surrender their modest gain. The troopers were supported by heavy artillery fire, and the exploding shells and grapeshot took a heavy toll on the besieged warriors. The Hunkpapas withdrew in defeat once more. They set fire to stacks of firewood work crews had been cutting for several months, but it was small satisfaction.

The winter turned bitter-cold, but Sitting Bull kept up the pressure. Between the presence of his warriors and the terrible weather, he was able to cut the fort off completely from contact with the outside world. No one dared come out, and it was impossible for anyone to make it through the deep snow. No one was foolish enough to try, anyway, with the mountains full of Lakota warriors.

But when the spring came, the Long Knives were still there. Sitting Bull kept sending messages to the fort through traders at nearby Fort Union that he intended to burn the fort to the ground and wipe every last trace of the stockade off the face of the earth. But all his bluster served only to galvanize support for the beleaguered soldiers, and as soon as the thaw permitted travel, Sully sent reinforcements and supplies, including a shipment of improved breechloaders, which made the Hunkpapa position even more difficult.

To make matters worse, the soldiers began building yet another fort. It was beginning to look as if there would soon be more Long Knives than Lakota warriors in the Missouri Valley.

Chapter 20 ═══════════

**Missouri River Valley
1868**

WHILE THE FIGHTING CONTINUED, the Hunkpapa, including Sitting Bull and Gall, another chief prominent in the war faction, continued to barter with the white traders at Fort Berthold. Most of the trading posts were surrounded by Lakota villages, some of them virtually permanent, as many of the people became what the war faction referred to as "hang-about-the-forts." But even those characterized by the government as hostiles were growing increasingly dependent on the forts for goods they could get nowhere else.

The Lakota were developing a taste for coffee and processed sugar, which they could not get except in trade. But their primary dependence on the traders was for ammunition and weapons. The government was trying to regulate Lakota access to firearms, but there was a legitimate need for rifles, which were used with increasing frequency in hunting buffalo. In addition, many of the traders knew that the Lakota would get weapons and ammunition from wandering bands of Canadian Indians, the Red River Metis, itinerant traders who were called Slota by the Lakota.

Rather than see the business for weapons go elsewhere, the traders tended to ignore regulations and make weapons, including some of the new breech-loading Spencer rifles and some Winchester and Springfield repeating rifles, available to the Lakota, without regard to whether the Indians in question followed Running Antelope or one of the other peace chiefs, or were adherents of the war faction under Sitting Bull, Crazy Horse, or Gall. Business, after all, was business.

Sitting Bull insisted on strict decorum whenever trading at one of the forts. He did not want to give the traders any cause for alarm, or the small army garrison reason to interfere. Rather than risk being cut off from access to Fort Berthold, it was better to swallow a little pride and get what was needed to pursue the war more effectively.

There were times when the war seemed pointless—and possibly endless—to Sitting Bull. As always, he confided in Four Horns, the one man among the Hunkpapa with whom he felt he could be completely honest, now that Jumping Bull was gone.

In early 1867, they were riding back from Fort Berthold to their village, twenty-five miles away. It was a beautiful evening in late spring, and the thick grass was already a brilliant green. The first flowers were beginning to bloom, and the rolling hills were draped in half a dozen different shades of purple, pink, and blue. It was so beautiful, and it made Sitting Bull's heart ache to think that all that beauty might somehow be taken away from his people. But it was beginning to seem increasingly as if there was nothing that could prevent that from happening.

"You know, uncle," he said, his voice barely audible, "sometimes I think perhaps I should try to make peace with the white man." He lapsed into a silence that seemed to hang in the air like a cloud, smothering all sound.

Four Horns gazed at him questioningly, but didn't press him, knowing that his nephew was trying to find the right words to say what was on his mind.

They had ridden nearly a mile before Sitting Bull continued. "I have fought so hard for so long against the white man that I don't think they would ever leave me alone now, even if we did make a treaty. I have killed so many whites. I think maybe it would be best if I died in battle. At least then I would die true to the old ways, the Lakota ways, that I have tried so hard to protect."

Four Horns tried to reassure him. "Other chiefs have killed whites, and they have managed to make peace."

"But not a good peace. And it is a peace on the white man's terms, a peace which takes everything from the Indian, leaving him nothing but memories. His freedom is taken away. He is told where to live, told to become a farmer instead of hunting the buffalo. I could never do that. It would weigh too heavily on me. It would be like being crushed under a thousand rocks. That is no way to live. Even when I just *think* about what it would be like, I find it hard to breathe. It is not a good way for any Lakota. Certainly not for me."

"Perhaps you could try. You could send a messenger to General Sully telling him you wanted to talk about peace. After you hear what he has to say, you could make up your mind whether it is something you could live with."

Sitting Bull shook his head. "I don't trust them. They tell us lies and when we tell them they have lied, they lie about that, too. You remember what Little Crow said about living on the reservation, how it was like being in a lodge that had no door, no way in or out."

"Little Crow is dead," Four Horns reminded him.

"True, but at least he died a free man, not a captive on a reservation."

"You have to decide whether it is better to die a free man, or live as one who is not quite so free but at least is alive."

"Crazy Horse and I have talked about this, and he thinks as I do. I think it would be worse than being dead—watching our lands ruined, watching our people give up the old ways, making themselves white on the outside. Soon they would be white on the inside, too. What would happen to them then?"

"Each man has to decide for himself."

"But he has to know what he is deciding. If only I could truly know what it would be like. I think I believe what Little Crow said. And what Inkpaduta said. That the reservation is a terrible place."

"If you believe that in your heart, then you have to keep on fighting. If you stop, there will be no one among the Hunkpapa who will continue."

"Gall would."

"Gall is like you. He wants to protect the people, but he has the same doubts. I have spoken to him more than once, and we have had a conversation very much like this one. No one knows what to do. But maybe that is part of being free. If you have no uncertainty, you also have no control. Everything is already decided, no matter what you think or want to do."

"Then I cannot stop fighting."

"Then you shouldn't. You know that I am with you, no matter what you decide. You have the respect of your people. You have the respect of the Strong Hearts and the Kit Foxes and the other warrior societies. They will follow wherever you lead. As I will."

"If only I knew where." Once more he lapsed into silence, and for the rest of the trip he said not another word. Four Horns looked at him once and thought he saw the silver rivulet of a tear on his cheek. He turned away. It was better not to talk about such things.

When they reached home, Her Holy Door pulled him into her lodge to tell him that news had come from the west. A Black Robe was coming on a peace mission. "The one they call De Smet is coming," she said. "He is coming to talk to us about peace with the white man."

Sitting Bull, like most plains Indians, knew of Pierre Jean De Smet. The Jesuit had been traveling across the plains for years, often going where no white man had ever been. And always, he treated the Indians he encountered with respect. He seemed to understand their ways as no other white man did, and he had a kind of courageous dignity the Indians respected. He did not talk down to them, and he did not lie to them.

Maybe, Sitting Bull thought, there is a way out after all. He listened while Her Holy Door told him the rest of what she had heard, then sent runners westward to try to learn more details. And while he waited to learn more, he continued his war.

A week later, messengers reached the Hunkpapa with news that the Great Father had established a peace commission, and that its members wanted to talk to Sitting Bull about settling the dispute over right-of-way for the railroads. But Sitting Bull was not interested in compromising just yet.

Gradually, more information about Father De Smet's visit was obtained from some of the peace chiefs, Running Antelope and Bear's Rib in particular, who had been kept informed by Charles Galpin, one of the traders with whom the Lakota did business, and a man they respected. Galpin was married to a Lakota woman who was half Hunkpapa and half Two Kettle, and he was trusted to tell them the truth.

A week after his latest raid, word reached Sitting Bull that De Smet was indeed on his way. While he waited for the priest, he tried to imagine why the Jesuit would want to talk to him, and what, if anything, the priest could do to ensure that this peace was somehow different from all those that had gone before—a fair one that would be upheld not just by the Lakota but by the white man, too.

They were camped on the Yellowstone, not far from the Powder, and on the edge of Oglala territory. Already, Sitting Bull was hearing news that Red Cloud was beginning to waver in his determination to continue his war against the white army, although he also heard that Crazy Horse was as determined as ever to drive the whites out of Lakota land.

The camp was a large one, including bands under the leadership of Black Moon, Four Horns, and Red Horn. Gall was there, and so was No Neck. At least, Sitting Bull thought, I will not be the only one who thinks as I do. And if I have doubts, I can talk to men who will understand.

Runners announced the imminent arrival of the mission and carried information that Running Antelope, Bear's Rib, and Two Bears were among the Lakota providing protection for De Smet and his followers. Sitting Bull also learned that Galpin was along, with his wife, and that they would serve as interpreters for the conference. At least he could feel confident that his words would be accurately explained to the Black Robe, and that he would know exactly what the missionary told him. But the presence of the peace chiefs was not reassuring.

On June 19, Four Horns sent dozens of warriors in full paint and regalia out to meet the missionary. As the procession drew close to the village, the lodges emptied as almost every man, woman, and

child in the nearly seven hundred tipis turned out
to witness the arrival. Many of them had heard of
De Smet, but few had ever seen him.

Sitting Bull stood in the rear ranks, watching the
approach of a fluttering banner, decorated with
gold stars and the figure of a woman in a long,
flowing robe. The vanguard headed straight for
Sitting Bull's lodge and stopped directly in front of
it. Sitting Bull stepped forward, edging through the
akicita who had been providing protection for the
Jesuit, and greeted him with a raised hand.

Orders were given to break up the crowd, and
the *akicita* sent the people scurrying back to their
lodges. The missionary was escorted into Sitting
Bull's tipi and food and water were brought in.

The chiefs let the weary travelers rest and talked
among themselves, trying to anticipate what he
might have to say. "I think we should let him tell
us, instead of trying to guess ourselves," Sitting
Bull suggested. "When he is rested, we will meet
with him, and then we will learn what he has to
say to us."

It was near sundown before De Smet was rested
enough to greet his hosts. Sitting Bull, Black Moon,
Four Horns, and No Neck comprised the official
greeting party, and they entered Sitting Bull's lodge
to find the priest prepared to talk, and the Galpins
ready to translate for them.

Sitting Bull took the lead and told De Smet how
the war between the Lakota and the white man was
the white man's doing. "I have killed many
whites," he began, "but not without provocation.
They have taken our land, they have killed our

women and children, they have come where they were not welcome and told those who have always lived there that they would have to leave. I am willing to listen to what you have to say, and I am prepared to be peaceful, but not if it means giving up everything my people need to live."

De Smet listened respectfully, occasionally asking a question or two, gathering information for the formal discussions scheduled to begin the following day.

As usual, the next day's ceremony began with a pipe. Four Horns lit it, raised it above his head, gestured toward the earth and the cardinal points, then handed it to Father De Smet, who smoked as if he had been doing it all his life. From the Jesuit, the pipe made its way around the council from chief to chief. They were meeting in a council lodge that had been built by combining several ordinary lodges into a single structure. Even so it was cramped, as there were so many participants.

Four Horns then invited De Smet to speak. The Jesuit framed his remarks carefully and delivered them with deliberation, pausing periodically to allow Galpin to translate for the Lakota.

"I am not here to make peace," he said. "I cannot do this, but it is something I want to see happen. I think it would be a good thing if you were to meet with the peace commissioners at Fort Rice."

At the mention of the hated post, Sitting Bull grew tense, but he said nothing. De Smet continued, "This war is a terrible thing. It is terrible for the whites and it is terrible for the Lakota. The cruelty is causing pain to everyone involved, and it would be a good thing if it could be ended now."

He paused to wait for the translation, looking around at the assembled chiefs. He did not seem afraid, only concerned that he be understood clearly, and Sitting Bull was impressed.

"I wish, I beg," the Jesuit went on, "that you bury your hatred. Try to forgive the white man for the cruelty he has shown you, as he will forgive you." He stopped then to look at the banner bearing the likeness of the Virgin Mary. Indicating it, he said, "I will leave this holy emblem of peace with you as a token of my sincere wish and a reminder that you must consider what is best for the Lakota people. And I think peace is what is best."

Black Moon took the pipe now, puffed it several times, then responded on behalf of all the chiefs. "I know you mean what you say. But you should know that there are many hatreds. There has been much suffering, and it is the white man who has caused it all. Every place we look, there are forts full of Long Knives. Our forest is destroyed, our buffalo slaughtered. The earth is stained red all across the plains, from both white and Indian blood. This is because we have been lied to again and again by the white man. If we could know for sure that we would be lied to no more, in time we might be able to forget what has gone before, and put it behind us. But I do not know if we can forget because I do not know if we can ever believe what the white man says."

Sitting Bull then took the pipe and made his speech. "I hope," he said, "that you are successful.

But I do not think so. We will send people to the council, and we will accept whatever is decided, so long as it is fair and the white man means to honor his promises."

He paid his respects then to De Smet and the Galpins and resumed his seat, only to jump up again immediately. "I have forgotten a few things I wanted to say," he told them. "I think the white man should know that we will not sell or surrender any part of our lands. The white man must stop destroying the trees along the Missouri River, and most of all, he must give up his forts and go back to his own territory. It is the forts, more than anything else, that insult us and provoke us."

The discussion went on for several more hours, but everything that mattered to either side had already been said. When the council session ended, De Smet once again slept in Sitting Bull's lodge, and on the following morning, with the *akicita* once more providing security, De Smet prepared to return to Fort Rice.

Sitting Bull rode in the procession only as far as the Powder River. De Smet paid his respects, and Sitting Bull reminded him of what had been said the day before. When the Jesuit continued on his way, he was not accompanied by any of the significant chiefs in the war faction.

Whether De Smet realized it or not, it was a clear signal from Sitting Bull and the other war chiefs that they held little hope for the advancement of peace by the commissioners.

Chapter 21 ══════════

Missouri River Valley
1868

GALL HAD BEEN SENT TO THE TREATY conference at
Fort Rice and he had stated the Hunkpapa case.
Then he had signed the treaty, without realizing
that not a single one of his concerns, and those of
the other Hunkpapa chiefs, had been addressed by
the agreement.

In effect, nothing changed. The forts remained in
place on the Missouri, and plans were taking shape
for a reservation for the Lakota people. The treaty
was concerned primarily with resolving the
Powder River war. The government agreed to aban-
don the forts in Oglala territory, including C. F.
Smith, but that meant nothing to the Hunkpapa,
whose lands were far to the east. Nevertheless,
Crazy Horse led a war party which burned the fort
to the ground while the whites who relinquished it
were still close enough to see the pall of smoke
from its ruin.

But the treaty was devastating in its implications. By signing on behalf of the Hunkpapas, Gall had bound them to settle on a reservation and to end all hostilities against the white invaders—or so, at least, was the government's interpretation. The white officials could not get it through their heads that Lakota democracy was far more comprehensive than their own version of government, and that no Lakota could bind anyone but himself to do anything, or to refrain from doing anything. Although it was doubtful Gall understood the implications of the treaty, since the peace commissioners themselves, in whose language the document had been composed, were not sure of its interpretation, it would eventually be used to justify continuing hostilities against the Hunkpapas for violating its provisions.

That Sitting Bull neither knew nor cared what the treaty said was made perfectly clear to the white occupiers when, less than two months after the treaty had been signed, he led yet another war party, this time more than one hundred and fifty warriors strong, against the hated Fort Buford. But, as in previous raids, the casualties inflicted on the Long Knives were light, only three soldiers killed. The Hunkpapa had to console themselves with the herd of beef cattle they ran off.

It was time to address questions of organization within the Hunkpapa councils. Four Horns was still the most influential and respected leader, but he was getting older now, and the younger warriors were beginning to look to someone closer to their own age for guidance. They preferred that their

leader be battle-hardened but not battle weary, a
man who would be willing to lead them against the
forts and wage war as the Hunkpapa had always
done, against all invaders, red or white.

Four Horns knew that he was probably due to
step aside, but he worried that the government,
which seemed cumbersome and nearly unwork-
able, had to be redesigned. He knew that peace was
going to be the central concern, as Running
Antelope and Bear's Rib continued to draw new
adherents. And since Red Cloud was increasingly
inclined to make some sort of peace with the white
man, Crazy Horse was growing more and more
influential among the Oglala.

What the Hunkpapa needed, as Four Horns saw
it, was someone like Crazy Horse, a man who could
lead by example, who was not afraid to fight, and
who could inspire others by his own conduct. That
man, clearly, was Sitting Bull, and Four Horns
decided that he would do what he could to persuade the other chiefs to recognize his nephew as
the principal leader of all the Hunkpapa.

Such a thing was almost inconceivable. The idea
of a single chief was alien to Lakota thinking, and
ran counter to hundreds of years of tradition. Four
Horns was contemplating nothing short of a revolu-
tion in Lakota governance, and he was not sure he
could pull it off. But more and more, he was
inclined to believe that it was the only hope the
Hunkpapa had.

Complicating matters further was the fact that of
the four Hunkpapa shirt-wearers, only Four Horns
himself had not fallen into disrepute. Running

Antelope had stolen another man's wife, Red Horn had outdone him in infamy by stealing two wives, and Loud-Voiced Hawk had stabbed another Hunkpapa to death. Since the institution of the shirt-wearers, they had been the primary source of authority for the tribe, but three of the four had forfeited their right to be shirt-wearers at all. Crazy Horse, an Oglala shirt-wearer, had married another man's wife without permission, and had thus relinquished his shirt in recognition of the strict code of behavior to which all shirt-wearers were expected to adhere. But among the Hunkpapa, things were so lax that none of the three miscreants had been removed from office, nor had they volunteered to step down.

That Running Antelope was a peace chief was all the more reason to remove him, because the highest councils of government had to speak with a single voice. If they were fighting among themselves, they would dissipate their authority, leaving the tribe directionless at the most perilous time in its history.

But his plan, no matter how well conceived, would not work if Sitting Bull would not go along with it. He had to convince his nephew first to accept the mantle with which he proposed to drape him. If Sitting Bull refused, then there was nothing more to be done, because as far as Four Horns could see, there was no one else capable of shouldering the enormous burden. Of all the Lakota, only Crazy Horse was Sitting Bull's match, but with increasing frequency, Crazy Horse went off into the wilderness by himself. Mystical by inclination, he was also solitary, and Four Horns knew that he would never consent to do what he had in mind. As a consequence, it was Sitting Bull or no one.

Four Horns waited for the right moment. He did not want to risk alienating Sitting Bull, because he might not be given another chance. When the two of them were off alone on a hunting trip, Four Horns saw his opportunity. They had been tracking a deer for nearly an hour, but the animal had gotten away, and Four Horns suggested they rest by the bank of a creek and let the horses graze a bit.

While they sat in the grass, Four Horns opened the discussion indirectly. "You know that all the Lakota people are divided on whether or not to honor the treaty with the white man," he began.

Sitting Bull pulled a fistful of grass and tapped it against his open palm. "I am not divided. The best thing for the Lakota would be for the white man to go away and never come back."

"That won't happen."

"We can make it happen."

"Not the way we are now. Not when we are fighting among ourselves. There is no one to unite us, to speak with one voice for all the Lakota. Red Cloud wanted to do that, but Red Cloud is already beginning to make his peace."

"Crazy Horse will never make peace. Crazy Horse thinks as I do, that the best way is the old way, *our* way. All he wants, and all that I want, is to be left alone. There would be no war if there was no one to make war against. If the white man were to leave tomorrow, then there would be peace."

"But the white man knows that we cannot agree among ourselves. He sees this and he makes use of it."

"It is our way."

"Maybe it is not the best way. Maybe we should try another way. You know that there is a Bear's Rib in every camp. He is ours, but the Oglala and the Blackfeet have theirs. So do the Sans Arcs and the Miniconjou, the Two Kettles and the Brule. As long as there is no one to stand opposed to them all, there cannot be one voice for the Lakota."

"What would you have us do, pick one man to speak for us all, the way the white man tried to make us do at Fort Laramie so long ago?"

Four Horns could not resist the opening. "Yes. That is what I would have us do."

Sitting Bull laughed. "You are dreaming, uncle. No one can do that."

"He could if he started with one group. The others who think as he did would follow, and those from the other camps would join him. Among the Hunkpapa, most of the people do not want to make peace with the white man. They just want him to leave them alone. So I think that the man to speak for all Lakota should be a Hunkpapa."

Sitting Bull leaned back in the grass, holding the torn blades overhead and letting them rain down over his chest. He liked the scent of the crushed grass. It smelled sweet and clean. "I don't think I would ever let any man speak for me as long as I can speak for myself. I don't see why another Lakota would feel any different."

"That would be true if things were different. But

already some let others speak for them. Some let
Running Antelope speak for them. Some let Bear's
Rib speak for them. Many Oglala let Red Cloud
speak for them. Why can't someone speak for the
others?"

"Who would you have be so bold as to try?"

"You."

Sitting Bull sat up as if he'd been stung by a
scorpion. "Me?" He laughed then, certain that Four
Horns was joking.

But Four Horns immediately made it clear that
he had meant exactly what he said. "Yes, you. It is
the natural thing. Already, you are the most
respected war chief among the Hunkpapa. The warriors listen to you. They follow you into battle.
They would follow you anywhere. You are the one
to lead them. Why not make it plain? Why not
invite all those who think as you do—Oglalas,
Miniconjous, all of them—to follow you?"

"I think it would be a dangerous thing. I think it
would divide us, instead of uniting us. It would
turn father against son, brother against brother."

"It has already come to that, Sitting Bull. You
know that as well as I do. Maybe the only way to
heal the division is to admit that it is there and let
people choose for themselves."

"The shirt-wearers would not permit it."

"The shirt-wearers are a joke. Running Antelope
is a shirt-wearer, and those who disagree with him
do not respect him. Even some of those who agree
with him think he is a fool and a bad man."

"Why not you for leader, then?"

"I am too old. I cannot ride into battle at the

head of a war party like I used to. But you are young enough to lead anywhere, including the warpath, if that is what it takes."

The idea was intriguing, and Sitting Bull did not dismiss it out of hand. Four Horns was hopeful. If he hadn't said no, then there was the chance that he might yet say yes. But Four Horns would not open the discussion with anyone until he had a commitment from his nephew. If he started trying to convince others, then Sitting Bull said no, the last chance was gone, for years if not forever.

"Will you think about it?" Four Horns asked.

Sitting Bull nodded. "I will think about it."

"There is no time to waste. Every day, things get worse. The sooner you make up your mind, the better."

"This is not an easy thing you are asking. I will have to be sure I want to do it. And sure that I think it is the best thing for the people."

"It is."

But Sitting Bull wasn't sure. It was a week before he made up his mind. He spent most of that time by himself, examining the proposal from every angle. He could find many reasons to reject the idea. But just as he knew the Lakota had to find a new way to fight against an enemy that did not fight as other enemies did, he understood that it might be necessary to change the way they governed themselves.

He thought that Four Horns might be overestimating the numbers of Lakota who were opposed to the peace treaty. There were times when he felt as if he were alone in that, or at the very best, one of a handful. Among the Oglala, it was much the same. The people were uncertain. They did not know what the future held for them, and they did not know what to do to give themselves a future they could live with. But while they waited, trying to make up their minds, the white government brought more Long Knives into Lakota land, the railroad went deeper, and the miners and settlers continued to flood across the land.

Already, the buffalo herds had been effectively divided by the railroad. The animals shied away from the railroad tracks, perhaps frightened by the smoke-belching monsters that traveled along the rails, perhaps having learned that they were too easily shot from the moving railroad cars. For whatever reason, the herds had split completely in two. Those south of the railroad never crossed to the north, and those to the north never went south. And the gap in the middle continued to widen as the numbers of buffalo continued to decline.

There were even rumors among the Lakota and Cheyenne that the white men planned to kill all the buffalo as a way to defeat the Indian resistance. It was difficult for a Lakota—even Sitting Bull—to imagine such a harsh extreme. The buffalo meant everything, and the possibility of exterminating them down to the last bull and cow seemed unthinkable. It is likely that the Lakota did not even believe it possible, because the numbers of the great beasts had been so huge and compared to the numbers of Lakota were still unimaginably large.

For a week, he continued to ponder the proposal

Four Horns had made to him. He went off to a hill-top one night and spent all the next day there, too, praying, hoping for a vision, for some sign of what he should do. But it never came. It seemed as if he was going to have to make this decision without any help from anyone, even *Wakantanka*.

He talked it over with Her Holy Door, and she thought it would be a good thing. "You are the only man who can do this thing that Four Horns thinks should be done," she told him.

"Are you saying so because I'm your son?" he asked, smiling at her.

But she did not smile back. "Of course," she said. Then, after waiting a beat or two, she added, "And because it is true."

He walked out to look at the stars on the last night before he made his decision. Each one of them looked like a brilliant glass bead. Some of them seemed so close he wanted to reach out and take them in his palm, but some seemed so far away he thought he could never hope to touch them at all.

That was the way his problem seemed to him. If you looked at it one way, it was a simple thing, a thing that any fool could understand. But when you looked at it another way, it seemed more com-plicated than anyone could understand, even the wisest of the holy men. Maybe, he thought, even *Wakantanka* doesn't understand it. But I will have to try.

It was like trying to unravel the mysteries of a spider's web. Each strand is connected to every other. Touch one and they all move. And no matter which one the fly touches, the spider knows and comes out of his hole. But with this web, the fly can't see all the strands, and he doesn't know where the spider is. Once he touches a strand, it will be too late to turn back.

Then, after a week of wondering, a week of sleepless nights and tortured self-doubt, Sitting Bull made up his mind. He would do as Four Horns asked. And he prayed to *Wakantanka*, hoping that he had not made a mistake. Because if he had, as with the fly and the spider's web, there would be no turning back.

Chapter 22 ═══════════

**Missouri River Valley
1872**

SITTING BULL SLOWLY CLIMBED the hill. On its top,
Crazy Horse sat cross-legged, waiting for him.
Sitting Bull stopped every so often to turn and look
at the thick grass rolling away like huge bolts of the
white man's green velvet cloth. His lame foot still
bothered him, and walking uphill was the worst.
He could still run when he had to, but he was no
longer like the wind. He kept looking around him,
his gaze flitting like a butterfly, never staying long
in one place, as if he wanted to see everything
there was to see, the way a man might look at the
world as he stepped onto a scaffold and waited for
the hangman's hood to shut it out forever.

It seemed to Crazy Horse that Sitting Bull was
not just looking at the world, he was absorbing it,
taking it into him and making it a part of himself.
The great medicine man was so intimately connected to the world around him that there was no

way to tell where one left off and the other began. That was what had drawn Crazy Horse to him in the first place. And the more time they spent together, the greater became the younger man's respect.

Sitting Bull knew that Crazy Horse admired him, and he respected the younger man, too, because like him, Crazy Horse understood the old ways. He knew them inside out, but more than that, he respected them. He saw why they were best. The relationship between the Sioux and the world in which they lived was more than a simple dependency. The way Sitting Bull saw it, the world needed the Lakota people as much as the Lakota needed the world and all that was in it. Each needed the other. The Lakota needed the plains, the open sky, the cold rushing waters of the rivers, and the buffalo. But all those things had special meaning in relation to the Lakota. It was the Lakota people who gave them their value. That was what made the Lakota so different from the white man. The white man looked at the world and saw only something to be taken. He had no respect for the earth. It was just something he stabbed and slashed and tore apart, ripping things from its insides the way a thief ripped things from a torn pocket.

Sitting Bull treasured his friendship with the young Oglala the way he valued no other human connection. Not even the love he'd had for Jumping Bull or Four Horns could come close. They were, in some way that Sitting Bull understood but could not quite articulate, the only two Lakota who saw things as they truly were. At night, lying in his lodge, worrying about the future, it was comforting to know that he was not alone. Crazy Horse didn't talk much, but Sitting Bull believed that the younger man felt the same way.

Sitting Bull was a brave man and a great warrior. He saw that Crazy Horse shared those qualities with him, and felt the same devotion to the old ways. It sometimes seemed to him that he and Crazy Horse were like two parts of the same organism, heart and brain of the same beast. Without either, the beast would die. And without either man, the Lakota themselves were doomed. What Sitting Bull feared, and what he had tried so hard to explain to Crazy Horse, was that the Lakota might be lost in any event. But Crazy Horse was fiercely determined, perhaps even more than Sitting Bull himself, to preserve what mattered. He would not accept the notion that the white man could not be defeated.

As he drew closer, Sitting Bull stopped once more, raising a hand to acknowledge the younger man, then turned again to look out over the valley, the blue-white curl of the river like a strip of the white man's shiny ribbon winding off to the southeast. A hawk cried high above the hill, and Sitting Bull looked up to watch it glide, its wings motionless as it rode the warm air rising from the valley floor. The great bird cried once more as Sitting Bull waved toward the sky. When he returned his gaze earthward, he saw that Crazy Horse was smiling at him. He knew that Crazy Horse was wondering whether man and bird were communicating, or if the wave was just a random movement that had nothing to do with the hawk. But if Crazy Horse asked, he would not know the true answer.

Sitting Bull climbed the last two hundred feet and sat on the grass beside Crazy Horse before saying anything. At forty-one, he was only a few years older than the great young warrior, but he seemed almost ancient by comparison. It was not that his physical powers had begun to desert him. Far from it—they were at their peak. He was still vigorous, his broad shoulders and solid trunk almost like a slab of granite. In some ways, he seemed so much more powerful than his young friend. But on some days he felt older than the ground he walked on. And this was one of those days.

"It's a beautiful day," Sitting Bull said. He lowered himself to the ground without another word, and they sat side by side for several minutes without talking. They sat this way often, when time and duty permitted, sometimes saying nothing, sometimes talking about whatever crossed their minds. Most of the talks had to do with the plight of their people, because neither warrior could afford to let his thoughts wander far from the impossible bind in which the Lakota now found themselves.

"The village looks so small," Crazy Horse said, finally breaking the silence. "When I was a boy, I used to make tiny tipis out of willow branches and scraps of buckskin. I could hold three or four in the palm of my hand, like a tiny village. I could make it float high above my head, where nothing, not even the dogs, could get to it. I wish that I could lift all the Lakota in my palm that way, to protect them from what is happening."

"We are in a greater palm," Sitting Bull said. "*Wakantanka* holds us in his hand. But sometimes I worry that he will forget that we are there and clap his hands together to kill a fly, or close his hand into a mighty fist. Maybe it will be something simple, as simple as a wave to a friend. But whatever it is, it will be the end of the Lakota people."

"I don't worry about *Wakantanka* or what he might do. I worry more about the white man. I can't interfere with what the Great Spirit will or will not do," Crazy Horse said. "Whatever he will do, he will do. I can't stop him, I can't change him. I just have to accept what he does, whatever it is. But the white man can be stopped."

"You have heard that the white man is building another iron road?"

Crazy Horse nodded. "Yes, I have heard. He is slicing open the Powder River country the way you cut open a bloated carcass. There are soldiers, too. Many of them. They are coming into the Yellowstone country, and soon there will be too many of them to stop or to drive away."

Sitting Bull was quiet for a moment, then said, "I have heard that, too. I think it is time we tried to do something to stop them, before they destroy everything. But it is hard to get the young warriors to listen. The young men have their heads full of foolishness. It is hard to teach them to do things in a way that the white man won't understand. They have no discipline. And Long Holy is filling their heads with his nonsense."

"Long Holy has strong medicine."

Sitting Bull nodded. "I know he does. I under-

stand medicine. You know that. But I don't think
he knows what he is doing. He tells the young men
he can make them bulletproof. All it will do is get
them hurt. And then they will distrust all
medicine, not just this silliness of Long Holy's."

"I have heard that he gave a demonstration."

"He did. I was there when he did it. He shot a
gun again and again. And the young men tried to
catch the bullets in their palms, like fools," said
Sitting Bull.

"And what happened? Did his medicine work?"

"The bullets bounced off. They made bruises,
but did not break the skin."

"But you still don't believe his medicine powerful enough to do what he says it can do?" Crazy
Horse looked surprised.

Sitting Bull snorted. "Always, the young men
want to think that they are bulletproof, or that a
knife cannot cut through their skins. They want to
think that their heads are so hard that a war club
will not break the bones like a woman breaks mel-
ons with a rock. And that is a good thing. It is
important to believe that you are powerful, that
you have strong medicine to protect you on the
warpath. It lets you do things that you would not
do if you were afraid of getting hurt. But Long
Holy's medicine is a fraud."

"You said the bullets bounced off."

"They did. But you and I know that we do not
put as much powder in our bullets as the white
man does. If there is not enough powder, the bullets don't travel as fast. They will bounce off skin.
You have seen it yourself—how sometimes we

shoot a bluecoat or a Crow and he does not bleed. Sometimes the bullet goes through his coat and stays there against his skin, and sometimes it does not even pierce the cloth. That is because we don't have enough gunpowder, and we weaken the bullets. But the white man has all the gunpowder he needs. If the young men ride in front of his guns thinking they will not be harmed, they will be killed."

"Have you told the young warriors this?"

Sitting Bull nodded his head. "Yes, I have told them. But they won't listen. They smile and shake their heads, the way you do when you listen to a foolish old man. Then, behind their hands, they say 'Sitting Bull is jealous of Long Holy.' I am not jealous. But I am not a fool. I am sure of what I know and what the young ones do not know."

"Maybe it is not a bad thing that they believe in Long Holy's medicine. It will give them courage, and that is something they will need."

"Sometimes I think that way, but then I remember what it will be like in the lodges when the women learn that their young men were wrong . . ."

Crazy Horse nodded his head. "How!"

Sitting Bull stood then and started to walk back down the hill. It was a long walk, and he limped every step of the way, even knowing that Crazy Horse was watching him. He felt a great weight on his shoulders and it seemed as if he were sinking into the earth with every step, as if he carried some invisible burden that made his shoulders sag under its weight.

When he started across the flats toward the
village, he turned to see Crazy Horse looking out
across the valley. Following his friend's gaze, he
saw the herds of ponies, their heads bobbing as
they tugged on the thick, lush grass. He saw the
dogs lapping at water by the river's edge. He saw
the children running along the riverbank, sometimes falling, sometimes slipping into the water
and kicking great silver arcs of spray into the air
with their bare feet. It made him sad to see these
images, each one so precious, each one so deeply
rooted in Lakota life. He wondered if he could preserve them, or if one day the valley would be full of
the white man's white-painted buildings, surrounded by sagging fences that carved the earth
into little square patches. He didn't know, but it
frightened him.

As he neared his lodge, Sitting Bull noticed
some movement on the ridge across the valley.
First one then two more riders broke over the crest
and headed down, pushing their warhorses at a full
gallop. Crazy Horse saw them, too, and started to
run. Soon he was going so fast that he dared not
stop for fear of falling over. The effort made his lip
hurt where the bullet scar was like a jagged slash of
lightning, and his lungs felt as if they were full of
fire. He saw Sitting Bull, with that distinctive limp-
ing run of his, heading toward the incoming
ponies.

Something was happening, and Crazy Horse
raced to the village, reaching the first lodge as the
riders slipped from their ponies.

The riders were scouts, and they were beside

themselves with excitement. They saw Sitting Bull and headed straight for him. "Bluecoats," they shouted. "Many Long Knives on Arrow Creek."

The word spread rapidly, and the Lakota warriors were infuriated by the invasion of their territory. Crazy Horse looked for Sitting Bull and saw him at the center of the widening circle surrounding the excited scouts.

Slipping through the throng, he eased in beside the medicine man. "We should make a good plan before we ride out to meet these soldiers," he said.

Sitting Bull nodded. "We should, but I don't think the hotheads will listen to us. I think we might have to lead without knowing where we are going. But that will be better than letting them go off on their own"

"We can make them listen to us," Crazy Horse insisted.

Sitting Bull shook his head. "No, all we can do is go with them and try to save them from themselves. They are reckless and spoiling for a fight. You'd better get your rifle and pony."

The war party rode for three days. Each night, around the council fire, Sitting Bull tried to convince the other men—with the help of Crazy Horse—of the need for restraint, for careful planning, for an understanding of the white man's way of fighting. And every night the council dissolved in argument. A few of the other warriors, like White Bull and Two Bows, were also in favor of careful planning. But most of the younger men, even Lone Bear, were too angry to listen or learn. Long Holy had filled their heads

with his foolishness, and they were determined
to prove that his medicine worked.

On August 14, word came back from the
advance scouts. There were many bluecoats, both
horse soldiers and foot soldiers . . . maybe four
hundred, maybe more. Sitting Bull and Crazy
Horse tried once again to devise a reasonable strategy, but the younger men were not to be deterred.
They pushed their mounts far ahead, and all Crazy
Horse and Sitting Bull could do was follow behind.

The advance party swept over the last ridge
above the mouth of Arrow Creek, a mile from
where it met the Tongue River, and galloped down
on the army herd. They succeeded in driving off
some American horses and cattle, but the attack
was too spontaneous to have much impact on the
soldiers. Under the command of Major E. M. Baker,
they quickly mounted a defense. Their superior
weapons drove off the Lakota, who retreated with
little to show for their efforts, and with any opportunity for a surprise attack swept away.

When the attackers rejoined the main body of
Lakota, Long Holy announced that he and seven of
his adherents were going to ride up to the army
lines and circle around them four times. He said
that all eight of them would return safe and sound.
"Maybe then," he challenged, "you will see that
what I have been saying is true. Maybe then you
will believe."

With a contemptuous glance at Sitting Bull,
Long Holy climbed onto his pony and led the
charge. He had taught his followers a medicine
song, and they shouted it at the top of their lungs

as they rode around Baker's men. A hail of gunfire poured out from the defensive positions. One by one the circling warriors were hit by bullets, until four of the eight were badly wounded.

Sitting Bull, unable to bear it any longer, charged into the open area between the Lakota and the soldiers. "Stop!" he shouted. "Stop this foolishness! You'll all get yourselves killed." He saw the blood streaming from the four wounded Lakota and could no longer contain his contempt for Long Holy and his false pride.

But Long Holy was not ready to give up. "I brought them here to make war," he shouted. "Let them do it!"

Sitting Bull paid no attention to the medicine man, and instead argued with the young warriors, trying to persuade them to be more cautious. Frightened by the results of their first charge behind Long Holy, and more than a little intimidated by the obvious anger of the great Sitting Bull, they listened.

For two solid hours, the two sides exchanged shots at long range, neither side causing much damage. Then, in an attempt to provoke pursuit, Crazy Horse galloped his pony down toward the bluecoats and rode slowly across the entire width of the soldiers' line. But not one soldier came out to chase him. Instead, the Long Knives continued to blaze away at long range, with little effect. When Crazy Horse returned to the Lakota line, Sitting Bull was annoyed. He felt that Crazy Horse was getting too much attention for his heroics.

Dismounting, he took his pipe and limped

slowly across the open field until he was about midway between the opposing forces, at the edge of the effective range of the army rifles. He sat down and, using a flint and steel, lit the pipe. Casually, Sitting Bull puffed away, until a wreath of smoke swirled around him. Turning to look over his shoulder, he shouted, "Anyone who wants to join me in a smoke, come on."

Several young warriors, anxious to prove their mettle, took the chief's dare and came out to join him. Soon, six or seven were arrayed in a line. Sitting Bull passed the pipe to his nephew, White Bull, who puffed hurriedly then passed the pipe along to the next man. The others smoked as fast as they could while bullets whistled around them, swarming like bees, tearing chunks of sod loose but hitting no one.

When the pipe had finally made its way back down the line to Sitting Bull, he took one more puff. One by one, the others who had smoked scampered back to safety, but Sitting Bull wasn't finished yet. He got out his cleaning stick, scraped the pipe bowl clean, and put the pipe into its beaded sheath. Then he got to his feet slowly and limped back to join the others, a broad smile on his face. The whole war party was in awe. This was certainly the bravest thing any Lakota warrior had ever done, they thought. Admiration spread throughout the group of warriors.

Then Crazy Horse played his trump card. Springing onto his pony, he called to White Bull, "Let's make one more pass," and he was off, charging across the open field toward one end of the army line. White Bull was behind him as he galloped the full length of the line, every soldier firing at him as he raced past. At the far end of the line, he turned back toward the Sioux, with White Bull, who had not gone as close, now in front of him.

Crazy Horse was almost back to the others when a bullet caught his pony, killing it outright, spilling him to the ground. Scrambling and crawling, he raced back unhurt, his face wearing a smile even broader than that of Sitting Bull.

Sitting Bull nodded his approval and returned the smile. "That's enough for today," he shouted. He might not have been outdone, but he had certainly been matched.

Chapter 23

Rosebud River Valley
1875

IN JULY OF 1874, A LONG U.S. ARMY column left Fort Abraham Lincoln and headed southwest. At its head rode Lieutenant Colonel George Armstrong Custer. The Lakota knew of him and his fearsome reputation. In 1868, Long Hair, as they called him, had led an attack on a Cheyenne village along the Washita River in Indian territory, attacking the very same camp that had been decimated by Colonel Chivington at Sand Creek. This time the chief of the Cheyenne, Black Kettle, who had survived Sand Creek, was not so lucky. Now Long Hair was leading his Long Knives into the very heart of sacred Lakota land, the *Paha Sapa*, the Black Hills.

The Lakota were already fuming over the intrusion of soldiers and survey teams and, when the surveys were complete, the construction crews building the Northern Pacific Railroad. The route planned for the new railroad would go through the

228

heart of the Yellowstone River country, just as Sitting Bull had predicted so long ago when Gall had signed the treaty at Fort Rice.

It was beginning to seem to Sitting Bull that only he and Crazy Horse saw just how far the white men were prepared to go to get what they wanted. Assurances meant nothing, treaties meant nothing, and now apparently even the agreement that the Black Hills would remain inviolate meant nothing.

The Lakota had been promised that the whites would not enter the Black Hills without their express permission, but Long Hair had not asked permission and he was heading a column large enough to suggest that he was not prepared to be dissuaded by anything short of total war. The justification for the expedition was the need to find a place to build a fort which would enable the military to supervise the treaty Lakota at the Red Cloud and Spotted Tail agencies. But Sitting Bull wasn't sure. There were plenty of places for such a fort that did not profane the sacred lands of the Lakota.

Scouts kept close watch on Custer for the two-month duration of the expedition, but there was no outright challenge to the column. When Custer returned, Sitting Bull was sorry that he hadn't taken a stronger stand as soon as the destination of the troops became known. Custer trumpeted to the world the discovery of gold in the Black Hills, and the announcement triggered a flood of prospectors, and later, mining crews. And where the miners went, the merchants went—towns springing up like weeds overnight to accommodate the needs of the miners and freighters.

Crazy Horse, incensed by the desecration of *Paha Sapa*, had taken to leading small bands of Oglala in hit-and-run attacks on mining camps and the supply trains that constantly wound their way through the hills. But it was like trying to stop a flood with a single sponge. There were just too many whites pouring in, and when the Indian attacks increased in frequency, the military presence was augmented. It was an ever increasing spiral.

Sitting Bull had his hands full with other troubles in the Yellowstone valley. Settlements were springing up, and the railroad crews were making progress. And to add to the irritation, the hated Crows, who had their reservation and agency nearby, were increasing their presence in Hunkpapa hunting grounds.

It was beginning to seem to Sitting Bull as if he and his people were being attacked from all sides, and it was difficult to know where to concentrate his attention. As a holy man, he was concerned about the Black Hills; as a traditionalist, he cared about the Crows, his bitterest enemies; and as a Lakota, he cared about the influx of whites into every corner of Sioux territory.

Sitting Bull had been warring with the whites for so long now that he seemed to understand them better than any other Lakota war chief except Crazy Horse. But Crazy Horse was too much of a mystic and too solitary by disposition to do what Sitting Bull knew had to be done. It was important to marshal as much manpower as possible, and that meant reaching out to other peoples. As the principal chief of the Hunkpapas, he had the prominence needed to approach other leaders, not just of the Lakota but of other tribes as well. With the number of Lakota now on the reservations, many of them disaffected but also many who believed as Red Cloud now did that accommodation was the only way to preserve themselves, allies had to be found to prosecute the full-scale war which Sitting Bull now believed to be inevitable.

The Hunkpapa had had the least to do with the whites, because of the seven Lakota tribes, their hunting grounds had, until recently, been the least disturbed by the invaders. As a consequence, the Hunkpapa had the greatest percentage of all Lakota bands living off the reservation. But Hunkpapas alone would not be enough. Even if all the disaffected treaty warriors were to band together with the nontreaty bands from all seven Lakota tribes, they would not be enough.

Sitting Bull knew that in order to wage the war on the scale he now believed necessary he needed as many warriors as he could get. The Cheyenne had long been allies, and with Sand Creek still a vivid memory, and the Washita a bitter reminder that being friendly and peaceful was no guarantee of protection against the predatory whites, they were likely candidates to join the alliance Sitting Bull planned to propose.

In early 1875, Sitting Bull sent word that there would be a grand sun dance and invited all those who wished to attend to meet on the banks of the Rosebud River near Muddy Creek. By early June,

hunting bands were pouring in from every direction. Four camp circles were established, one each
for the Hunkpapa, the Oglala, the Miniconjou and
Sans Arcs, and the Cheyenne.

As the bands arrived one by one, Sitting Bull
was heartened by the turnout. Not only were the
numbers of warriors greater than he had hoped, but
the best of the war chiefs were there, too. The
Oglala had Crazy Horse and Black Twin among
their number, while the Miniconjou and Sans Arcs
had Spotted Eagle, and the Cheyennes had Little
Wolf and the famous warrior and holy man Ice.

These were the kind of men he needed, men
who believed as he did and were as fiercely committed as he was to the preservation of the old
ways and the defense of Lakota lands. As confident
as he was in his own skills, he knew that he could
not do what needed to be done by himself. He
needed help, and these chiefs were the men he
would have chosen himself to give that help.

When the people had gathered and the sun
dance lodge had been constructed, Sitting Bull prepared to make his appeal to the assembled chiefs
and warriors for intertribal unity. He knew that the
future of his people depended on his success. He
wanted to make an impression. They all knew of
him, of his exploits in battle, of his accomplishments as a singer and musician, of his dedication
as a holy man. But reputation alone would not be
enough to sway his audience; he needed to seize
them in a way no one ever had.

Ice had presented him with a magnificent black
stallion, and Sitting Bull decided that it would be

just the right horse to ride for his grand entrance. He took great pains getting himself ready, applying his ceremonial paint and wearing a new warbonnet with a full trail of eagle feathers. The black stallion was daubed with white paint in bands and spots. Then Sitting Bull mounted up and rode toward the sun dance lodge, making a great circle.

The people began to press in from all sides as he made another circuit, then dismounted and leading the magnificent horse by the bridle began to dance. He sang songs he had composed especially for the occasion. By now the lodge was filled to overflowing, and Sitting Bull, knowing that he had the full attention of his audience, announced that he wanted two ceremonial pipes filled, one for the Lakota and one for the Cheyenne.

When the pipes were ready, he took both and resumed his dance, miming battle with the enemy. By now the audience was itself singing, and with a grand flourish, he wrapped his arms across his chest to signify that he had captured his enemies. A roar went up as Sitting Bull raised the pipes overhead in offering to the heavens.

Afterward Sitting Bull, Ice, Crazy Horse, and some of the other chiefs gathered in a council lodge. They all knew that war was coming soon, that it would be big, and that it would be pivotal. They were not yet sure when it would start or with whom it would be waged, but there was no doubt at all that it was coming.

"We all know," Sitting Bull declared, "that we cannot trust the white man. He has said that we would have the Black Hills forever, and yet Long

Hair has gone there without our permission. He has said that we would have the land of the Powder River valley as long as the buffalo run, and now he builds his railroad there and kills the buffalo. He has said many things, but he has never said a true thing to the Lakota."

The assembled chiefs nodded their heads in agreement as Sitting Bull continued, "If we want to save our lands, to have them—as is our right—for ourselves, we will have to work together. If it means making war on the white man together, then that is what we should do. I want nothing better than for the white man to go back where he came from and leave me in peace. If he would do this, then I would forever be a friend to him. If he did not bother me, he would never see me, never even know I am here. But always he makes promises and always he breaks them. He is like a child who misbehaves. You tell him to stop, and he says yes, he understands, and then he disobeys again. Again you tell him, and again he says yes, he will stop. And again he misbehaves."

Once more, the chiefs indicated their agreement with a chorus of "How!"

But Sitting Bull was not finished yet. "Now he wants to take away not only our hunting grounds, but our sacred lands of *Paha Sapa*. This time, I think, it will not be enough to say stop. This time, I think, we will have to *make* him stop. We will have to do whatever we can to keep what is ours."

But even as he spoke, the government was attempting to acquire the Black Hills. Pressure was brought to bear on the agency chiefs in an effort to induce them to sell title to the area. If this could be managed, then the government would simply claim that the agency chiefs had acted on behalf of all the Lakota people, and that the land had been fairly acquired. But there was no real interest in being fair. Any excuse would do, and if no one could be persuaded to sell the Black Hills, then they would just have to be taken by force.

Red Cloud and Spotted Tail, long since ensconced in their own separate agencies, had been willing to make the deal proposed by the government. Red Cloud had tried to get more than the government offered, but even what he was asking was a pitiful fraction of the true worth of the territory in question. And any deal would ignore the fact that the land was sacred. But Red Cloud suspected that the Black Hills would be taken one way or another, and that the Lakota should get whatever they could. Anything at all was better than nothing. In the eyes of Crazy Horse and Sitting Bull, though, the Black Hills could not and must not be sold, not at any price.

Sitting Bull learned of the maneuverings. He was depressed by the news, and beginning to wonder if it was possible to hold onto the land, even if he managed to enlist every nonagency Indian on the plains.

He spent much time alone, trying to find some way to prevent the white man from taking the land. During long nights, sitting up on a hill overlooking his village, he mulled over his options, but they were few and unpredictable. He knew that some Indians had gone north, to Canada, where they seemed to be well treated, left alone by the government of the Grandmother Country, allowed to live as they had always lived. The weather there was harsher, and the buffalo fewer, but at the rate the buffalo were disappearing from the plains south of the border, there was little reason to think that would continue to be the case much longer.

He also knew that the Cheyenne had occasionally gone as far south as Mexico, but what he heard of the land there did not appeal to him. It was hot and barren, the buffalo few, and such a move would imperil the Lakota way of life every bit as much as capitulation to the demands of the United States would. It seemed that no matter which way he turned, he found himself staring at a blank wall. And he felt as if he were virtually alone in his understanding of just how dire the circumstances were. It was true that other chiefs were opposed to the treaties, opposed to the white man taking the land, dedicated to the old ways. But only Crazy Horse seemed to see things as clearly as Sitting Bull himself, and two men, no matter how valiant, could not stem the white tide.

Desperate for an answer to a question that only he and Crazy Horse appeared to be trying to address, he rode off to be alone in late summer. He spent several days in isolation, fasting and building a sweat lodge for himself, spending hours at a time trying to pierce the veil of uncertainty that seemed to hide the way into the future.

On the fourth day of his fast, he climbed to the top of a nearby hill before daybreak and watched the sun climb over the horizon. All day long he watched the sun, hoping that somehow it would communicate to him the right path to follow.

By late afternoon, thirsty and hungry, his eyes filmed over by a brilliant, gauzy haze, he heard a sound like thunder. It seemed that the sky was clouding over, and the haze grew dark and thick. For a moment he thought it was going to rain, but as he listened, he realized the sound was not thunder at all but buffalo, thousands upon thousands of them, and they were heading his way.

Rubbing his eyes with the back of his wrist, he tried to see them, but instead watched as the sun disappeared in a cloud of thick dust swirling up from the advancing herd. A moment later a bull broke over the next ridge, and he watched in awe as wave after wave of the huge animals followed the great bull in the lead. Then he felt stark terror grip him as he realized that the bull was a skeleton, and as the waves of animals followed it down the hillside into the valley below, the flesh seemed to melt from their bones and vanish in puffs of thick, black smoke. It was this smoke, rather than dust kicked up by the buffalo hooves, that was blotting out the sun.

He knew that he was watching the end of the Lakota people, and that that end would come soon unless he could find a way to prevent it.

Chapter 24 ═══════

Rosebud River Valley
1876

BY 1875, SITTING BULL WAS well known in
Washington. Men he had never heard of had heard
of him and regarded him as something akin to the
devil. His reputation among the enemies of the
Hunkpapa, such as the Crows, Shoshone, and
Arikara, was such that they too regarded him as
death incarnate. His reputation among the Lakota
was more accurate, but no less awe inspiring. This
complex set of factors had combined to make him
the focus of policy making among the politicians
and the Indian Bureau.

That he deserved his notoriety is beyond dispute. It is only the accuracy of these impressions
that can be called into question. The Indian
Bureau, under constant pressure to resolve the
"Indian Problem" by any means necessary, quite
naturally looked for a reasonable alibi for its fail-
ures. Rather than examine the reasonableness of

its own policy and that of the government in general, the Bureau chose to make Sitting Bull the scapegoat for virtually every incident involving the Lakota. Similarly, the Crows and other enemies of the Lakota who had been dealt with rather harshly by Sitting Bull, and who had reason to hate him, blamed him for their misfortunes, never losing the opportunity to blame him for violent confrontations between whites and Indians.

Sitting Bull was not without enemies among the Lakota themselves, either. Some, such as Red Cloud, had decided that the path of least resistance was the only way to ensure Lakota survival. In order to maintain their own influence among the treaty Indians and with the white politicians and soldiers, such men availed themselves of every chance to paint Sitting Bull in the worst possible colors. Defaming him ensured their own continued power, and while there is no doubt that some of these chiefs were motivated by the best of intentions, their methods are somewhat less than admirable. Other Lakota were envious of his power and influence and did their best to undermine him.

For whatever reasons, Sitting Bull was widely believed in the East to be the single most influential leader among the so-called hostile Indians. Crazy Horse was as highly regarded by the non-treaty Lakota bands, but he was not nearly as well known among the whites, and his own band of followers was considerably smaller, largely as a consequence of his reclusive nature. That Sitting Bull had become the first among equals in keeping with the plan that Four Horns had devised cemented the war chief's notoriety.

By the end of 1875, the government leaders concerned with the maintenance of peace on the western plains, civil and military alike, were convinced that all-out war was the only solution to their problems. The War Department was actively engaged in drawing up plans for an offensive the following spring, one that was intended to put an end for all time to the Sioux wars and bring civilization at long last to the plains.

There was constant pressure from the railroads, which were having great difficulty completing their construction because of the incessant harassment of work crews. Where the track had ben successfully laid, trains themselves were subjected to attack without warning, which made them less attractive to potential customers. Raids by Lakota bands were costing the railroads money, and they wanted the raids stopped at any cost. Ever sensitive to the concerns of business, the government was determined to do everything in its power to give the railroads what they wanted. If peace meant breaking promises made to savages, then that was a small enough price to pay, and certainly one that no one would object to—no one whose opinion counted, in any event.

President Grant had convened a meeting of his principal advisers on Indian policy, including Zachariah Chandler, the Secretary of the Interior; E. P. Smith, the Commissioner of Indian Affairs; and William Belknap, the Secretary of War. The result of the meeting was a foregone conclusion, and everyone in attendance knew it. They knew, after all, what was expected of them, and Chandler drafted an order that served as the opening shot in the great war to pacify the western plains. It was sent to the Commissioner of Indian Affairs, and read: "Referring to our communication of the 27th ultimo, relative to the status of certain Sioux Indians residing without the bounds of their reservation and their continued hostile attitude towards the whites, I have to request that you direct the Indian agents at all Sioux agencies in Dakota and at Fort Peck, Montana, to notify said Indians that unless they shall remove within the bounds of their reservation (and remain there), before the 31st of January next, they shall be deemed hostile and treated accordingly by the military force."

The directive, which did not even reach the Standing Rock Agency until December 22, was silent on several relevant questions, however. It did not explain how the so-called hostile bands were to be notified in time to make the deadline, since the directive left less than sixty days, not only for the word to be passed, but for compliance. Nor did the Secretary much bother with the questionable assumption that the Lakota who had signed no treaty even had a reservation to go to.

Also overlooked in the Secretary's desire to solve this most vexing of problems was the reality that even treaty Lakota strayed beyond the perpetually shrinking boundaries of the Sioux reservation in order to track buffalo herds. Hunting was absolutely essential to supplement the meager rations authorized by the government, which more often than not were short-weighted and inedible if they were delivered at all.

Sitting Bull could no doubt have disabused the Secretary of the Interior of several mistaken assumptions, but as usual the Indians were not consulted about their own lives. And both Red Cloud and Spotted Tail, each of whom had his own agency, could and frequently did testify as to the futility of attempting to go through official channels in order to correct these abuses.

The military was more than happy to see this retreat from the abortive and frequently sabotaged "peace policy" President Grant had tried on first coming to office. The officer corps had a few scores to settle, such as the Grattan and Fetterman affairs, and the lower ranks were full of would-be Grattans, anxious to settle things at gunpoint.

But the government moved slowly, and it was months before the full significance of the decision would become apparent to either side in the slowly escalating conflict.

Sitting Bull was more than two hundred and fifty miles from Standing Rock on December 22. The winter, which promised to be more severe than usual, had already begun in earnest. Messengers had to carry the news hundreds of miles through snowdrifts, howling winds, and subfreezing temperatures. Off and on for the next few weeks, the snow mounted, making those bands even further away than Sitting Bull's

Hunkpapas inaccessible until spring. By that time, were they disposed to honor the requirements, they would already be in violation of the directive and months beyond the unreasonable deadline.

But Sitting Bull was in no mood to observe any limits the white government meant to impose on him. He knew that there was no food at the agencies, because his own camp was full of treaty Indians who had left them rather than starve. Despite the government's inability to determine whether or not Sitting Bull had even been apprised of the directive, he was declared hostile on February 7, 1876, and orders were issued to subdue him by force.

Unfortunately for the army, however, the snows were so deep and the weather conditions so inhospitable that a punitive expedition was unable to penetrate into the northwestern reaches along the Powder, where Sitting Bull was camped, by marching up the Missouri River valley. In view of the weather, the commander of the expedition, General George Crook, whom the Lakota called Three Stars for his rank insignia, decided to pursue other bands declared hostile and then living off the reservation by approaching them from the south, where the weather was more moderate.

On March 1, 1876, Crook led his column out of Fort Fetterman, Wyoming. Crook's initial target was not Sitting Bull but Crazy Horse, and he had information—mistaken however—that Crazy Horse was camped a few miles above the mouth of the

Little Powder River. Crook did not realize that the camp in question was actually inhabited by Cheyennes under Chief Two Moon.

It took the column nearly three weeks to reach its destination, and the battle, which began on March 17, would complicate the war still further by bringing the Cheyennes into it. Colonel J. J. Reynolds, who led the attack, managed to take the camp for a short period, capturing a large number of Cheyenne ponies as well, but he panicked and was unable to hold the camp or the horses for long once the Cheyenne regrouped. All he managed to do was provoke Two Moon and ensure that Sitting Bull and Crazy Horse would have another powerful and respected ally. He was court-martialed for his failure, but the damage was done.

The weather continued to be severe. Bands of Oglala and Cheyenne drifted into Sitting Bull's camp during the rest of March and early April, and when he heard the news of the unprovoked attack on Two Moon's Cheyennes, he knew that he could no longer postpone the inevitable. Haunted by his vision of the herd of skeletal buffalo, and fearful that he might be leading his people into a war that would bring about their destruction, he realized that he had no choice; the white man would not let his people live as they chose, or where they chose, and the alternative proposed by the representatives of the Great Father was no choice at all.

Sitting Bull was incensed by the attack on the Cheyennes. He knew that the moment he had been dreading was now at hand. As soon as the weather broke, he sent runners all across the plains, to every Lakota camp, and to the Cheyenne, as well. He even reached out to the Arapaho. The messengers rode until their ponies dropped, and at every camp the message was the same: "It is war. Come to my camp on the Rosebud River and we will have one big fight with the Long Knives."

Roving bands of nontreaty Indians began to pour into Sitting Bull's camp, swelling it to hundreds of lodges, then to more than a thousand. It became a flood as some bands of treaty Lakota, off the reservation for a buffalo hunt made necessary by the near starvation they suffered on the agency's meager rations, joined the Hunkpapa and Oglala hostiles. By early June, Sitting Bull knew that the fight would be soon, and that its outcome might very well determine the future of his people.

This was the chance Sitting Bull needed to impress upon his allies the need to organize their forces in a way that would enable them to fight more effectively against the Long Knives with their centralized command structure. But such an understanding could not be accomplished by an act of will. It was necessary to persuade, cajole, even bargain—whatever it would take to make the other chiefs see things as he did.

It was nearly time for the sun dance, and Sitting Bull wanted to have his ducks in a row before the great ceremony. A council was called, and a huge council lodge erected by combining several

dwellings. All the great nontreaty chiefs were
there: Crazy Horse and Low Dog from the Oglala,
Lame Deer and Black Moon from the Miniconjou,
Spotted Eagle and Black Eagle of the Sans Arcs,
Four Horns and Black Moon from the Hunkpapa.
The Cheyenne were represented by Two Moon,
Ice, and Little Horse, and there was a sizable con-
tingent of warriors from Spotted Tail's Brules, as
well as Two Kettles, Blackfeet Sioux, and
Yanktonais. Even Inkpaduta was there with his
Santee Sioux.

Once the pipe had been smoked, Sitting Bull
took the floor. He looked at Ice and smiled. "Our
Cheyenne brothers are here with us, and we welcome them. As our guests, they should have the
honor of choosing their leader for the coming war
before we choose our own leader."

The Cheyenne chiefs did not hesitate. Two
Moon, whose camp had been hit by Crook's column in March, was named the war leader for all
the Cheyennes. Now came the difficult moment of
choosing an overall leader for the Lakota.

One after another, each Lakota chief spoke his
piece. Crazy Horse, in his intense way, seemed to
set the tone. He was not in a mood for wasted ora-
tory. "The man to lead the Lakota is the man who
called us here," he said. "Sitting Bull." And he sat
back down without another word. Four Horns
agreed, and Black Moon merely added his own
endorsement. When all the Lakota chiefs who
wished to speak had spoken, there was still only
one name under consideration.

Two Moon got to his feet then and said, "It

does not seem as if you will have trouble making your decision. You have the right man—the man who called us here. He is your war chief, and you follow him where he leads. I don't see any reason for you to choose another. It is Sitting Bull."

The vote was unanimous, and word spread like wildfire among the warriors. There was some grumbling among those who were affiliated with some chief other than Sitting Bull, but no one seriously objected. Sitting Bull was well known to them all, and his reputation was formidable. The consensus seemed to be that if they had to follow one man into a battle that might determine the future of their people, they had the man they wanted to follow.

It was time to prepare, and Sitting Bull set to work immediately. He sent the warriors out in every direction with instructions to gather horses. He cautioned them to be conservative, taking just a few head at any one location. He did not want his men to be caught, and he knew that bands of Lakota were seldom followed for a handful of stolen horses. Any raid large enough to draw the attention of the army might accidentally reveal the existence of the huge camp and compromise the war plans before he was ready.

And he told each and every band of warriors dispatched for horses the same thing: "If you meet a white man, kill him. Spare no one. Let not one live. Not one."

Some of the treaty bands were getting nervous and wanted to leave, but Sitting Bull could not permit it. The Blackfeet Sioux chief Kill Eagle approached Sitting Bull one evening a few days after the election, and Sitting Bull scowled at him. "I know why you are here," he said. "You and your people want to go home. But you cannot. No one can leave. We cannot let the Long Knives know what we are planning, and you know that if you are allowed to leave, someone in your band will talk. Word will get out no matter what you do."

"But my people are afraid of the Long Knives, they . . ."

Sitting Bull cut him off with a glare. "If the Long Knives come, it will not be your people alone who will die. And if the Long Knives learn of our plans before we are ready, we cannot win. This is our last, best chance to send the white man back where he came from. I won't allow you to take that chance away from us."

Kill Eagle started to bluster. "I am a free man. I go where I want. I . . ."

Sitting Bull gave him a baleful smile. Then he shook his head. "No. You are not a free man now. You and your people will stay. Until I say you can leave." And before Kill Eagle could object, Sitting Bull dispatched *akicitas* from the Strong Heart Society to see to it that the Blackfeet stayed put.

Sitting Bull was now the most powerful war leader on the plains, with more men under his direct command than any other war chief before or since. And he knew that he could not afford to be soft. What he did from now on would determine whether the Lakota lived free or as prisoners on the reservation. The odds were against him, overwhelmingly so, and he knew it. But he'd never backed down from a fight, not with the Crows or the Shoshone or the Hohe. And he was not prepared to shrink from the challenge of the Long Knives, either.

Chapter 25 ═══════════

Rosebud River Valley
1876

FOR SITTING BULL, NO ENDEAVOR as significant as the
coming war could be undertaken without supplication to *Wakantanka*, and there was no better way to
solicit assistance than the sun dance. Sitting Bull
resolved to hold the greatest sun dance ever, with
participation from all of the allied tribes—not just
the bands of Lakotas, but the Cheyennes and the
Arapaho as well.

He planned to dance himself. He had done so
before, but never when so much was at stake. It
seemed to him that sacrifice was in order. Once
more, he turned to his friend Crazy Horse for counsel, and the two men went off alone, ostensibly to
hunt, but really because Sitting Bull felt that he
had to get the best advice he could—and there was
no better man for that than Crazy Horse. Four
Horns wanted to come along, but Sitting Bull for-
bade it. "Someone has to be here to speak for me

until I get back," he said. "The people know you and respect you. They know that words from your lips come from my own."

The two great Lakota chiefs rode all day long and camped well up the Rosebud, in a broad valley surrounding a winding creek. Far up either slope, thick pine forests turned the hills a green so dark it was almost black. They built a fire and settled down for the night, not expecting to sleep, but to talk.

"You have never danced the sun dance, have you?" Sitting Bull asked.

Crazy Horse shook his head. "No."

"Why not?"

"I don't know. I am not really a holy man like you. I know only what I know, and I am willing to wait for tomorrow to come to see what it brings."

"Is it because you don't believe in *Wakantanka*? Is that why you have never danced?"

"No. I have visions, just as you do. When I was a boy, I made my vision quest, just as you did. I was so hungry for it that I did not go through the usual preparations. I went off by myself without studying with a holy man, and without going to the sweat lodge for purification first. I stayed on a high rock overlooking a lake for three days. And I was out of my head with thirst and the blazing sun. I was beginning to think that I had done something wrong, that I had offended *Wakantanka*, and that because of this I would not have a vision."

Crazy Horse fell silent for a long time, and Sitting Bull waited patiently for him to continue. While he waited, he watched the clouds high overhead. One great black mass rushed toward the valley, and in the early evening sun, Sitting Bull could see its huge shadow spreading over the grass, darkening it, and as the wind picked up, seeming to flatten its blades under an invisible weight.

Looking up at the cloud again, he saw it catch fire at its edges as the sun was hidden behind it; then a single blade of brilliant light burst through its heart and swept like a burning sword across the valley. A moment later, the cloud began to disintegrate, its fragments swirling as they separated.

Only when the cloud was gone did Crazy Horse resume, and Sitting Bull realized his friend had been watching the cloud as intently as he had. "I wish," he began, "that the war would go away so easily, but I know that it will not."

Then, as if he had never changed the subject, Crazy Horse picked up where he had left off. "My vision has never failed me. And for some reason that I don't quite understand, I know that it is enough. It is for other, better men to speak to *Wakantanka* on behalf of the people. I am here only to do what I can do to feed them and to protect them."

It was Sitting Bull's turn to grow silent. He understood what Crazy Horse was saying, and there were times when he felt the same way. But he knew that his path and that of his friend were very different, and he had to do what his heart told him to, just as Crazy Horse did. It was not a matter of what you thought, it was what you felt inside, and you ignored it only at great peril.

"I will dance at the sun dance," he said, breathing

a heavy sigh. "I am not a young man, and it will be a hard thing, but I have to do it."

"I wish it was something I could take on my own shoulders, but I cannot," Crazy Horse said.

"I know that. And I know you would do it if it were the right thing for both of us . . . and for the people. But a man who picks and chooses what he is willing to do for the good of the people is no friend to them. I cannot say, 'I will do this thing, because I don't mind, but this other thing is too much, let someone else do it.' I would not deserve to be a leader if I were to do such a thing."

"The war will be bad, we both know this," Crazy Horse said, shaking his head slowly. "And we need strong medicine if we are to have a chance. I think the sun dance is powerful medicine, and I know that men who dance get close to *Wakantanka* in a way I have never been able to do. Sometimes I wish I were different, but I cannot change what I am."

"You should not wish to change," Sitting Bull assured him. "Each man does what it is set out for him to do. You have done well for the Lakota people."

"You know," Crazy Horse said, "that it has been foretold that I will not be killed in battle, but that I will meet death from behind, while my hands are being held by a friend. It was part of my vision, and I believe it."

Sitting Bull nodded gravely. "Yes, I know. I have seen things in my own visions, and all of them have come to pass except one. And that one I will not talk about to any man. But I know that when I dance the sun dance this time, I will see the future in a way that will be true, and what I see will come to be. I have never been afraid of any man. I have fought the Crows and the Shoshone, the Arikara and the Hohe. I have fought the Long Knives, and I have never turned away from a good fight. But I am frightened of what I might see now. I fear for the Lakota in a way I have never feared anything before in my life."

Crazy Horse clapped a hand on his friend's shoulder. "Maybe you will see a good thing. Maybe you will see the Long Knives turning to dust and blowing away in a great wind off the plains. Maybe you will see the buffalo coming back, until they cover the earth as far as you can see in any direction. That would be a good thing."

Sitting Bull thought about the herd he had seen in his vision, the flesh melting like fat in the sunlight, turning to smoke and covering the sun with a great cloud, and he shook his head. "I hope so," he said. "But I don't think so."

Neither man slept, but neither said another word. They sat beside the fire all night long, each wrapped in his own thoughts, his own private terrors dancing in the shadows just beyond the reach of the firelight. The night was so black that the stars looked close enough to touch, and the wind hissed through the cottonwoods beside the creek, its whisper broken only by the hoot of a distant owl.

When the stars began to fade and the sky turned gray again, they were ready for the long ride home. Before mounting their ponies, Crazy Horse took Sitting Bull in his arms. "We will do what we have to, you and I," he said. "And it will be up to *Wakantanka* to decide if we have done enough."

It was near nightfall when they reached the camp on the Rosebud, and they sat on a hill overlooking the lodges that stretched out of sight in either direction. The camp was even larger than it had been the morning before, and the great lodge for the sun dance was already in place. Sitting Bull had things to do before his dance, and he wanted to get ready. As they rode down the hill, the two men separated; Crazy Horse headed for the Oglala circle and his own people, while Sitting Bull went directly to the Hunkpapa lodges.

When he reached the circle, he rode directly to his tipi, where Four Horns was waiting for him. He searched his nephew's face, looking for some indication that Sitting Bull had accomplished his purpose, learned something perhaps, or found some peace of mind. But there was no evidence of what, if anything, had happened in the immobile features.

"Uncle," he said, "I have vows to make, and I will need witnesses. Find White Bull and Jumping Bull for me." At the mention of the second name, Four Horns grew solemn. The name was now used by the Assiniboin Sitting Bull had adopted, taken in honor of Sitting Bull's father. As an afterthought, he asked for the son of Black Moon to join the party, too.

When Four Horns had gathered the witnesses Sitting Bull had requested, the four men rode out of camp again, to a high butte, where Sitting Bull lit the ceremonial pipe and made an offering. Raising the pipe overhead, he pleaded with *Wakantanka* for assistance. "Have pity on me and my people. Bring the wild game for us to hunt. Let all good men be more powerful, so that they can have the peace that comes only from strength. If you do this, and grant my people safety and happiness, I will dance for two days and two nights and give you a fat buffalo in offering."

Sitting Bull then smoked the pipe and passed it to each of his three witnesses in turn. It was time to hunt now, and Sitting Bull was looking for the buffalo he had pledged. They found a small herd, and Sitting Bull succeeded in bringing down three large animals. With White Bull's help, he chose the best, a fat cow, and prepared it for offering, rolling it upright and stretching its legs out to the four directions. Then he called upon *Wakantanka* to accept the offering in fulfillment of his promise.

He returned to camp full of hope. It had been a promising beginning, and he was now starting to think that perhaps things were not as bleak as they seemed. He told Jumping Bull that he planned to offer one hundred pieces of flesh at the sun dance and asked his adopted brother if he would be willing to do the cutting.

Jumping Bull, honored by the request, agreed. When Sitting Bull was ready, sitting against the base of the ceremonial cottonwood, Jumping Bull knelt beside him, a sharp metal awl in one hand and a razor-sharp, thin-bladed knife in the other. Starting at the wrist, he worked his way up one arm and down the other, raising pieces of flesh with the point of the awl and using the knife to slice them off.

It was time for the dance now and Sitting Bull made himself ready. He approached the sacred pole, arms outstretched. Staring at the sun, he danced ceaselessly, pleading to *Wakantanka* to hear his prayers for his people. He was still bleeding from the wounds in both arms, and at the first intermission, the blood was wiped away with sage leaves.

Four Horns was worried about his nephew. The sun dance was rigorous even for a man in the prime of life, and Sitting Bull was forty-five years old. The medicine man feared that Sitting Bull might be pushing himself too hard, demanding more of his body than it could possibly deliver. With the war coming, the Lakota needed him more than ever. It would serve no good purpose for Sitting Bull to prostrate himself, risking debilitation and even death, if it meant he would not be there to lead the people when he was finished. He knew that Sitting Bull was proud, so Four Horns would not mention his concerns. And he consoled himself with the thought that *Wakantanka* would not let any harm come to a man who had always shown nothing but respect for the Great Spirit, and had never failed to place the needs of the people ahead of his own needs.

When the dance resumed, Sitting Bull sprang to his feet and plunged back in. He was exhausted and he was thirsty, but he pushed aside any thought of stopping. Too much depended on him, and if he broke his vow, he would never be able to face his people again. Late into the night he danced on, and by the following morning he was nearly drained. But he would not hear of stopping, even though White Bull had whispered to him at an intermission that it might be a good thing. "You have danced enough," he said. "You have kept your vow, as everyone can see. You should stop now."

Sitting Bull shook off the concerns of his nephew. When the dance resumed, he staggered to his feet and danced on. It was near noon before the next intermission, and Sitting Bull was nearly dead on his feet. White Bull and Jumping Bull carried him to the shady arbor and poured water on him to revive him.

He was slow to respond, and only when he started to sputter and slap at the water skin, did they leave off.

"Are you all right?" White Bull asked, kneeling beside his uncle.

Sitting Bull nodded. "I am fine. Tired, but that is nothing. I have had a vision."

"What? What did you see?" White Bull asked, leaning closer.

"Get Black Moon. I will tell him."

White Bull rushed off to find the holy man, and when Black Moon came hurrying back with White Bull, he knelt beside the exhausted chief and leaned close. "White Bull says you have had a vision," he prompted.

Sitting Bull nodded. "Yes. At first I heard a voice, deep, coming from no one I could see, maybe the sky itself. 'I give you these because they have no ears,' it said. And I looked up at the sky and I saw men and horses, mostly Long Knives and a few Indians, and they were falling from the sky upside down. Their hats were falling off. The soldiers were falling right into our camp."

Black Moon nodded as if he understood. By now the people were pressing in around the chief, trying to hear what he was saying. Black Moon got to his feet and ordered the people back to give Sitting Bull some room. "Let him breathe," he shouted. "Let him breathe." Then he announced the vision to the gathering, and a hush fell over them. They knew what it meant. It meant the Long Knives were coming to them, and because they were falling upside down, it meant they were dead, killed in a battle with the Lakota.

Black Moon called an immediate end to the sun dance. "We have had the word we sought," he announced. *"Wakantanka* has spoken to us through Sitting Bull. It is time to make ready."

Chapter 26 ═══════════

Rosebud River Valley
1876

WHILE ATTENDING TO THE sun dance, Sitting Bull had
not neglected more mundane matters. Scouts had
been sent in every direction on a daily basis, in
parties numbering anywhere from half a dozen to
sixty or more. When they could, they would flash
their information back to camp at long range by
using mirrors, and when that wasn't possible, one
or more of the scouting party rode all the way back
to the main camp.

After the close of the sun dance, on June 14, the
main village moved a few miles to Reno Creek, in
a valley between the Rosebud and Little Bighorn
rivers, a move made necessary by the sheer size of
the encampment. The huge herds of horses were
stripping the grass rapidly, and it was essential to
keep them well fed and rested because no one
knew when the Long Knives would come, only
that they were sure to do so. The prophecy of

Sitting Bull's vision left no room for doubt on that score.

The Long Knives were closer than anyone realized. General Crook, at the head of a column of more than one thousand soldiers and nearly three hundred Indian scouts, all Crows, Shoshones, and Rees, all deadly enemies of the Lakota, were moving inexorably closer.

On June 16, scouts finally stumbled on Crook and his men and dashed back to the village to alert Sitting Bull. Yellow Nose, a Ute captive now living among the Cheyenne, led the scouting party that finally made the discovery. It was late afternoon by the time he rushed to Sitting Bull's lodge with the news.

"The valley of the Rosebud River is alive with Long Knives," he said. "They are like ants, everywhere you look."

Sitting Bull did not seem upset by the information. He believed in his vision, and he had been waiting patiently for the Long Knives to arrive. Their numbers did not matter. What mattered was the truth of the vision. As soon as Yellow Nose left the lodge, Sitting Bull got to his feet and went outside. He looked at the village stretching away up and down the creek bank, farther than he could see in either direction. He looked up at the sky, his lips pursed. So, he thought, they have come at last.

With the enemy that close there was no time to lose, and he called the chiefs together to tell them what Yellow Nose had reported. Word spread through the camp that something was happening. The chiefs were hurrying to see Sitting Bull; that was all anyone knew for certain. But it must mean soldiers were coming. Nothing else would get them to move so fast.

By the time all the chiefs had gathered, Sitting Bull knew what had to be done. He wanted a war party, a large one, a thousand men or more. But he wanted a large force kept in reserve at the village. He had seen too many times what havoc could be visited on defenseless lodges, seen too many slaughtered women and children. He was not going to let that happen again. This was a time for discipline, a time to fight as the white man fought.

Some of the best chiefs were to lead their men in the war party, chiefs who thought as he did, chiefs who understood that a new way to fight was their only chance to protect the old way to live. Crazy Horse was the principal chief, and he waited patiently for the warriors to paint themselves and their horses, gather their weapons, and mount their ponies. By the time they were ready to ride, it was after sundown.

The following morning, Crazy Horse and his Oglalas ran into a band of Crow scouts, and the first shots were exchanged. The Crows retreated, awed by the huge war party. Crook and his men were camped along the Rosebud, their horses unsaddled even though it was eight o'clock in the morning. Both men and animals were exhausted from the steady march which had begun on June 1. And they had risen at three that morning for yet another leg.

Surveying the deployment, Crazy Horse decided that he had the perfect opportunity to practice what he and Sitting Bull had been so fervently preaching. Rather than sending his entire force in a headlong charge against the massed weapons of the Long Knives, he would try to decoy them, sending small groups of his own men out to probe, make contact, and lure smaller bands of soldiers in pursuit. The decoys would lead their pursuers toward larger masses of hidden warriors. This was the best chance to neutralize the overwhelming advantage in firepower belonging to Crook's column.

In addition, Crazy Horse took advantage of his knowledge of the terrain, deploying a significant number of warriors downstream, along both banks of the Rosebud where it passed through a narrow channel between high rock walls on both sides. The land atop the ravine on both sides was studded with boulders and fallen timber and patches of pine forest that gave his warriors ample cover, both to conceal themselves while they waited and for safety once the shooting started.

He had two things in mind in this deployment. If the Long Knives tried to move on the village, either as a way to escape or because they managed to defeat the initial assault force, the trap would safeguard the village. Similarly, if he could force the column in that direction, he could close in on it from both sides and from the rear, making escape all but impossible. But it remained to be seen whether the warriors had enough discipline to work toward the larger goals he had in mind.

When Crazy Horse and his warriors made their first contact, they were driven back by heavy rifle fire, and rather than hurl themselves at the enemy as they usually did, they seemed disposed to follow the plan. Crook, surveying the land around him, realized that there was a bit of high ground that would give him a commanding sweep of the entire valley, and dispatched Colonel William Royall with instructions to capture the hill.

But Crazy Horse had seen how the white men fought. He knew what Royall wanted, and he was determined that he would not have it. A quick charge by the Lakota nearly cut Royall off from the rest of the column. But Royall managed to take the high ground without losing direct contact with the main body of soldiers. Crazy Horse tried three times to retake the hill, but the combination of the soldiers' vantage point and rapid fire was more than the Lakota could cope with.

Fewer than half of the warriors had guns at all, and those who did were more often than not armed with museum pieces forty or fifty years out of date, many of them held together with wire and rawhide thongs. Ammunition was limited, too, and much of it was short-loaded, reducing both range and impact. Gunpowder was scarce and expensive, and the Lakota had learned to stretch it as far as it could be stretched. The consequences were few when you were shooting at buffalo, but when you were facing a large force of trained soldiers who were fully equipped with vastly superior weaponry, the disadvantage was all but insuperable.

Nevertheless, Crazy Horse stood his ground. And he was pleased to see that the warriors were less interested in counting coup than they used to be. As Sitting Bull had so often noted, the Long

Knives fought to kill, and they did not stop fighting to cry or to celebrate. If the Lakota were going to withstand the white assault, they were going to have to forget about glory and concentrate on disposing of the enemy, soldier by soldier, until they were forced to withdraw.

The plan seemed to be working. Again and again, Crazy Horse led a charge toward the army line, baiting the Long Knives, teasing them, daring them to follow him and his warriors. And again and again the Long Knives took the bait, chasing after him, extending their lines to the breaking point, making them vulnerable to counterattack. But they always stopped just in time, before the Lakota could cut them off and surround them.

General Crook seemed to realize what was happening, but he was powerless to do anything about it. He knew that there were two more columns in the field, under General Terry and Colonel Gibbons, but he did not know where they were. Worse still was his ignorance of the exact size of the Lakota force facing him. The relentless hit-and-run tactics which Crazy Horse had devised made it impossible for Crook to guess how many warriors were in the field, and he had no idea whether there might be more lying in wait on the far side of the hills. He had no choice but to fight a conservative, defensive battle.

For the moment, he would not characterize his situation as desperate, but difficult it certainly was, and the longer it lasted, the more danger there was of being overrun. If there were more warriors in the field and they joined the fight, the soldiers' advantage of firepower, already largely neutralized by Crazy Horse's generalship, would be rendered totally ineffective. As the day wore on, he considered one plan after another, dismissing each in turn, until he finally decided that he would have to break the stalemate no matter what it took.

Crook decided that he had to bring pressure to bear on the main village, which he knew to be somewhere downstream, although he did not know exactly where—or how large it might be. He sent a detachment under the command of Captain Anson Mills down the river, intending to follow with the balance of his command after first feinting in the opposite direction.

But once Mills left, the tide turned. Crook's command was stressed to the breaking point now. Every move he made was countered by Crazy Horse; any attempt to charge the massed Lakota warriors was swiftly repelled. And Royall had his hands full keeping his hilltop.

Mills was having his own difficulties. The valley of the Rosebud suddenly narrowed, and the sheer walls on either side made defense against attack from above difficult, and in some places, impossible. The Lakota waited patiently along both sides of the ravine downstream, but before Mills could reach the trap, he received word from Crook that he had to return to relieve the main command, which was under serious attack.

Mills led his men up out of the ravine and found himself behind and on the flank of the Lakota line. But as soon as he pressured them, the warriors broke off their attack and vanished into the hills and ravines surrounding the Rosebud. The Lakota knew the terrain better than the soldiers, and better than the Crow and Shoshone scouts attached to Crook's column.

With his forces reunited, Crook made one more attempt to fight his way downstream to take the village. But when the column reached the narrow ravine, the Crow and Shoshone refused to enter it. The general was angry, but decided that if the scouts would not take the risk, it was with good reason.

The general took stock and realized that his men were worn out. Their ammunition was low, and their supplies of food virtually exhausted. He had intended to replenish food stocks from the captured village, but that was now impossible. He had no choice but to retreat. Returning to the scene of the battle, he issued orders to camp for the night. Rest was essential for his men, and it gave the command the opportunity to treat the wounded and bury the dead.

Crook hated to give up, but there were so many wounded men, and the only way to move them over the rough terrain was by travois. Rather than subject the wounded to such agony, he decided to give up the field. Splitting the command was out of the question. Split into equal parts, neither half could hold off the Lakota. A small detachment charged with transporting the wounded would be torn to ribbons as soon as it separated from the column.

As soon as Crook reached his main camp on Goose Creek, all but a handful of his Indian scouts defected. The Crows were angry that he had been slow to support them in their first encounter with the Lakota and fearful for their families, who were not far away. The Shoshone, too, were disaffected, resentful, and concerned for the safety of their families, who were living on the Wind River Reservation. Both groups feared that the vengeful Lakota might turn their wrath on the Indian allies of the Long Knives, and they were not willing to take that chance.

The Lakota returned to their village, where Sitting Bull anxiously awaited news of the battle. Crazy Horse paid him a visit, and the two discussed the battle in great detail well into the night.

Crazy Horse was pleased that the new tactics had worked, but disappointed that they had worked only to a point. "If we could have surrounded the Long Knives on the hill, we could have beaten them," he said. "But their guns shoot so much faster than ours, and they kill at greater distance."

"But you lost very few warriors," Sitting Bull reminded him. "And you forced the Long Knives to turn back. That is a victory."

Crazy Horse nodded. "Yes, one victory, but not the war. They will come again. And we have to find a way to control them. I had set a trap for them, and it was working well. They had sent some soldiers down the Rosebud, and they were almost where we wanted them, but then another soldier came and they turned back."

"That is because they have discipline. This is something the Lakota still do not have, something we have to teach them. If one warrior came up to a band and told them to follow him back the way they had come, some would follow and some would not. That is the difference between the Long Knives and ourselves. You see it and I see it, but we have to make the others see it—especially the younger men. They are so anxious to make a name for themselves that they think only of themselves in battle. Unless we can change them, we will not win."

"What about your vision? Don't you believe it is true?"

Sitting Bull thought for a moment before answering. "Yes, I believe it is true, but I do not know *how* it is true. Just as you say you won the battle today but not the war, my vision could be one battle. We should be glad that we won that battle, and it should give us heart for the war, but still the war must be fought; it is not won in dreams alone."

"There are rumors that more Long Knives are coming this way."

"I have heard them. But we will not run, not now. I don't know what will happen, but I know it is better to let it happen. A man can't run away from what is meant to happen, even if he wants to. We are here, and we will stay here. This is our land, and if the Long Knives want to take it from us, they will have to pay for it in blood."

Chapter 27 ══════════

**Little Bighorn River Valley
1876**

THEY HAD MOVED THE CAMP AGAIN. It was so big now
that no one, not even Sitting Bull, knew exactly
how large it was. There could be two thousand
warriors and there could just as easily be five thousand. But the victory over General Crook's column
was filling the camp, especially the younger warriors, with a sense of euphoria. The sheer size of
the village, something none of them had ever seen
before, and none could have imagined, combined
with the defeat of Crook to create a sense of invin-
cibility. Some even thought that the battle on the
Rosebud had been the great victory that Sitting Bull
had prophesied at the sun dance, and that the Long
Knives had been defeated once and for all.

But Sitting Bull was worried. He knew that other
Long Knives were coming, but until his scouts
were able to find them, he would not be able to
convince the warriors that they had to be vigilant.

And while the Lakota and Cheyenne celebrated prematurely, General Alfred Terry and Colonel John Gibbon, the second and third prongs of the three-column assault, continued to push deeper and deeper into Lakota territory. They were already closing in on the village, because a scouting party led by Major Marcus Reno had discovered a trail made by several hundred lodges being dragged to a campsite. As soon as Reno was certain of what he had discovered, he headed back to the main column under General Terry with the news.

Reno met with Terry as soon as he reached the commander's camp. "As near as we can tell, General," he told Terry, "there were about three hundred and fifty lodges. We did a rough count of the number of campfires. The Crow scouts think the trail was about three weeks old when we came across it. We followed the trail up the Rosebud River for nearly forty miles, but we didn't see a single Indian."

"And you're sure which direction they were moving?"

"Yes, sir, absolutely sure. They were headed toward the Little Bighorn River. My guess is that that's where the village is now."

Terry, armed with Reno's information, called for a conference among his staff. They met on June 21 aboard the steamboat *Far West*, where he outlined his strategy for the next phase of the campaign. Terry was reasonably sure he knew where the Lakota camp was—if not precisely, then within a few miles—but in any event close enough to move on them.

Spreading his maps out on a table, he indicated the point along the Rosebud where Reno had discovered the trail of the lodges. "Here," he said, "is where I want you to start, Colonel. This is where Major Reno found the signs. Follow the trail wherever it leads you. I suspect that it will take you to the Little Bighorn, and you should come out somewhere to the south of the Sioux village."

Lieutenant Colonel George Armstrong Custer frowned. Still pining for his brevet rank of major general, he was, as usual, prickly with authority. "I still think that Major Reno should have followed it all the way. He let them know we're here, and it's going to be more difficult to get close now."

Reno was annoyed. "They didn't know we were there. We never saw one Indian. We never saw one fresh sign that any Indian had been there for weeks."

"Just because you didn't see them doesn't mean they didn't see you," Custer argued.

Terry was in no mood for squabbling among his commanders. "Whether they saw you or not, it is too late to worry about it, Major," Terry snapped. "And it doesn't alter what I want you to do, Colonel Custer. The point is, we know where they are; now all we have to do is hit them. While you come in south of the village, Colonel Gibbon and his men will move in from the north. We'll have them in a vise, and all we have to do then is turn the screws and squeeze them until they say uncle."

"We'll have to move quickly," Custer said. "The Sioux don't stay in one place too long. As soon as the grass is chewed up, they'll move the village."

"I don't imagine we'll have any trouble finding them again, even if they do," Terry said. "They've been in this general area for several weeks, and I see no reason to expect them to stray too far."

Custer nodded. "Even so, I'll want to travel light. Minimum rations for fifteen days, so we can follow them wherever they go. But we'll leave the tents and sleeping gear behind."

"Don't stint on your ammunition, Colonel," Terry warned.

Custer laughed. "No need to worry about that, General. My men like to fight more than they like to eat."

"I can let you have the Gatling guns . . ."

Custer shook his head. "They'll just slow us down. That's rough country."

Terry looked at the two, his jaw set in anticipation of an argument. "Any questions, gentlemen?"

Neither man had any, so Terry concluded, "You know your orders, gentlemen, and I expect you to follow them, unless you see sufficient reason to deviate from them."

Custer wasted no time. His command moved out on the morning of June 22. Fearful of giving away his position by unnecessary noise, he issued orders that the men leave their sabers behind.

In the Lakota village, Sitting Bull was uneasy. No one had seen the Long Knives since they had withdrawn from the Rosebud, but he couldn't shake the feeling that they were not far away. He redoubled his scouting expeditions, but still they came back with nothing to report.

Sitting Bull was not alone in his concern. On the

evening of June 23, he left his lodge to get some fresh air, and to get away from the pressures of family matters. In his lodge he had two wives, two daughters, two sons, his brother-in-law, Gray Eagle, and a set of newborn twins—sometimes he needed to get away, to have a little silence just to clear his head.

As he watched the sunset, he heard a voice crying out, and he stood on tiptoe to see who it was. Moving through the camp was a Cheyenne herald, and as he moved closer, his words finally became clear. "Tie your horse outside your lodges. Soldiers are coming."

Sitting Bull walked into the crowd gathering around the herald and pulled him aside. "Why are you stirring up the people?" he asked.

"Box Elder has had a dream," the Cheyenne told him.

Sitting Bull knew Box Elder as a revered holy man among the Cheyenne, and he pressed the herald for more information. "What kind of dream?"

"He saw soldiers coming to our camp," the herald explained. "That's all he told me."

For a moment, Sitting Bull was tempted to dismiss the warning as Box Elder's attempt to keep the warriors alert. Everyone knew the soldiers were still in the field, but the only ones they knew about for certain were Crook's column, which was still moving away from the village, and some Long Knives camped on the Rosebud. Neither group posed a threat to the Lakota and Cheyenne encampment. But Box Elder was not a man to dismiss lightly. If he had dreamed the Long Knives were coming, then they were coming.

He sent the herald on his way, knowing that few would listen to him, but more worried than ever about the day ahead. Just the night before, a Cheyenne warrior had howled at a wolf, and the wolf had howled back, a sure sign that there would be meat for the wolves . . . and soon.

On the evening of the twenty-fourth, Sitting Bull stripped to his breechcloth and painted himself, took a pipe, then waded across the Little Bighorn and walked to the bottom of a hill just across from the village. He stood watching the sun beginning to set behind the snowcapped peaks of the Bighorn Mountains. For a moment, he felt a pain in his chest, as if a fist had closed on his heart and begun to squeeze it. The land was so beautiful, and the mere thought of losing it was almost too painful to endure.

He climbed up the hill, the village behind him now. He could hear the sounds of the camp, and as the sunlight faded, the firelight flickered, casting long shadows on the walls of the lodges. Holding the pipe high overhead, he pleaded with *Wakantanka*, "My people wish to live," he cried. "Save us from danger. Wherever the sun and moon are, there you are, too. You are everywhere. Watch over the people and let them live."

His voice sounded strange to his own ears— strained, raw, as if the words had to struggle from somewhere deep inside him. He watched the sun set, and when it was gone, waited for the stars to come out before walking slowly back to his lodge.

Inside, he lay down and closed his eyes, but sleep would not come. He tossed and turned all night long, every now and then sitting up to listen. Anything might be a signal that the Long Knives had come; the bark of a stray dog, the nicker of a pony, the snap of a twig, the call of an owl. But each time, straining his ears to hear the meaning behind the sound, he heard nothing more. He lay back down, his eyes fixed on the smoke hole over his head, through which he could see a handful of stars flickering in the wavering plume of smoke.

Sitting Bull was up at dawn and watched Gray Eagle and his nephew One Bull, White Bull's brother, turn the picketed horses loose, then drive the animals down to the water's edge to drink. Later they would bring them to the grass behind the camp for grazing. It was hot, the air thick and humid already, as Sitting Bull walked to the council lodge to visit with some friends.

After an hour or so of conversation, the men in the council lodge heard a shout and a young warrior burst in, his words tumbling from his lips. Sitting Bull raised a hand, "Wait until you can say what you have to say," he said. "Take a deep breath, then let the words come."

The young man started babbling again, but this time the sense of his words was unmistakable. "Two boys, they were walking in the hills, and they found a soldier bag. They opened it up and found bread. They sat down to eat it, and some Long Knives came and started shooting. They killed Deeds, but Hona got away."

Every man in the tent knew what the news meant—the Long Knives were getting close. Sitting Bull got to his feet and ran to his lodge for his weapons. As he neared his tipi, he heard a shout and turned to see a warrior pointing south, downstream from the camp. There, Sitting Bull saw a cloud of dust and at the bottom of it, the blue shirts of the Long Knives and the heads of their horses.

He ducked into his lodge and found that One Bull was already there, grabbing his own weapons. "Uncle," One Bull said, "I am going to fight the Long Knives."

Sitting Bull hugged him. "Good. Don't be afraid. And take this. . . ." He grabbed his shield, the same one his father had given him so long ago, and draped it over One Bull's chest, then sent him out of the lodge. Sitting Bull, his hands full of weapons and a cartridge belt, was right behind him.

Vaulting onto his warhorse, which someone had caught and held by its picket rope, Sitting Bull worked his way through the milling throng of women, children, and old men who were preparing to flee the village. By the time he reached the south edge of the camp, it was clear that the Long Knives knew exactly where they were heading. The Hunkpapa camp, as the southernmost of the camp circles, was going to take the brunt of the assault.

Sitting Bull turned to see his mother on horseback, already riding away from the oncoming soldiers, then turned back to the business at hand. The Hunkpapa warriors, some on horseback and others, who had given their horses to women and children, on foot, poured out of the village. They were already firing their guns, trying to slow the advance of the Long Knives long enough for the noncombatants to make their escape.

More and more warriors were filling in the gaps in the Hunkpapa lines, and they now had enough men to bring the cavalry charge to a halt. The Long Knives dismounted and took cover, firing their weapons incessantly. Sitting Bull was out front, rallying his warriors. With the Long Knives on foot, it would be easier. He formed two lines, one on the north and one on the west side of the river, and started to press the soldiers, who began to drop back, still firing, but seemingly more concerned with their own safety than with pressing their attack. In dismounting, they conceded an advantage; that puzzled Sitting Bull, who began to suspect a trap.

But the Hunkpapa continued their attack, and the Long Knives pulled back away from the river and took refuge in the thick timber. Falling back still further, the soldiers formed a rough line along a cutbank that ran through the trees, and the Hunkpapa advanced on them from all sides.

Small bands of warriors now began to probe the line of the Long Knives, charging forward until they drew fire, then falling back. The soldiers had good cover now, and their weapons gave them the advantage. Several young warriors were cut down in the middle of headlong charges against the army line, and Sitting Bull shouted for the others to hang back.

Puzzled by the behavior of the soldiers, Sitting Bull wanted to be certain he understood what was happening before sacrificing any more men. For the time being, the village was safe, and he was content to hold the Long Knives off at long range. No sooner had he made that decision, however, than the soldiers climbed back on their horses and turned to run. They were no longer in good order; they were running for their lives. This much, at least, was no trick, he realized. They had been waiting for someone to join them, and whoever it was had not come.

Immediately, the Hunkpapa swarmed through the trees, cutting off small groups of fleeing soldiers, chasing others in headlong flight. But Sitting Bull was more concerned now about the other Long Knives. They were out there somewhere. But where?

He saw a handful of horse soldiers plunge into the river, still running away from the camp. One Bull started after them, rallying several warriors for the chase, but Sitting Bull stopped them with a shout. "Let them go, let them live to tell the truth, to say how it was the Long Knives and not the Lakota who started this fight!"

Heading back to the deserted village, Sitting Bull spotted more Long Knives on the ridge to the east across the river, hundreds of horse soldiers, riding flat out, and he knew that he had been right—there had been a second force. But now, with the first attack beaten back and the soldiers fleeing for their lives, the Long Knives on the ridge had no one to help them.

Sitting Bull moved closer, riding his black warhorse and holding his quirt. He was surrounded

by warriors, some of whom headed across the river
to join the fight shaping up there. It looked as if the
Long Knives were heading for the ford, planning to
cross the river. As Sitting Bull watched, several
Cheyenne warriors cut them off, and the horse soldiers stopped. A moment later, the hillside
exploded in gunfire, and the thick banks of gun-
smoke mingled with the clouds of dust from the
army horses and the Lakota and Cheyenne war
ponies.

At first it was possible to see what was happening, but only dimly through the thickening haze.
The warriors had surrounded the Long Knives
now, and the horse soldiers dismounted. More gunfire erupted, and it sounded to Sitting Bull as if it
would never stop. At first the heavy fire drove the
warriors back, but a hail of arrows poured in on the
troopers from every side, and one by one their guns
began to fall silent.

The smoke and dust were too thick to enable
him to see anything clearly now, and Sitting Bull
had to gauge the progress of the fight by sound
alone. He could tell that the warriors were capturing rifles and pistols from the fallen Long Knives,
and the tide was turning in the Lakotas' favor.

The sound of the battle had changed. There was
still shooting, but it was no longer steady, as if
most of the guns were empty, or the soldiers who
manned them no longer able to shoot. Isolated war
cries echoed across the river now, and a sporadic
shot cracked here and there, until at last there was
total silence.

Sitting Bull urged his black into the river and

rode across. On the far side, he saw White Bull coming back from the battle.

"Are they all dead?" Sitting Bull asked.

White Bull nodded. "Yes. They are all dead."

Sitting Bull did not know it then, but among the dead Long Knives on the hill was the man who had stolen the *Paha Sapa*, the hated Long Hair, George Armstrong Custer. And his prophecy had come true.

Chapter 28 ━━━━━

Slim Buttes, Dakota Territory
1876

THE BATTLE AT THE LITTLE BIGHORN was the high
point of Lakota resistance, but few of the chiefs
seemed to realize it. In the immediate aftermath of
the defeat of Custer, the huge Lakota/Cheyenne village fragmented as the chiefs took their bands off
for the summer buffalo hunt. Dozens of bands of
varying sizes crisscrossed the northern plains, their
sporadic contact with one another used to
exchange information about the movement of the
army units in the territory. Three Stars Crook was
on the march again, and Terry was still eager to run
down and subdue both Sitting Bull and Crazy
Horse.

For Sitting Bull, the months of July and August
were an anxious time. He knew that the destruction
of Custer's entire command would only make the
Long Knives more determined than ever to find
him and, if they could, destroy him. Despite his

understanding that the Lakota had to continue to fight to defend their land and their way of life, he had more immediate concerns, foremost among them being food and other supplies for the coming winter.

He continued to maintain that he had no interest in waging war against the whites if they would just go away and leave his people alone. But deep down inside, he knew that was not about to happen. And if he had to fight, he would fight; not because he wanted to, but because the Long Knives gave him no choice.

Everything was colored by the events of June 25. The strain on his nerves was tremendous and unrelenting. Every time a scout broke over a ridge and headed for the camp, it might mean the Long Knives were coming. While trying to lead a normal life, the members of Sitting Bull's band had to be prepared for war at a moment's notice. There was no doubt in the chief's mind that the Little Bighorn battle had been a great victory for the Indians of the northern plains, but there could be no doubt, either, that the army would not rest until it had avenged Custer and his men.

As the weeks went by, news of Crook's column— sketchy, vague, and far from complete—drifted in, often days or weeks old. But short of direct contact with that column, or General Terry's forces, it was all the news he was likely to get. And it was better to have no news at all than to have the Long Knives come thundering down on his camp yet again.

Despite the fact that he was the foremost Hunkpapa chief, and the most influential nontreaty

Lakota chief, his command of the widely scattered bands was tenuous, based more on his reputation than on any direct contact or control. The Lakota simply lacked the kind of centralized government Crook and Terry had behind them. Channels of communication did not exist. The democracy of the Lakota was in many significant ways their biggest handicap, and Sitting Bull knew it.

As usual, when he needed a sounding board he turned to his uncle, Four Horns. In early September, having received yet another vague report of army movement on the plains, he went to his uncle's lodge.

Sitting across the fire pit from Four Horns, he rubbed his hands together and sighed. Four Horns watched him closely, waiting patiently for his nephew to say what was on his mind; although he thought he could guess what he was thinking, because he had been there when the Oglala hunting party had passed on its information. The wait was taking a toll on Sitting Bull, and he seldom smiled now . . . and almost never thought of anything but the war.

"I don't understand," Sitting Bull began, "why the white men will not leave us alone to live as we want to live. Whenever I have had the chance to tell them, I have told them: go away and leave us alone and then we will be friends instead of enemies. But they have no ears."

Four Horns smiled sadly. "They have ears, nephew, but not for you. They want the land, and they will not rest until they have it."

Sitting Bull nodded. "Always they have some

new excuse. They say to Red Cloud, 'We will take this much land and leave you the rest. In exchange, we will give you this and that.' Then the next winter or the winter after that, they come back and Red Cloud says, 'Where are those things you gave us in exchange for the land?' And they say, 'Those things are coming. But we want more land now, and we will give you this and that for it.' Always, Red Cloud agrees, because he doesn't know how to refuse them any more."

"Red Cloud has made a bad bargain," Four Horns agreed. "He meant well, but he let the white man take advantage of him, and it is the people who suffer."

"I have never agreed to give them any land, and still they say that they have bought it out from under me, and that I must leave the land even though it still is mine. All I want is for the people to hunt the buffalo, to feed themselves and live as they have always lived. This does not seem to be so much to ask."

"I saw Running Antelope," Four Horns said, "and I asked him why he was out hunting if life on the reservation was so good. And he said that he just wanted to do what he had always done. But I know he was not telling the truth. I talked to people in his camp, and they told me that there is no food on the reservations. Always there is some excuse, but though the white man does not seem to know it, not even an Indian can eat excuses."

"I have heard how they bought the Black Hills," Sitting Bull said. "Men came from the Great Father and said that they would pay so much for them, and even Red Cloud said no, that was not enough. The Black Hills are sacred land, he told them. And they said this is all the Great Father wants to pay. If you don't accept it, the Great Father will take the Black Hills anyway, and you will have nothing for them. That is a strange way to buy something."

"It is a sad thing that has happened to Red Cloud," Four Horns sighed. "He was a great warrior when he was young. And when the Long Knives went into the Powder River country, nobody except Crazy Horse fought them harder or better. But they have covered his eyes and spun him around and now he walks like a dizzy man, stumbling from place to place, not knowing which way to go. He listens to them and like a fool he believes what they tell him."

Sitting Bull reached into the fire and grabbed a stick to poke at the coals. "He never should have listened to them the first time. That was his mistake. He believed them once, and then he could not stop believing them, even though his eyes saw the rotten food they gave him and his ears were filled with the cries of hungry children and the wailing of the old people who died like flies."

"But it is hard to know what else to do. As long as we stay off the reservation, the Long Knives will come after us. That is no way to live," Four Horns said.

Sitting Bull replied, "I have been thinking that we should leave this place, go to the Grandmother Country. The redcoats there will leave us in peace, as they do the Blackfeet."

Four Horns did not look happy. "It would be a

hard thing to leave our land. And if we go to the Grandmother Country, we might not ever be able to come back."

"What is better—to go there and live as we have always lived, or stay here and be hunted like wolves for as long as we live? The Long Knives will never leave us in peace, and there are so many of them. You have heard the stories, just as I have, of the war between the bluecoat Long Knives and the graycoat Long Knives. There were more soldiers than there are buffalo, and they died in numbers too large to count. In one day, I have heard, more soldiers died than there are Lakota now living. For men who are so comfortable with death, what are the lives of a few Indians?"

"It is something we will have to think about, Sitting Bull. It is not a decision that will be easy to make," cautioned Four Horns.

"But it must be made . . . and soon. Already we know that the Long Knives are crawling over the plains like the white worms that eat a buffalo carcass."

Sitting Bull poked at the fire again, then sat and watched the sparks rise up toward the smoke hole. He was about to continue speaking when a shout distracted him. He turned toward the lodge entrance and listened. He heard the shout once more, and got up quickly to go outside, Four Horns right behind him.

He saw Eats-the-Bear, an Oglala he knew from Iron Shield's band, hanging off his pony and bleeding from a wound in his shoulder. Warriors swarmed around him and Sitting Bull pushed through the crowd to help the man from his horse.

With Four Horns helping him, he carried the wounded man into his uncle's lodge. He turned to a woman who was peering through the entrance and said, "Go to my lodge and ask Four Robes for my medicine bags. Then bring some soup."

As soon as the woman had gone, Sitting Bull turned his attention to the warrior. "What happened, my friend?" he asked.

"Three Stars," the warrior gasped. "He is attacking Iron Shield's camp. There are hundreds of Long Knives, and they are shooting everyone."

"Where?"

"Slim Buttes," the Oglala replied.

To his uncle, Sitting Bull said, "See to him."

"Where are you going?"

"To help Iron Shield."

"But that is a long ride. You will not get there in time," Four Horns warned.

"If I don't help, who will?"

Four Horns nodded. "Then go," he said.

Sitting Bull sent runners through the camp to summon the warriors, then ran to his lodge to get his weapons. Within a half hour, they were ready to ride, more than a thousand warriors strong. But Slim Buttes was a long way off. They rode hard, passing more refugees along the way. The first reports were heartening. One old man estimated that there were only two hundred Long Knives and said that most of the people had managed to get away, but that the Long Knives had captured the camp and were burning the lodges.

It was well into the afternoon by the time Sitting Bull's war party reached Slim Buttes; in the meantime, the rest of General Crook's column had arrived, and Sitting Bull's forces were outnumbered almost two to one. And once again, the firepower of the soldiers was more than a match for Lakota determination.

Sitting Bull and his warriors swarmed over the buttes, taking the high ground and trying to force the soldiers to relinquish what was left of Iron Shield's camp. But it was no use. The two sides squared off in long lines and exchanged fire for much of the afternoon, but to little effect. The damage to Iron Shield's small village had already been done, and all Sitting Bull could hope to do was provide cover for the escaping fugitives.

Some of Iron Shield's men were holed up in a makeshift cave with their chief. The soldiers knew they were there and fired relentlessly into the cave. Crook, impressed by the courage of the warriors, offered them a chance to surrender, but Iron Shield would not surrender.

Crook's forces resumed firing, and the warriors, supported by Sitting Bull and his men on the bluffs, did their best to return fire. But their supplies of ammunition were all but exhausted, and Crook seemed to have no end of bullets for his guns.

Crook again called a cease-fire, and this time Iron Shield agreed to surrender if Crook would promise to spare his warriors. The general, moved by the chief's courage and concern for his men, gave his word, and the small band of warriors

staggered out of their cave. Iron Shield himself
had been gut-shot and was mortally wounded, but
he refused help and walked on his own to surrender his weapon to Three Stars.

Sitting Bull, outnumbered and outgunned, was
powerless to intervene. As the sun set, both sides
dug in for the night. Crook's men were exhausted.
They had been on a forced march for nearly two
weeks, subsisting on the meat of their own horses
and mules because rations had been so depleted.
And they were angry both at Iron Shield and his
warriors, and at Crook himself for having given his
pledge to let them live.

A search of the captured camp had revealed the
presence of articles belonging to Custer's cavalry-
men, including a glove marked with the name
Myles Keogh, a captain in Custer's command. In
addition, several of the Lakota horses wore the 7th
Cavalry brand on their flanks. In the days since
Little Bighorn, a kind of frenzy had swept the
country. The powers that be in Washington were
determined to snuff out Sioux resistance, no matter
what the cost. Crook's men felt they had had a
chance to exact a little personal revenge and
resented their commander's interference, but Crook
would not yield.

When the sun came up, Sitting Bull once more
rallied his warriors, but there was nothing left to
be done. All he could do was watch as Crook's
column reformed and started its march, bearing
with it dozens of captives from Iron Shield's village. Iron Shield himself had died during the
night. Sitting Bull and his warriors shouted

encouragement to the captives, and he led an abortive charge that cut off several soldiers and a handful of captives—only to learn that the captives were going along willingly. They had had enough of war.

As the column moved out of sight, Sitting Bull oversaw the burial of the dead. Every body was like a knife through his heart. There were old men, women, children—even a newborn baby dead in its mother's arms, shot through the head. The mother, too, had been shot to death. These were the bodies of people he knew, the children of friends, the parents of men who had ridden beside him, and between his grief and his rage, he felt as if his heart were breaking.

And as the great chief climbed back onto his horse and headed home, he kept looking northward, as if his gaze were drawn by some irresistible force. He was going to the Grandmother Country. He knew that now. Because there was no place else to go . . .

Chapter 29

Saskatchewan
1880

LIFE IN THE GRANDMOTHER COUNTRY was not what Sitting Bull had hoped it would be. He and his people had freedom, of sorts, but it just wasn't the same. Almost from the first, the people had begun drifting away by the handful, back below the border to turn themselves in at the agency.

It was hardest for the young men, because the old ways, the ways that had allowed them to attain prominence, were gone. No more war parties against the Crows or the Arikara. No more stealing horses from the white settlers, or thundering down out of the mountains on a wagon train or brigade of Long Knives. The buffalo in Canada were fewer, and the hunt was not the same, either. Nothing was the same; nothing was as good as it had been.

Sitting Bull did his best to adapt. He was more than a chief now, he was a statesman, and he took his responsibility seriously. He had hundreds of people depending on him, and he knew that he was there in the Grandmother Country by sufferance of the redcoat representatives of the Grandmother herself, Queen Victoria. But that sufferance was thin ice on which to skate. He knew that the redcoats were just waiting for an excuse to expel him, and he knew, too, that if he were expelled from Canada, the soldier chief they called Bear Coat, Nelson Miles, would be waiting for him. Bear Coat himself had told him so—to his face.

He could still remember the meeting with Miles in 1876, just after Slim Buttes. At first Bear Coat had been open and conciliatory, speaking to him with respect, warrior to warrior, and Sitting Bull had thought they had worked everything out. But on the second day of the council between them, the itchy Long Knives flexed their trigger fingers and the boisterous Hunkpapa warriors had been looking for trouble, even expecting it. And as Sitting Bull knew only too well, if you are looking for trouble, it finds you.

So Miles had gotten angry and tried to blame Sitting Bull for things he had not done, and for breaking promises he had not made. The truth was that Miles had made promises he could not keep, and both men knew it. The council had broken off and Sitting Bull had headed for the border, taking his time in order to show that he was not afraid of Bear Coat or anyone else.

The next winter, news reached him that Crazy Horse had been murdered. It had happened just as

Crazy Horse had told him it would, the way it had been foretold in the great Oglala's vision. Held by the arms by two Oglala policemen at Fort Robinson, he had been stabbed in the back by a soldier with a bayonet. That news, more than any other, had crushed Sitting Bull's spirit. He had loved Crazy Horse like a brother, and with him gone, there was no one else left to speak for the people. Spotted Tail was just a pale shadow and Red Cloud was no better than a white man now. Only Sitting Bull was left.

The redcoats did not trust him. They watched him like hungry wolves, just waiting for him to do something wrong, or maybe not even wrong, but something they could use to send him home. They were frightened of him. His reputation as a fearsome warrior had preceded him to Canada, and they were wary of him—as if they expected him to go on the warpath at any moment; as if he would be foolish enough to make himself unwelcome in his last refuge on earth.

But it meant he had to be hard with his people, harder than he had ever been, harder than he wanted to be. He didn't like it, but he did it because if he were not hard on them, the agents and redcoats of the Grandmother would be harder still, and that was one thing they could not afford.

When his brother-in-law, Gray Eagle, had helped three other warriors steal horses from the Slota, the Slota had complained to the redcoats, and the redcoats came to Sitting Bull's village. They knew what had happened to the horses, that some young warriors had taken them. The redcoat chief had demanded that the men be found and punished, warning that if Sitting Bull did not punish them, he would do it himself.

So Sitting Bull had found the men, including Gray Eagle, and punished them, because he knew that if the redcoats punished them it would be much worse. He took the responsibility seriously, because he was chief. That is what it meant to be chief—to do the hard things that no one else wanted to do. And the punishment was severe, so severe that Gray Eagle still had not forgiven him.

He could remember the time when they heard the Nez Percé were coming, when Joseph, with a thousand people and all they owned, tried to join him. That had been a tricky time, because the redcoats did not want every Indian in the United States coming to live in their country. Joseph had failed. It was Bear Coat Miles who stopped him at Bear Paw, just forty miles from the border and safety. That was a terrible time . . . so many Nez Percé killed, and all they had wanted was to be left alone. It had seemed especially harsh because Joseph was leaving his land, letting the white man have it, and even that was not good enough. Nothing the Indians did was ever good enough for the white man.

The white men wanted the land and they wanted the Indians too, and it made no sense at all. It was as if they were saying, "You can't stay here because this is not your land, now. It is ours." And you said, "Fine, then I will leave." And they said,

"No, we won't let you leave. You will go and live on land that we don't want, land that is not good for anything. Except Indians." It was so hard to understand what the white man really wanted. And just when he thought he did finally understand, it seemed to change. There were times when he thought the white man himself did not know, or maybe that the white men were fighting among themselves.

Even in his confusion, Sitting Bull was homesick. White Bull had already gone to the reservation. One Bull was still with him, along with Jumping Bull and Four Horns. But the young men were drifting away, and soon there would be no one left—no one but old men to hunt the buffalo and to feed other men now too old to hunt for themselves. It seemed as if the Lakota people were withering away, drying up like leaves on a dying tree, just waiting for the wind to blow them off and carry them away.

Sitting Bull did not want it to end that way. He did not want to be chief of a nation of old men with wrinkled skin and flabby arms, begging for food in a country that did not care whether they lived or died. But he knew that war was no longer feasible. There were too many Long Knives and too few warriors. And ahead of him lay one hard winter after another.

Sometimes he led a hunting party south of the border to hunt buffalo in Montana, but Montana was filling up with settlers and there were complaints about the Lakota hunting. They were bothering no one. There were no raids on settlements or even on isolated farms. Just the buffalo, that's all they wanted. And every summer there were fewer and fewer of them. Soon they would be gone altogether, and there would be no one left to mourn their passing except Sitting Bull and a handful of old men who remembered when the earth used to tremble with the pounding of a million hooves.

Maybe, Sitting Bull thought, maybe what I should do is go back, cross the border, go home. They want me to live like a white man, think like a white man, maybe I can do this. And even if I can't, the young ones can. The children can learn to do what an old man might not be able to learn. At least then they will have a chance, as long as there is someone to look out for them, the way Red Cloud is supposed to and does not, the way Crazy Horse wanted to and was not allowed to.

He and Four Horns talked sometimes, an old man and an older man, and it seemed that maybe the world had changed too much for both of them, made them lost, strangers in a place that only looked familiar, but was not. Then he would talk to One Bull or to Jumping Bull, and they would say No, uncle, or No, brother, it has not changed so much that there is no place for you. But your place is here, not at Standing Rock. If you go home, they said, the Long Knives will kill you as they killed Crazy Horse.

He knew that One Bull and Jumping Bull were probably right. But he knew, too, that sometimes you have to stake your life on something that is important, and if the people were not important, then nothing was. That was why Joseph, the Nez Percé, had risked everything. He had lost, but he had tried.

I can try, too, Sitting Bull told himself. There was a time when I ran like the wind, when no one, not even Crawler, could catch me. There was a time when I would ride into a Crow village by myself, count coup, and ride out again. I was afraid of nothing. I was there when we stood up to Long Hair and punished him for stealing the *Paha Sapa*. I looked Bear Coat in the eye and told him I would not let him stop my people from going where they wanted, whenever they wanted to go. There was a time when I would have looked the Great Father himself in the eye until he blinked, and I would say to him, This is my land, and you cannot take it from me because I do not wish to sell it. And I think I would still do that today, if I had the chance.

He would look at the sky then, at the vast expanse of unclouded blue, then at the green sweep of the plains stretching out in every direction, the purple smear of the hills, and the white-capped mountains sharp as the teeth of a wolf, and he would think, The world is so big, why can't there be a place in it for me and my people to live the way we want to live?

Some of the Canadians, like the Frenchman, LeGare, looked at him as if he were trade goods, something to be sold for a few dollars. There was enough traffic back and forth across the border, small groups of warriors leaving the reservation to hunt and visiting relatives in Canada, that Sitting Bull knew what the agents in the United States were thinking; that it would be useful to them if the great Sitting Bull could be induced to come back, to take his place in line with all the other Lakota, to stand with his hand out, waiting like a beggar for the Great Father's annuities. They wanted to take his rifle and his lance and give him a rake. Instead of riding a buffalo runner behind a herd, they wanted him to walk behind a team of oxen and break the ground to raise corn.

Every day it got harder and harder to resist. Without his land, without the right to roam from the *Paha Sapa* to the Bighorns, up the Missouri and down the Yellowstone, what was he but just another man without a country, an unwelcome presence in a country that wished he would just go home. But he had no home to go to, not now. The reservation was not home. It was more like a prison. And some of his people, he knew, they tried to put in real prisons. That had happened to Crazy Horse, and when he said no, they killed him, stabbing him in the back because they didn't have the courage to look him in the eye. He wondered if that was what waited for him at Standing Rock.

They sent commissioners to see him, men in stiff collars with wax on their mustaches, to paint him pretty pictures of reservation life. They told him how they would build him a house like the one they had built for Red Cloud. But what was wrong with a tipi? It kept him warm when it snowed. In the summer, when the air was thick and the heat enough to squeeze the breath from his chest, he could roll up its sides and let in the breeze if there was one. Could Red Cloud do that? Could Red Cloud roll up the sides of his house? And if the grass was used up, could Red Cloud pack up his house and move it to some other place?

They told him that he would have to give up his horses and his guns. You will live in one place, they told him, and when you do that, you don't need a horse. And you don't have to shoot corn, so you don't need a gun. They told him that, too. But it didn't matter, because that wasn't what he wanted.

But when he thought of the people, how they had no one to look the white men in the eye and say no, it made him sad. He knew that he could do that, and there were times when he thought that he was the only one who could. Maybe, he told himself, maybe I have to go back, even if I don't want to. Maybe I can learn to live in a house that stays in one place like a tree.

There were long days and longer nights when he turned these thoughts over and over in his mind, like stones tumbling in a swift creek, until they were smooth and polished and pretty to look at. But after all, they were just stones like any other. It depended on what you wanted to see when you looked at them, that was all.

He prayed to *Wakantanka*, but there was no answer. These questions were too hard even for the Great Spirit to answer. He knew then that he would have to decide for himself, and for the people. And he knew what he would have to do, because there was only one thing *to* do, just as there was only one man to speak for the Lakota, and he was that man. He could stand on the highest hill in the Grandmother Country and shout until his throat was raw, but no one would hear him.

If he wanted to be heard, he would have to go back.

Chapter 30 ═══════

Fort Buford, Dakota Territory
1881

JEAN LOUIS LEGARE, A FRENCH-CANADIAN TRADER, had been working on Sitting Bull so hard for so long, trying to convince him to turn himself in at Standing Rock, that the chief accused him of wanting to sell him by the pound. It was a joke, but only partly. Sitting Bull knew that LeGare stood to profit if he were the one who succeeded in bringing in the last and most significant of the Lakota chiefs.

The Canadians had refused to feed the Lakota, hoping their hunger would lead them to return to the United States. LeGare had been supplying food, not out of humanitarian concern but as a business investment. With nowhere else to turn, Sitting Bull had taken the trader's food because he did not want to go to the reservation.

The future seemed to be shrinking around Sitting Bull like a skin drying in the sun, squeezing the life out of him, and in early July, LeGare finally got his wish.

They left LeGare's trading post on July 10 and headed south. To make certain the Lakota followed him, LeGare packed all the food and other supplies from his warehouse in wagons and brought everything along. He did not want anything to tempt the chief to think there was any point in staying behind. Many of the impoverished Lakota were themselves packed into wagons because they no longer had their own horses. Those few who had mounts went on horseback, as they had always done; although the horses, too, were worn to a frazzle.

As the wagons crossed the border and rolled south through buffalo country, with the melancholy procession of warriors with a few lodges trailing in their wake, Sitting Bull saw the ruins of the old way of life lying in the grass. The bones of long-dead buffalo, almost hidden by the summer growth, the plains dotted with flowers, the way the white man decorated the graves of his dead, as if in memory of Lakota freedom, stretched in every direction. These were not buffalo the Lakota had killed, but the picked-over remains of herds slaughtered by the hide hunters and soldiers. Lupine and columbine sprouted inside the rib cages of the huge beasts, looking for all the world as if they had been imprisoned in the bones. Sitting Bull could not help but wonder if these chalky hulks were all that remained of the skeletal herd of his vision; if perhaps it was here those stampeding dead had finally fallen still and silent.

Ahead lay Fort Buford, the trading post where Sitting Bull had so often gone to trade skins for guns and ammunition. He tried not to think about it, about those days when he had ridden to a post knowing that in a day or two or three, whenever he chose, he would climb onto his horse and ride away again. Those days were gone now, dead as the buffalo whose skeletons lay all around him. But he could not think of another way. There was no other place to go, and he set his jaw, trying to hold back the flood of emotions welling up inside him.

Looking at the pathetic column straggling along in the wake of the wagons, he shook his head. It was hard to believe that it had come to this; that a life so rich, so full, and so free could have been reduced to this bedraggled procession. He wanted to shout out his defiance, but there was no one to hear, no one to quake at the sound of his voice, and if it were to be a prayer, no one to answer it.

They reached Fort Buford on the afternoon of July 19 and set up camp. Some of the Long Knives, like curious children, came to gape at the man whose very name had once made their skin crawl. He could see it in their faces—the wonder, the disbelief, the question . . . could this tired and ancient-looking man in tattered clothes once have been the scourge of the plains? When camp was established, Sitting Bull retired to his lodge to rest.

He was feeling his age. At fifty, he could no longer do what he had done at thirty . . . or even at forty. The years had taken their toll, wearing him down.

It seemed to him as if the ravages of time on his body replicated in some symbolic way everything that had happened to his people. They too were worn down, old and tired. Not just the older ones who had come with him to Fort Buford, but all of them. The faces of the young men at the fort looked haggard and drawn as if they, too, had been worn out, made old before their time.

When they had rested overnight, it was time to turn in their horses and their guns. The ragged and hungry Lakota lined up before the officers and, one by one, surrendered everything that had made them free—the buffalo runners and warhorses, of which they had managed to retain only fourteen, then their pistols and revolvers.

Sitting Bull, as befitted his station, went last, accompanied by Crow Foot, his eight-year-old son. He set his treasured Winchester repeater, which had been a gift from White Bull so long ago, on the floor, nodded to it and to Crow Foot, then looked Major David Brotherton in the eye . . . still proud, bent but not broken . . . but no longer free.

Afterword

AFTER HIS SURRENDER, SITTING BULL was taken to Fort Randall, where he was interned as a prisoner of war. The officers at the fort treated him well, and those who came to know him admired his courage and intelligence. His health improved, and he began to recover his old vigor. And, as could be expected, he never lost his concern for his people.

When he was finally released to the agency at Standing Rock, he became active in the affairs of the Lakota reservation, working unstintingly to improve conditions there, and waging an uphill battle against the indifference of the Indian Bureau, the treachery of the United States government, and the greed that continued to fuel westward expansion and piecemeal subjugation of his former country.

But the biggest threat to his influence, which remained considerable and actually seemed to increase, was the backbiting and jealousy of other chiefs, including former friends like Gall and Running Antelope. The Lakota knew they had been given a raw deal, but powerless to throw off the white yoke, they turned their bitterness inward, many of the chiefs competing with one another for influence that no longer counted for much.

The agent at Standing Rock, James McLaughlin, tried repeatedly to undermine Sitting Bull's authority, refusing to acknowledge his status as chief and constantly trying to sabotage Sitting Bull's efforts to improve conditions on the reservation.

For a time, the chief joined Buffalo Bill's Wild West Show and became a celebrity. Everywhere he went, people lined up for his photograph, which he sold by the hundreds, almost always giving the money away to poor children he encountered on his travels. Generosity was—and for Sitting Bull remained—one of the four cardinal virtues for a Lakota, especially for a chief.

The government remained uneasy about Sitting Bull. When another Lakota, the dreamer and medicine man Wo-vo-ka, began to preach his Ghost Dance religion, that uneasiness quickly turned to paranoia and then to hysteria. The Ghost Dance cult believed that all the great chiefs would come back, and that the white man would be driven away. The buffalo would return, and the Lakota would be able to return to their old way of life.

Sitting Bull was not a member of the cult, but he thought the Ghost Dance itself harmless. Nonetheless the government, concerned about a possible uprising, overreacted. Several Indian policemen were sent to arrest him, rousting him out of bed in the middle of the night. When friends grabbed weapons and came to his assistance, a gunfight broke out. Sitting Bull was shot once each by Bull Head and Red Tomahawk, two of the policemen. Like his friend Crazy Horse, probably his only rival for preeminence among the Lakota chiefs, Sitting Bull met his death while unarmed, at the hands of his own people.

There are several biographies of Sitting Bull, but the most recent, and by far the best, is by Robert Utley, *The Lance and the Shield.* For those who wish additional reading, two other biographies, by Stanley Vestal and Alexander Adams, are helpful, as is Vestal's *Warpath*, a biography of Sitting Bull's nephew, White Bull. There is, of course, a multitude of works available on the Sioux War of 1876, but one of the most comprehensive overviews is *Centennial Campaign: The Sioux War of 1876* by John S. Gray. For a broader acquaintance with Lakota society, Royal Hasrick's *The Sioux* is excellent, and the work of James Walker, published in several volumes by the University of Nebraska Press, is comprehensive and invaluable on Lakota myth, ritual, and belief.

Bill Dugan is the pseudonym of a full-time writer who lives in upstate New York with his family.

She felt exposed, yet safe. It was an intoxicating combination.

The sharp sound of crunching gravel nearby roused Olivia. She froze, acutely aware of her semidressed state. A woman's voice cut through the night air. "It's cold out here. Let's go back inside." A man murmured something intelligible and the sound of retreating footsteps left Olivia alone with Adam once again.

Olivia had no intention of squandering even a minute of this night. She smoothed her palms over Adam's chest, and rising on tiptoe, she whispered in his ear, "I don't think it's cold at all. In fact, I think it's very, very hot."

"Honey, you're killing me." Adam's low murmur stirred her hair and her feminine self-esteem.

Her thighs quivered and clenched in response to the need in his voice. She reached between them and touched him. "We could go to my house."

"Are you propositioning me, Olivia?" Was that a hopeful note underlying his incredulity?

She knew she'd stepped—make that leapt— beyond her self-imposed boundaries. But it was just for one night. Hopefully one *incredible* night. She drew a fortifying breath. "Yes, I believe I am."

"Thank God," he whispered roughly, just before he crushed her lips with his.

Dear Reader,

I've had the time of my life writing my first book for Temptation. Especially since it offered me the chance to combine two of my favorite things—sizzling sensuality and humor. After all, it's not every day a girl finds herself in the wrong bed. Or, in this case, the right bed. With the wrong brother. Or is he?

Olivia Cooper, daughter of the town drunk, has spent a lifetime trying to rise above her inherited reputation. She's carved a respectable niche for herself as the local librarian and head of the literacy council. And as long as she manages to control her occasional reckless impulses, all is right with her world. But not for long....

Luke Rutledge is the black sheep of his family and the local bad boy. As a rule, the lofty Rutledges don't sport earrings or tattoos, and they definitely don't ride around on a Harley. Except for Luke, that is.... So when Olivia finds herself having the best sex of her life with the resident rebel, it's the last place she should be. And it's exactly where her wild side urges her to go—again and again!

I hope you enjoy Luke and Olivia's story. I sure enjoyed writing it and I'd love to know what you think. You can write to me at: P.O. Box 801068, Acworth, GA 30101. And don't forget to look for my next book, *Barely Decent*, coming out in November.

Enjoy,

Jennifer LaBrecque

Books by Jennifer LaBrecque

HARLEQUIN DUETS
28—ANDREW IN EXCESS
52—KIDS + COPS = CHAOS
64—JINGLE BELL BRIDE?